Changeling Press, LLC

ChangelingPress.com

Azrael (Devil's Boneyard MC 13)
A Dixie Reapers MC Bad Boys Romance
Harley Wylde

Azrael (Devil's Boneyard MC 13)
A Dixie Reapers MC Bad Boys Romance
Harley Wylde

ISBN: 978-1-60521-952-3

Publisher:
Changeling Press LLC
315 N. Centre St.
Martinsburg, WV 25404
ChangelingPress.com

Printed in the U.S.A.

Editor: Crystal Esau
Cover Artist: Bryan Keller

The individual stories in this anthology have been previously released in E-Book format.

Table of Contents

Azrael (Devil's Boneyard MC 13)
A Dixie Reapers MC Bad Boys Romance
Harley Wylde

Sometimes, to find yourself, you have to get lost in the shadows. Are you ready to embrace the darkness?

Zara: My mother has vanished without a trace, and no one seems willing to help. Except for one enigmatic figure whispered about in hushed tones: the Angel of Death, Azrael, a guardian of justice who ensures bad men meet their fate. I set out to find him. I didn't count on finding him to be the sexiest man I'd ever met -- or falling for him. In his arms, I find an unexpected sanctuary. I should be terrified of his violent world, but he offers me safety and ignites a passion I've never felt before.

Azrael: I live in the shadows, doing whatever I must to protect those who have lost all hope. It's no place for a woman. Then I met Zara. Her fierce spirit and unwavering courage break down my walls. I'll stop at nothing to bring her mother home, even if it means I leave a trail of bodies in my wake. For Zara, I'd do anything, even walk through hell itself. I never wanted to fall in love... but now that I have, I'll do anything to keep my new family safe. I'm the monster who hunts other monsters, the one who defends those who can't protect themselves. Now I need to make sure that darkness doesn't touch those I love or die trying.

Lose yourself in a world where love conquers fear, and courage fights against the darkness.

Chapter One

Azrael

I tracked my target for six blocks, keeping to the shadows as he moved through the decaying part of town. The streets had names but nobody used them anymore. This was just the bad side, where even cops wouldn't patrol after dark. Perfect hunting ground for a man like me. The dealer was nervous, his head swiveling every few steps, fingers twitching. He never looked up or behind. If he had, he might have noticed me.

Charming had been crystal clear when he'd slid the photo across the table this morning. "Devil's Minions are arming up. Find out what they're buying and send a message."

Ever since we'd gotten word another club had moved in too close to home, we'd been more vigilant than usual. Charming was on edge, which meant we all were.

The alley came up on my right, narrow and stinking of piss and rotted food. The man ducked into it without breaking stride. I counted to ten, checked my surroundings, then followed. My boots made hardly a sound against the damp concrete. Years of practice had taught me how to move like a ghost when needed.

Twenty yards in, the alley bent sharply left. I pressed my back against the brick wall and tilted my head just enough to peek around. There they were. Three men, my target and two others I didn't recognize. Between them sat a black duffel bag, unzipped enough to show the gleaming metal inside.

"This all of it?" one asked, his voice carrying the distinct edge of someone who thought he was more important than he was.

"Half," my target replied. "You get the rest when I see the money."

The third man knelt and pulled back the zipper farther. "Six Glocks, four AR-15s... What about the ammo?"

"In the truck. Once we --"

I shifted my weight and a discarded bottle clinked against the brick. All three men went silent.

"The fuck was that?" the kneeling one said, already on his feet and reaching behind his back.

I could've disappeared, come back another day when they weren't so alert. But Charming wanted a message sent, and waiting wouldn't accomplish that. I stepped around the corner, keeping my stance loose. Ready.

All three pulled guns immediately. Someone else might have been scared. Not me. Wasn't the first time I'd had a gun pointed at me. Wouldn't be the last.

"Who the fuck are you?" my target demanded, his pistol wavering slightly.

"Private party," the one who'd checked the weapons added. "Get the fuck out of here if you want to live."

I smiled. Not the kind that reaches your eyes. The kind that makes smart people run. "Private? An alley? Not hardly. You boys picked the wrong town to do business in."

"The hell you talking about? We got permission to be here."

"From who?" I asked, genuinely curious. "Because the Devil's Boneyard don't remember giving it."

The name landed like I knew it would. Their eyes widened, and the one farthest from me took a half-step backward before catching himself.

"Devil's Boneyard can fuck off," my target spat, though his voice cracked. "This is Minion territory now. Everyone knows the Devil's Boneyard have lost their bite."

I shook my head slowly. "No such thing. Never will be. My President asked me to deliver a message."

"Yeah? What's that?" the farthest one asked, trying to sound brave.

I looked each of them in the eye. "This is the only warning. Pack up and leave, or we'll burn everything you've built to the ground."

The one nearest the bag laughed. "There's three of us and one of you, asshole. Only message getting delivered is your body to the morgue."

I didn't bother responding. Words were done. I moved.

The first shot went wide as I closed the distance, ducking low and driving my shoulder into my target's stomach. The air left his lungs in a rush as he folded over me. I grabbed his gun hand and twisted until something snapped. His scream echoed against the brick as his pistol clattered to the ground.

The other two were already firing. One bullet grazed my arm, hot pain slicing through me, but I shook it off. I spun my target around, using him as a shield. Two shots thudded into his chest, and he jerked against me.

"Fuck! Stop shooting!" he screamed at his friends.

I shoved him forward and drew my own weapon from inside my cut. My first shot got the farthest man in the throat. He dropped his gun and clutched at the sudden fountain of blood, eyes bulging in shock. He'd be dead shortly after he hit the ground.

The third man emptied his clip at me, but panic

made him sloppy. I felt one bullet tug at my jeans, but it didn't bite into my flesh. When his gun clicked empty, his face went slack. "Wait --" he started, fumbling for another magazine.

I crossed the distance in three strides and drove my fist into his face. Cartilage crunched under my knuckles. Blood sprayed from his shattered nose. He stumbled back against the wall, ammo forgotten. I hit him again, this time in the gut. As he doubled over, I brought my knee up into his face. More crunching. More blood.

My target was trying to crawl away, leaving a dark trail behind him. The one I'd shot in the throat had stopped moving, eyes fixed on nothing. The third man slid down the wall, consciousness fading as blood poured from his ruined face.

I turned back to my target. "Where's the Minions' President? Or your boss. Who the fuck do you answer to?"

"Please," he gasped. "I got kids."

"So do a lot of people. Answer my fucking question."

"Strip club… Velvet something. My boss is there most nights, same for their President."

I nodded. Information secured. Now for the message.

I pulled my knife from its sheath. The blade caught what little light penetrated the alley, gleaming darkly. My target's eyes fixed on it. "No, man. Please. I told you what you wanted."

"You did," I agreed. "And I appreciate that. But a message needs sending."

I grabbed him by the hair and yanked his head back, then dragged my blade in one smooth motion across his throat. Hot blood spilled over my hand and down my wrist. He made a horrible gurgling sound as he tried to breathe through the new opening in his neck.

The third man had regained enough awareness to see what was happening. He tried to scramble away, but his legs weren't working right. I walked to him calmly, knife still dripping.

"I'll tell the Pres," he pleaded, hands up.

"You won't be telling anyone anything," I said, and drove the knife up under his ribs. Once. Twice. A third time. His body jerked, then went still.

I wiped my blade on his shirt before returning it to its sheath. The alley had gone quiet except for the distant sounds of traffic and my own breathing. I checked the duffel bag, confirming what I'd seen. High-quality weapons, not the cheap shit usually found in street deals. The Devil's Minions were serious about arming up.

I zipped the bag closed and slung it over my shoulder. Evidence secured. Message delivered. And hell, we got some new toys free of charge out of the deal. Not bad.

Blood was already drying tacky on my hands as I walked away from the carnage. I felt nothing but the satisfaction of a job well done. This city had enough problems without a one percent club trying to muscle in. Sometimes cleaning required getting your hands dirty.

I left the alley the same way I'd entered, invisible to anyone who might be watching. Just another shadow moving through a city full of them. But unlike most shadows, I left something behind. Something that would make the Minions understand exactly what happened when you tried to set up shop in Devil's Boneyard territory.

A warning written in blood.

I secured the weapons to the back of my bike and then hauled ass back toward home. But I needed to clean up before I hit the more respectable side of town. I pulled into the Gas-N-Go at the edge of what could only be considered the ghetto. It was the kind of place where the security cameras had been broken for years and nobody cared enough to fix them. Perfect.

The neon sign flickered pathetically, casting sickly blue light across my bloodstained knuckles. I parked around back, away from the single streetlight. The bathroom key hung on a piece of splintered wood labeled "RESTROOM" in faded black marker. The attendant barely looked up from his phone as I dropped a twenty on the counter. He pocketed it without a word. No questions. That's why I came here.

The bathroom door protested with a screech as I pushed it open. The stench hit me immediately -- bleach barely covering the reek of piss and something worse. One bulb dangled from the ceiling, threatening to plunge the room into darkness at any moment. The tile floor might have been white once, decades ago. Now it was a patchwork of stained gray squares, cracked and broken in spots.

I locked the door behind me. The mirror, spotted with age and what looked like old toothpaste flecks, fractured my reflection into disconnected pieces. Blood had dried in the creases of my knuckles and under my fingernails. More had splattered across my forearms. A few drops darkened the front of my shirt.

I turned the hot water tap. It groaned and sputtered before a weak stream emerged, lukewarm at best. I squirted some pink soap from the dispenser into my palm and began the methodical process of washing away the evidence.

Pink foam turned red as I scrubbed, the water swirling crimson down the drain. Three men dead in an alley. Three lives ended by my hand. I should have felt something -- regret, guilt, horror at what I'd done. Instead, I felt the same calm I always did after a job. The blood washing away felt like cleansing, not just my hands but the town itself.

The Devil's Minions were cancer, spreading through neighboring towns and now trying to infect ours. They'd started with drugs, then guns. Girls would be next. Always was. I'd seen enough clubs go down that road to know the pattern. First you supply the town with its vices, then you own the town.

Not here. Not while the Devil's Boneyard stood watch.

I scrubbed harder at a stubborn spot on my thumb, the skin raw underneath. The water ran clearer now, only faint traces of pink swirling down the drain. That spiral reminded me of something else. Something older.

My mother's blood snaking down her face from a cut on her temple. One of the regulars had gotten drunk and broken a glass against her head. She'd plastered a smile on her face and assured me she was fine, but even then I'd known she was lying.

I grabbed some paper towels and wet them, wiping at the blood spatters on my shirt. Better to have a wet shirt than one covered in red. When I was done, I washed my hands once more then dried them. As I stared at my reflection, I tried to see my mother in me. I'd never known my dad, but I liked to think I didn't have a damn thing in common with him.

My mom had been dead a long-ass time. Cancer took her slow, gave me time to say goodbye, but not enough time to become the man she'd wanted me to be. College educated. Safe job. Family.

"Sorry, Mom," I whispered. "Didn't quite work out that way."

Instead, I'd found the Devil's Boneyard. Or they'd found me. Stripes had seen something in me. Potential, he called it. Cinder had given me purpose. The club had given me family.

Would she understand? I'd like to think so. Mom had been pragmatic about the world. "Sometimes good people have to do bad things to protect what matters," she'd told me once, after I'd gotten suspended for breaking a bully's nose. She hadn't approved, exactly, but she'd understood.

The men in that alley weren't good people. They would have brought poison into our town, destroyed lives, all for profit. I'd stopped that. Three lives against how many I'd potentially saved?

The math made sense to me, even if it wouldn't have to her.

I checked myself in the mirror one more time. No visible blood. Nothing to attract attention. I ran my fingers through my hair and practiced looking normal. Not too hard. I'd gotten good at it over the years.

Before leaving, I wiped down everything I'd touched. The Devil's Boneyard had friends in the police department, but certain habits kept you alive in this business. Attention to detail. Never get sloppy.

I unlocked the door. The attendant glanced up as I passed, his gaze moving over me in assessment.

"You look better," he said, voice gravelly from years of cigarettes.

I stopped. "Better than what?"

He shrugged. "Than when you came in. Like maybe you found what you were looking for."

Something about his stare made me take a closer

look. The tattoo peeking out from his sleeve wasn't just any ink. I recognized the style. Prison work.

"Maybe I did," I said carefully. "You work here long?"

"Long enough to know when to mind my own business." He tapped his finger against the counter. "Long enough to know what kind of men come through here needing to clean up."

I felt my muscles tense, ready for trouble. "That right?"

He nodded toward my cut. "Devil's Boneyard. You boys do good work. Kept my sister's kid off the shit when the Undead Serpents were running it through here. I respect that."

I relaxed slightly. "Just doing what needs doing."

"Heard there's new players moving in. Minions or some shit." He spat into a cup beside the register. "Bad news, those boys. No respect."

"No respect," I agreed. "And not long for this world if they keep pushing."

He nodded, understanding passing between us. "Good hunting, brother."

I pushed open the door, night air cool against my face. The town spread out before me, lights glittering in the darkness. Most people out there had no idea what happened in the shadows to keep them safe. They didn't know about men like me, or the lines we crossed so they wouldn't have to.

That was fine. Let them sleep easy. I'd carry the weight of what I'd done tonight. Add it to all the rest. It wasn't a burden anymore -- just the price of the life I'd chosen.

I started my bike and pulled onto the empty street. The compound waited, and after that, more work to be done. The town needed cleaning, and I was just getting started.

I rolled through the gates of the Devil's Boneyard compound just past midnight, the tension easing from my shoulders as I passed under the skull-adorned archway. Home. Or the closest thing to it I'd had in years. Floodlights illuminated the lot where dozens of bikes stood in neat rows, chrome glinting like scattered stars. Two Prospects snapped to attention as I pulled up.

"They're waiting for you," one of them said, not meeting my eyes directly. Smart kid. He'd learn the rules fast enough -- never look too eager, never too scared. Balance was everything in this life. After the shit we'd dealt with, we'd cracked down on the rules when bringing in Prospects. Too many rotten apples.

"How long they been in there?" I asked.

"'Bout an hour. Stripes came in with news from town, then Samurai showed up. Charming's still in his office."

I nodded and headed for the clubhouse. The two-story building had been renovated recently. Now it was somewhere between a fortress and headquarters.

The heavy door opened to the sound of classic rock and the smell of whiskey, smoke, and leather. Our main room sprawled before me, all exposed brick and worn hardwood floors. The long bar against the far wall gleamed with decades of polishing. Trophy pipes and old photos covered the walls, history and legacy looking down on each new generation.

Three of my brothers played pool in the corner, their laughter cutting through Lynyrd Skynyrd's "Simple Man" pumping from the speakers. A couple of club girls lounged on the couches, one stretching like a cat as I walked in. She smiled, inviting. I gave her a nod but kept moving. Business first.

Stripes and Samurai sat at the bar, hunched over amber-filled glasses, their heads close in conversation. Stripes spotted me first.

"The hunter returns," he said, his Russian accent thick as always. "Was beginning to think you'd fallen into trouble, brother."

I slid onto the stool beside him. "Takes more than a few Minion punks to cause me trouble."

The Prospect behind the bar, Harland, had a glass of Jack in front of me before I could ask. Smart kid. I took a long swallow, the burn a welcome friend after the night's work.

"You find what Charming sent you for?" Samurai asked, his voice quiet.

"Found it and handled it." I set my glass down. "Three of them doing a weapons exchange in the alley behind Murphy's. High-end stuff -- Glocks and AR-15s. Not street-level shit. Bag is on my bike."

Stripes whistled low. "They're arming for war, then."

"Looks that way. I sent the message Charming wanted delivered." I flexed my hand, knuckles still tender beneath the skin. "Left them where someone will find them."

"Good." Samurai nodded once. "What else did you learn?"

"Looks like the Minions' base of operations is some strip joint. Velvet something. One of them spilled before I cut his throat."

"*Velvet Cage*," Stripes supplied, his face darkening. "*Da*, we know this place. Very bad business happening there."

"What kind of bad business?" I asked, already guessing.

Samurai glanced around, then leaned closer.

"Girls. Young ones. Word is they're not all working by choice."

My stomach tightened. Human trafficking. The line no respectable club crossed. Even in our world, there were rules. Lines you didn't step over unless you wanted war. Hadn't always been that way, but there were more and more of us ready to put our lives on the line to keep this shit from happening. Not just here, but across the country.

"We're sure about this?" I asked.

Stripes nodded gravely. "My contact in sheriff's office, he says three girls reported missing last month. All last seen at this club. Deputies go to investigate, suddenly they find nothing wrong. Girls who made complaints withdraw statements, say they just went on vacation." He held my gaze. "Meanwhile, one of the deputies buys new boat. Very convenient timing, *da*?"

"Fucking bought and paid for," I muttered. "So the cops are useless."

"Worse than useless," Samurai added. "They're protecting the Minions' operation."

I drained my glass and gestured for another. "What does Charming want to do about it?"

"That," came a deep voice from behind us, "is what we're about to discuss."

We all turned as Charming strode into the room. At sixty-three, his hair had gone mostly gray, but he moved with the same authority he always had. The club president's patch on his cut commanded immediate respect. The room went quiet, even the music seeming to drop in volume.

"Church," he announced. "Now."

The three brothers at the pool table immediately set down their cues. The club women stood and headed for the door without being told. They knew it was time to get the hell out. Church meant members only, and it meant serious business.

I followed Stripes and Samurai through the door at the back of the main room, into our chapel. The long wooden table dominated the space, scarred from decades of meetings just like this one. The horned skull carved into its center stared up at us, silent witness to all our decisions, good and bad.

Charming took his place at the head of the table. I sat in my usual spot halfway down, watching as the rest of the club filed in. We waited until everyone had a chance to get here, since some had been at home or out having fun. The door closed with finality after the last brother walked in, and Charming brought down the gavel.

"We've got a problem," he began without preamble. "Devil's Minions have moved from inconvenience to threat."

Murmurs of agreement circled the table.

"Azrael," he continued, looking my way, "report."

I laid out everything I'd seen and done -- the weapons deal, the quality of the merchandise, the information about the *Velver Cage*. I didn't sugarcoat the violence. These men had seen worse, done worse. Hell, most would probably think I'd gone easy on them. In truth, I had. I'd needed to make sure they could be recognized when they were found.

When I finished, Charming nodded. "Good work. The message needed sending." He stood and leaned forward, placing both hands flat on the table. "But it's worse than we thought. I had a visit today from someone you all know -- Melissa Carter."

The name sent a ripple through the room. Melissa had been a friend to the club for two years now, running the new women's shelter on the eastside. We provided security, donations, and made sure her ex-husband -- who'd put her in the hospital twice -- stayed far away.

"Her shelter took in a girl last night," Charming continued. "Seventeen years old, beat to hell, track marks up both arms. Says she was held at the *Velver Cage* for three months after answering an ad for waitress work. They got her hooked on heroin, then put her to work in the back rooms." His knuckles went white against the wood. "When she tried to leave, they made an example of her."

"Jesus Christ," someone muttered down the table.

"It gets worse," Charming said grimly. "She says there are at least a dozen girls in the same situation. Some as young as fifteen. And the guy running the whole operation personally samples the merchandise before putting it on offer to customers."

"Marco," I said, the name tasting like poison.

"Marco Delgado," Charming confirmed. "Ex-military, dishonorable discharge. Rumor says he was trafficking girls in Afghanistan before Uncle Sam caught on. Now he's set up shop here, thinking we won't notice or won't care. And he's the current President for the Minions in this area."

Stripes slammed his fist on the table. "We should burn the place to ground. With him inside."

"Not yet," Charming cautioned. "We do this right, or we don't do it at all. The girl says they move the merchandise every few days between the club and other locations. We hit too soon, those girls disappear forever."

"Do we know when they were last moved? If it's already been several days, waiting means we'll lose them," I said.

"Intel says they won't be moved again for another two days."

"So what's the play?" Samurai asked, ever the strategist.

Charming's gaze found mine. "Azrael, you and Stripes will do recon on the *Velver Cage*. I want to know security, layout, patrol patterns, everything. Samurai, you and Phantom work your contacts. Find the clean law enforcement, the ones we can trust when this goes down. We'll need them on our side."

He looked around the table. "Make no mistake, brothers. This is war. Not just for territory, not just for business. This is about what kind of men we are. What kind of club we are." His voice hardened. "The Devil's Boneyard does not allow this shit in our town. Not now, not ever."

Nods of agreement spread around the table. On this we were united.

"We meet back here in forty-eight hours with intel," Charming continued. "Then we plan the hit. If there are girls in that club, we get them out. And then --" his eyes went cold --"then we send Marco Delgado straight to hell."

"And his whole fucking operation with him," Stripes added darkly.

I thought of the men I'd killed tonight. A warm-up for what was coming. The Devil's Minions had chosen the wrong town, the wrong enemy. They'd crossed a line that couldn't be uncrossed.

Charming brought the gavel down with finality. "Church dismissed. Azrael, Stripes, Samurai -- my office. We need to talk details."

As the others filed out, I caught Samurai's eye. He gave me the slightest nod, a silent acknowledgment of what we all knew. The coming days would be bloody. But sometimes blood was necessary to wash away the filth.

I followed Charming toward his office. This wasn't just club business anymore. This was about something more fundamental.

Some lines you didn't cross in our world. Those who did paid the price.

And the Devil's Boneyard would be collecting in full.

Chapter Two

Azrael

The rain pelted against my face as I leaned into the curve of the road. My bike responded like it was an extension of my body, the engine's rumble vibrating through my chest as I cut through the empty streets. Nights like this were my sanctuary -- dark, wet, and desolate. The kind of night where decent folks stayed inside, leaving the streets to predators like me. Or so I thought, until a scream sliced through the steady drumming of rain on pavement.

I jerked my head toward the sound, my muscles tensing. Screams in this part of town weren't uncommon, but this one -- this one had the sharp edge of genuine terror. I throttled down, my tires hissing across the wet asphalt as I made a quick decision. The club patch on my back meant something in these streets. It wasn't just for show -- it carried weight and responsibility.

The alley mouth loomed dark between two abandoned storefronts, a black slash in the neon-tinted night. I killed the engine and dismounted in one fluid motion, my boots splashing into a puddle that soaked my jeans to mid-calf. The cold barely registered. My hand automatically went to the knife at my hip as I moved forward, staying close to the brick wall where shadows offered cover.

Another scream, choked off this time, followed by male laughter and the sound of something -- or someone -- hitting the ground hard.

I rounded a dumpster, and the scene unfolded before me: three men surrounding a woman who'd been forced to her knees, her clothes torn at the shoulder. Broken glass crunched under their boots, reflecting the distant streetlight in wicked little sparkles. One man held her hair in his fist, yanking her head back at an unnatural angle. Another had his hand over her mouth. The third was unbuckling his belt.

The woman's gaze found mine through the darkness -- blue eyes, startlingly bright against her darker skin. They weren't filled with fear but with fury, a rage so pure it nearly matched my own. Only one choice I could make.

"Evening, gentlemen," I said, stepping into the alley fully now. "Seems like the lady isn't interested in your company."

The men turned, the one with his hand on his belt pausing mid-motion.

"Fuck off," the largest one snarled, his face half-hidden beneath a scrappy beard. "Mind your own business."

I smiled, knowing it was the type that would send a chill down their spines. At least, if they were smart. "This is my business. Everything that happens in this neighborhood, in this fucking town, is my business."

The dim light caught my cut, and I watched recognition dawn on their faces. The smart ones would have backed off then. None of them were smart.

"There's three of us and one of you," said the one holding the woman's hair. Seemed to be a common theme these days. Why did assholes like these think that would make me give a shit and back down? "And we're just having a little fun. No harm in that."

"No harm," I repeated, taking a step closer. "We'll see about that."

The first one rushed me -- drunk, clumsy, confident in his size. I sidestepped, letting his momentum carry him past me before driving my elbow into the base of his skull. He stumbled forward, his feet sliding on the wet concrete before he face-planted into the wall. The crunch of cartilage told me his nose wouldn't be the same again.

The second attacker was warier, circling as his friend groaned and slid down the bricks. He pulled a switchblade, the metal catching the light filtering into the alley.

"You're gonna regret this," he promised, flicking the blade open with practiced ease.

"I doubt it," I replied.

He lunged, slashing wildly. I caught his wrist, twisting until I heard the *pop* of tendons and his knife clattered to the ground. His scream was high and thin as I drove my blade into the meat of his upper arm, not deep enough to kill, just enough to make sure he remembered this night every time the weather changed.

The third man, the one who'd been holding the woman's hair, shoved her aside and backed away, hands raised. "Hey, man, we didn't know she was with someone. We're just --"

My boot connected with his groin before he could finish the sentence. As he doubled over, I grabbed the back of his head and brought my knee up to meet his descending face. The impact sent vibrations up my leg, and he collapsed into a heap of limbs and whimpers, blood gushing from his nose.

Three down, none of them moving to get up. Pathetic little fuckers. The only sounds now were the rain, their pained breathing, and the distant wail of a siren that had nothing to do with us.

I turned to the woman, who had pushed herself to her feet, leaning against the dumpster for support. Her breathing was ragged, but her eyes were clear and focused. Blood trickled from her hairline where one of them must have struck her, mingling with the rain on her face. Her dark hair clung to her cheeks and neck, and despite her torn clothing, she stood with a dignity that seemed out of place in this filthy alley.

"You okay?" I asked, wiping my blade on my jeans before putting it away.

"I am now," she said, her voice steadier than I expected. She wasn't from around here -- not with that hint of an accent I couldn't quite place.

I approached her slowly, holding my hands where she could see them. "Need a hospital?"

She shook her head, wincing slightly at the movement. "No hospitals. No police."

That was something we could agree on. I glanced back at the men on the ground. None of them were dead, though the one with the knife wound was bleeding heavily, clutching his arm and cursing. They wouldn't be bothering anyone else tonight.

"Got somewhere to go?" I asked.

She straightened up, pushing wet hair from her face. "I found exactly where I need to be."

That wasn't the answer I expected. I narrowed my eyes, suddenly wary. Random women in alleys weren't usually looking to find people like me unless they were working for someone else.

"What's that supposed to mean?"

She took a step closer, and I noticed she was smaller than she first appeared, barely reaching my shoulders. Her clothes -- what was left of them -- were expensive, not the kind you usually saw in this neighborhood.

"My name is Zara Colton," she said, looking up at me with those blue eyes that didn't match the rest of her features. "And I've been searching for you."

My hand instinctively moved back toward my knife. "How do you know who I am?"

"I didn't," she admitted. "Not until just now. They call you the Angel of Death in some circles. Azrael. The one who punishes men who hurt women and children." She gestured to the groaning men on the ground. "I've heard the stories, but I needed to see for myself."

"You got yourself attacked on purpose?" I asked incredulously.

She looked away, her jaw tightening. "No. That was… unfortunate timing. But perhaps fortunate too, since it led me to you."

"Why?" The question came out harsher than I intended, but strangers with agendas made me nervous, especially pretty ones who knew things they shouldn't. Wouldn't be the first time a man was betrayed by a woman. I didn't trust people blindly.

Zara looked back at me, and something in her expression shifted, a vulnerability showing through her composed facade. "Because I need your help. My mother is missing, and I believe you can help find her."

The rain continued to fall around us, washing the blood from the concrete into the gutters. In the distance, the siren grew louder, then faded as it turned down another street. One of the men at our feet groaned and tried to roll over. I placed my boot on his chest, pressing down just enough to keep him still.

"This isn't the place to talk," I said finally. "Can you ride?"

She nodded, a ghost of a smile touching her lips. "Yes. Although it's been a while."

"Then let's go. The club will want to hear whatever it is you have to say." I gestured toward the alley entrance where my bike waited. "After you, Zara

Colton."

She moved past me, her steps uneven but determined. I gave one last look at the three men before following her. They wouldn't be the only ones remembering this night. So would I, though for entirely different reasons. Something told me that the woman walking ahead of me was about to change everything, and in my experience, change was rarely for the better.

I stepped toward Zara, noting how she swayed slightly despite her tough facade. Up close, I could see the bruise forming at her temple and the way she cradled her left arm against her side. Tough as she might be trying to act, she was hurt. I reached out slowly, giving her plenty of time to back away if she wanted to. She didn't.

"Let me see," I said, my voice low as I gently took her arm.

She winced but allowed me to push up what remained of her sleeve. An ugly gash about three inches long ran along her forearm, still seeping blood.

"Deep enough to need stitches?" I asked, examining it in the dim light.

Zara shook her head. "I don't think so. It's not that bad."

I pulled a bandana from my back pocket -- clean enough to serve as a temporary bandage. I wrapped it around her arm, tying it just tight enough to slow the bleeding without cutting off circulation.

"Thanks," she murmured, watching my hands work with a curious intensity.

"Don't thank me yet. We still need to get out of here."

I didn't miss how she gritted her teeth against the pain, but I respected her enough not to comment. I walked beside her, close enough to catch her if she stumbled, but not touching her. Rain continued to fall, softer now but persistent, soaking through her torn shirt and plastering her dark hair to her scalp. By the time we reached my bike, she was shivering.

"Here," I said, shrugging off my leather jacket. It was wet on the outside but still dry and warm inside. "Put this on."

For a moment, I thought she might refuse, but then she took it with a small nod. The jacket swallowed her, the sleeves extending well past her fingertips, but at least it covered the worst of her torn clothing and offered some protection from the cold.

My bike gleamed under the streetlight, water beading on its polished surface. I straddled it first, then held out my hand to Zara.

"You said you'd ridden before, right?" I asked as she approached.

"Yes." She took my hand. Her palm was smaller than mine but calloused in places that suggested she wasn't a stranger to physical work.

I helped her onto the back of the seat, steadying her as she settled in. "Hold on tight. The streets are slick, and so is the bike. I don't want you sliding off."

There was a moment of hesitation before I felt her arms wrap around my waist, her front pressed against my back. The intimacy of it wasn't lost on me, but this wasn't the time or place to dwell on how her body felt against mine. I started the bike, and the engine roared to life, vibrating beneath us.

"Ready?" I called over my shoulder.

Her answer was a tightening of her arms around my middle. I eased the bike into first gear and pulled away, moving slower than I typically would.

Rain streaked past us as we moved through the

abandoned streets. I kept to the back roads where traffic was always sparse, avoiding the main drags where cops might pull us over.

As we rode, I felt Zara gradually relax against me, her grip loosening just enough to be comfortable without becoming dangerous. It was strange having someone on the back of my bike. I usually rode alone -- it was safer that way. Fewer complications, fewer liabilities. But there was something about Zara that had made me break my own rules.

Maybe it was the way she'd stood in that alley, bloody but unbowed. Maybe it was the mention of her missing mother. Or maybe I was just getting soft in my old age. Whatever the reason, she was here now, her breath warm against my shoulder blade even through my wet shirt.

After a few minutes of riding, I called over the engine noise, "Are you injured anywhere else?"

I felt her shift behind me. "I'm okay," she replied, her voice close to my ear. "Just some scrapes and bruises. Nothing broken."

There was a catch in her voice that told me she was downplaying her pain, but I didn't push it. She was conscious and alert, and that would have to do until we reached somewhere safer.

We turned onto a narrow street that wound through the industrial district, flanked by shuttered warehouses and chain-link fences. The streetlights were fewer here, pools of orange light separated by stretches of near darkness. Zara's hold on me tightened as we passed through one of these dark patches.

"Where are we going?" she asked, her lips close to my ear to be heard over the engine and the rain.

"Somewhere safe," I answered, not ready to tell her exactly where until I was sure of her intentions. She was still a stranger, no matter how compelling her story.

She fell silent after that, her face pressed against my back as we rode. I could feel her shivering despite my jacket, and I pushed the bike a little faster, eager to get her someplace warm and dry.

The city gradually gave way to the outskirts, buildings becoming more sparse, the darkness between streetlights growing longer. Zara's gaze remained fixed on the passing darkness -- I could feel her head turn occasionally as she took in our surroundings. She wasn't just along for the ride. She was paying attention, memorizing the route. Smart girl.

We passed beneath a highway overpass, the sound of the engine amplified by the concrete above us, then emerged onto a stretch of road that ran parallel to an abandoned railway. The rain had tapered to a misty drizzle, but the night had grown colder, the wind cutting through my wet shirt like tiny knives.

I felt Zara's body tense as we approached a crossroads. Her hand moved from my waist to my shoulder, squeezing gently.

"I need to stop for a minute," she said, her voice strained.

I slowed and pulled onto the shoulder, bringing the bike to a halt beneath the shelter of a massive oak tree that hung over the road. The engine ticked as it cooled, the only sound besides the drip of water from leaves overhead.

Zara dismounted awkwardly, wincing as her feet hit the ground. I followed, keeping a hand on her elbow to steady her.

"What's wrong?" I asked, scanning her for signs of hidden injuries.

She flexed her left arm, the one with the

makeshift bandage. "It's starting to throb. And I'm a little dizzy."

Under the diffused moonlight breaking through the clouds, I could see that the bandana around her arm was soaked through with blood. Too much blood for a superficial wound.

"Let me see," I said, already reaching for the knot.

She offered her arm without protest, another sign that she was feeling worse than she let on. I unwrapped the bandana carefully, revealing the gash beneath. It was deeper than I'd initially thought, the edges clean but wide, showing the pale glimpse of fat tissue beneath the skin.

"This needs stitches," I said firmly. "And probably antibiotics. Those alley rats who attacked you might have had all kinds of shit on their knives."

Zara shook her head. "No hospitals. I told you."

"We have someone at the club who can take care of it," I said. "He's got medical training."

She looked into my eyes, searching for something -- trustworthiness, maybe, or deception. Whatever she was looking for, she must have found it, because she nodded slowly. "Okay."

I wrapped her arm again, tighter this time, using a clean section of the bandana. "We're not far now. Can you hang on for another ten minutes?"

"I've been hanging on for several days," she said with a grim smile. "Another ten minutes won't kill me."

I helped her back onto the bike, noting how she sagged against me as soon as we were settled. Her arms encircled my waist again, but there was less strength in them now. Blood loss and shock were taking their toll.

The engine roared back to life, and I guided the bike back onto the road, pushing the speed higher than was strictly safe on the wet pavement. Zara's head rested between my shoulder blades, her breath warm but increasingly shallow against my back.

"Stay with me," I murmured, though I knew she couldn't hear me over the wind and engine. "Almost there."

The road curved around a wooded area, and then the club's compound came into view -- a collection of buildings and homes surrounded by a high fence topped with razor wire. Security lights mounted on tall poles cast harsh white light over the lot where several bikes and trucks were parked despite the late hour.

The main gate was closed, but a figure emerged from the guard shack as we approached. One of our Prospects, a young kid called Ash, watched us. He recognized my bike immediately and hurried to open the gate, his eyes widening as he noted the woman clinging to my back.

I rode through without stopping to explain, heading straight for my house at the far end of the compound. As I pulled up into the driveway and stopped in front of the porch, Zara stirred against my back.

"We're here," I said, cutting the engine. The sudden silence was heavy around us, broken only by the distant sound of thunder and the steady drip of water from the eaves.

I dismounted first, then turned to help Zara. She tried to swing her leg over the bike but faltered, nearly falling before I caught her around the waist.

"Easy," I murmured, supporting most of her weight as her feet touched the ground.

She looked up at my face. "I'm not usually this helpless," she said, a note of defiance in her tired voice.

"I know," I responded simply, because I did know. I'd seen how she'd faced those men in the alley, seen the fire in her eyes even when she was on her knees. This woman was a fighter, not a victim. The fact that she was allowing me to help her at all spoke volumes about how bad she must be feeling. I'd met her type before. They didn't accept help easily.

I guided her up the three steps to my front door, unlocked it, and ushered her inside, flipping on lights as we went. The house wasn't much -- living room, kitchen, bathroom, two bedrooms -- but it was clean and secure. Right now, that was all that mattered.

"Sit," I instructed, steering her toward the couch. She sank onto it gratefully, her gaze already scanning the room, taking in the sparse furnishings and the exits. Always assessing, always planning. I was beginning to like this woman.

"I'll call Doc," I said, reaching for my phone. "He'll fix up that arm properly."

Zara nodded, letting her head fall back against the couch cushions. In the harsh overhead light, I could see the full extent of her injuries -- the bruise at her temple had darkened, her lip was split at the corner, and there were defensive marks on her hands.

"Thank you," she said, her gaze meeting mine with unexpected intensity. "For what you did back there. For bringing me here."

I shrugged uncomfortably. Gratitude always made me uneasy. "You said you've been looking for me. Well, now you've found me. Once we get you fixed up, you can tell me exactly why you think I can help find your mother."

She held my gaze steadily. "I don't think you can

help. I know you can."

"Rest," I said, heading for the bathroom to get the first aid kit. "We've got a lot to talk about, but it can wait until that arm is taken care of."

Zara closed her eyes briefly, her hand clutching the edge of my jacket around her. "It's waited this long. I suppose it can wait a little longer."

I paused in the doorway, looking back at her -- this strange, fierce woman who'd appeared in my life out of nowhere. I had a feeling that nothing would be the same after tonight. Whether that was good or bad remained to be seen.

Chapter Three

Zara

He hadn't yet asked the details I'd heard about him, or why I'd come to this town, certain I'd find him. I knew he had to have questions, but so far, he seemed more interested in making sure I was okay. It only proved to me I'd made the right choice to come here. I hadn't met anyone like him before.

Truth be told, a lot of women had heard about Azrael. Even though I lived several hours from the Devil's Boneyard territory, I'd heard whispers about him. When the police hadn't seemed interested in doing their job and finding my mom, I'd known I had to at least try to reach out to him. He'd been my only hope of ever seeing my mother again. I had no way of knowing if she remained in Florida, or if her abductors had taken her elsewhere.

Of course, I hadn't counted on getting jumped and dragged into that alley tonight. It had worked out in the end, but he'd been right when he said I could have died. I'd done my best to sound and appear tough. Honestly, I'd been terrified until he'd shown up. I'd caught sight of the name on his cut, and I'd known he would help me. It had given me the courage I needed.

Being in his home didn't make me as nervous as it should have. I was alone with a man I'd never met before, one who was part of a motorcycle club. From what I'd heard, while his club didn't harm innocent people, there had been a time when things were different. Of course, everything I thought I knew was based on rumors. The truth could be vastly different. But desperate times called for desperate measures... and I was as desperate as a daughter could get. My mother was the only family I had left, at least out of the ones I knew. I'd never met her family. She'd been born in Egypt, but she'd once told me her family was from Israel.

Azrael had stepped away a few minutes ago to call the man he'd referred to as Doc, then moved me to the kitchen table. Better light for Doc, he'd said. When he'd gone to answer the knock at the door, I'd assumed it was Doc. An older man entered the kitchen with Azrael, carrying a bag in his hand, like the type doctors used to carry for house calls. He gave me a kind smile and spoke softly to Azrael, low enough I couldn't hear what they were talking about.

When he approached, I noticed he moved slowly. He eased down onto a chair next to me and assessed me with gentle eyes. "I hear you've had a rough night."

I nodded. "Azrael thinks I need stitches."

He pursed his lips. "Well, he should know. I've put him back together enough times."

I glanced at the man who'd saved me and wondered how often he got hurt doing what he did. And yet, he'd likely heard me scream and come to save me just the same. Most people would have kept walking. Best case scenario, they might have called the police, but I'd never met anyone who would dare enter the alley to try to save a stranger. Until today.

"Let me take a look," Doc said. I held out my arm and he unwrapped the bandana. His face remained blank, as if he hadn't a care in the world. He'd either dealt with much worse, or he was doing his best not to show his emotions so I would remain calm. Either way, I appreciated his bedside manner. "It seems Azrael is correct. I think five or six should close it up. I can numb the area, but the injection is going to burn something awful. Nothing I can do about that."

"It's okay. Not my first time having stitches. Although, the last time I was in the Emergency Room."

He smiled faintly. "All right. Let me prep everything I'll need."

* * *

Azrael

"So," I said conversationally, trying to distract her as Doc treated her wounds, "you said you've been looking for me. How'd you know where to find me?"

Her gaze shifted to my face. "I didn't, not exactly. I knew the general area your club controls. I've been watching, asking questions, putting things together. Women talk, especially when they or someone they know has been saved from being attacked or worse."

"And you met some of those women?" I asked.

"Yeah. I made it to your town but wasn't entirely sure where you'd be once I got here. That alley tonight -- pure coincidence. Bad luck turning good."

"Those men could have killed you," I pointed out, as Doc tied off the second stitch.

"They could have tried," she replied with a hardness that made me reassess her. This woman had more to her than I'd initially thought.

Doc finished the stitches -- five in total -- then dressed the wound with antiseptic ointment and a clean bandage. Zara flexed her arm experimentally, testing the pull of the sutures. She'd said she'd gotten them before. Looked like it was true.

"Thanks," she said, inspecting his work. "Clean stitches."

"Lots of practice." Doc packed away the supplies, then stood. "I'll leave you in Azrael's hands, but if you need me, I'm a phone call away."

"What about antibiotics or pain meds? Can she shower? I'm sure she'd like to clean up," I said.

"She'll be fine without meds. Tylenol if the pain is too much. I put a waterproof bandage over the stitches. If you want to make doubly sure, cover it with plastic wrap or a trash bag. She'll be fine for now."

Doc let himself out and I went over to the coffeemaker and started some coffee. Zara remained at the table. There was still a lot I didn't know about her or the situation, but I doubted I would resolve anything tonight. She'd been through hell and probably needed some sleep. The coffee was more for me than her, but maybe a few sips would warm her up at least. It finished brewing, and I pulled down two mugs, filling hers halfway and mine to the top.

I slid her mug over to her. "It's not some fancy flavor, and I don't have creamer, but it's hot."

She took it gratefully, wrapping both hands around the mug. I hadn't thought about the fact she might have a bag or car somewhere. I'd just focused on getting her out of the alley and away from those men. Now I had time to sit and think.

She looked so innocent under the bright kitchen lights. Wasn't likely she was underage, but it wouldn't hurt to check. "How old are you?" I asked.

"Twenty-two," she replied. "Old enough to know what I'm doing, if that's your concern."

I raised an eyebrow. "And what exactly are you doing, Zara Colton? Besides getting yourself attacked in alleys and stitched up by strangers?"

Her gaze never leaving mine, she said, "Looking for my mother. She disappeared about five days ago. The police say she probably ran off, but they don't know her. She wouldn't leave without telling me, not voluntarily."

"And you think she was taken by... whom? Human traffickers?" Probably not a leap most people would make, but if she'd been looking for me, that had to be the case.

Zara nodded. "I've been doing my own research. Following leads. There've been a lot of missing women, and they fit a certain profile -- exotic-looking, between thirty and forty-five, most with some connection to the Middle East or North Africa."

"Like your mother," I said, seeing where this was going.

"Like my mother," she confirmed. "She's Egyptian. Or rather, that's where she was born. Apparently, her family is actually from Israel. I'm not sure where exactly. I've never met them. Mom met my father when she was only seventeen. The two fell in love and were inseparable. He died a few years ago. In case you were wondering about my eye color, he was an American. Blond-haired and blue-eyed. Everything else I inherited from my mother."

"My mom was also born in the Middle East," I said. "No clue who the fuck my father is, but if I ever find out, I'll be sure to send him straight to hell."

Her eyes widened slightly. I'd said more than I should have. Just the same, I'd meant every word. I leaned back in my chair, studying her.

"Daddy issues?" she asked, probably trying to lighten the moment.

"Mom was gang-raped by three men. I'm the result." I saw her pale, and figured I should have found a better way to tell her. Or kept it to myself.

"You used past tense when saying she's from the Middle East. Does that mean she's gone?" she asked.

I nodded. "Cancer."

She pushed her mug aside, and I noticed she hadn't taken so much as a sip. At least it had warmed her hands. If she was going to stay here, I'd have to find out what she liked. I was a fairly simple man. I kept coffee on hand, occasionally grabbed a soda, but otherwise I drank water.

"You should get cleaned up, then get some rest." I stood up. "We can talk more in the morning. The club will want to hear your story."

She stood as well, swaying slightly before steadying herself on the back of the chair. "I need to know if you're going to help me or not."

I looked at her -- this small, fierce woman with her stitched-up arm and determined eyes. She'd tracked me down, survived an attack, and was still standing, still fighting for her mother. How could I turn her away?

"We'll help you," I said finally. At least, I hoped the club would agree. If not, I'd do what I could on my own. "But understand something -- once you're in, you're in. There's no backing out halfway through. Think you can live with yourself if I have to spill blood in my pursuit of bringing your mom back?"

Zara lifted her chin, a flash of pride in her expression. "I'm not the backing out type. And whoever took my mom would have done it against her will. As far as I'm concerned, they deserve to die."

I liked this woman. More than I should. "I'll lend you something to sleep in. I'm assuming you have clothes stashed somewhere?"

"Yeah. Motel across town." She sighed. "And thank you. For the rescue, the medical care, listening to me. All of it."

I shrugged, uncomfortable again with her gratitude. "Get some sleep, Zara. Tomorrow's going to be a long day."

"Shower, then sleep. You were right. I do want to get cleaned up. I feel grimy after being in that alley."

"Bathroom is across from the spare bedroom. It's the only one in the house, so if the door is closed, it's occupied. Towels are under the sink. There's a spare toothbrush in the drawer."

"I never asked your name," she said softly. "Just know you as Azrael."

"It's better if you don't know it. Around here, I go by my road name. That's all you need for now."

Something like understanding flickered in her eyes. "Fair enough, Azrael, Angel of Death."

She disappeared into the bathroom, closing the door behind her. I fetched a shirt and pair of boxers, then knocked on the door. She cracked it open, the shower already running. I passed them to her, then went to the kitchen, wondering what the hell I'd gotten myself into. Bringing a stranger into the compound was risky enough, but getting involved in her personal issues was another level of complication. The club would have questions, and I didn't have all the answers.

But there was something about Zara Colton -- her determination, her courage, the fire that burned behind those blue eyes -- that told me she was worth the risk. And if her mom had been trafficked, maybe it would tie into the Devil's Minions somehow. I knew the club wouldn't turn her away then.

I settled on the couch, my gun within easy reach, and listened to the quiet sounds of the house. The water in the bathroom shut off, and a few minutes later, I heard the door open and she quietly padded to the bedroom.

She was safe for now, under my protection and

that of the club. Tomorrow would bring its own challenges, but for tonight, at least, the demons had been kept at bay.

For both of us.

Although, I had a feeling Charming would have a few choice words for me. I hadn't exactly asked for permission to bring her here or informed him yet. It actually surprised me he hadn't called or dropped by. Between the Prospect at the gate who'd seen me come here with Zara, and Doc stopping by to treat her, someone should have ratted me out by now. Either they hadn't, or Charming was giving me time to come clean.

"No time like the present," I muttered. I pulled my phone from my pocket and shot off a text to him. If the kids were asleep, no fucking way I was waking them up with a call this time of night.

Saved a woman from getting gang-raped. She's at my house for tonight.

It only took a few minutes for him to respond. *Seems like you're leaving a few things out.*

Shit. Looked like he'd already spoken with Doc. I called Charming's phone, hoping his eleven-year-old twins, Misha and Alek, weren't going to wake up. Those boys would give their dad hell, which meant his wife, Dakota, would be pissed as well.

He picked up before it even finished ringing once.

"Any reason you waited until now to tell me about your houseguest?" he asked, not even bothering with a simple hello.

"She just went to bed. Not mine, just so we're clear. Her name is Zara."

"Not what I asked."

Fucking hell. "I was out riding, heard a scream

- 41 -

and went to check it out. Found her in an alley with three men intent on doing whatever they wanted with her. She was a bit banged up, had to get stitches in one arm. Turns out she was searching for me. I guess I've made a name for myself."

"Angel of Death?" he asked.

"Does everyone but me know about it?"

Charming chuckled. "Most likely. Did she say what she wanted with you?"

"Her mom is missing. I don't have all the details yet. Just know her mom was born in Egypt, but apparently her family is from Israel. Dad was American. Died a few years ago. Sounds like it's just her and her mom."

I heard Charming walking through his house, then a door open and shut. I was willing to bet he'd gone outside so he wouldn't bother his family. "How old is she?"

"Says she's twenty-two. It's not like I asked for her ID." I tipped my head back and closed my eyes. "Now you know as much as I do. I'll see what I can get from her, but I'm probably going to need some help on this one. She wants me to find her mom."

"We'll talk more in the morning. But you know damn well she can't move in with you."

Before I could say anything in response, he ended the call. I stared at the phone a moment before I got up. After I made sure all the doors were locked, I went to the bedroom and stripped out of my clothes, then flopped back on the bed. I had a feeling things were about to become complicated.

Chapter Four

Azrael

I didn't invite many people into my home. There was a reason for that -- plenty of them, actually -- but I'd made an exception for Zara. Completely out of character for me, but I hadn't been able to just leave her in that alley.

I'd let her sleep in this morning, but apparently the smell of bacon had woken her. Of course, I still didn't know about her food preferences. My mother had been raised Muslim, but she hadn't raised me in the faith. Bacon had been on our table when we could afford it. But I wasn't sure about Zara.

She padded into the kitchen, looking rather adorable in my clothes. I fought not to smile.

"Sit," I told her, pointing to one of the wooden chairs at my kitchen table.

She didn't sit. Instead, she paced, her hands twisting in front of her. Her blue eyes darted around the space, taking in the sparse furnishings, the worn countertops, the tidy sink. She hadn't really gotten a good look at my house last night. Now, in the broad light of day, everything was laid bare. I wondered what she'd expected. Probably not this -- not a simple house at the edge of the Devil's Boneyard compound, tucked away from the noise and chaos.

I turned on the faucet, letting cold water wash over my hands. "It's time to talk. I need all the details you can give me. Start at the beginning. Pretend we didn't speak last night."

"My mother's been taken."

I studied her face carefully. I remembered her saying she was twenty-two. She was young -- too young to be mixed up in the kind of shit that usually found its way to my doorstep. Pretty in a way that was hard to ignore, with skin a few shades darker than mine and those startling blue eyes.

"What makes you think that?" I asked.

"She's been missing for days. She wouldn't just leave. Not without telling me." Zara's fingers tightened on the chair. "I went to her house, and there were signs of a struggle. A broken vase. Her purse was still there, her phone."

"You call the cops?"

She let out a bitter laugh. "Yeah. They took a report. Said they'd look into it. Then they asked if my mother had any 'male friends' she might have gone off with. Asked if she was the type to do drugs, to disappear on benders."

"Even with the scene laid out the way it was?"

"Yeah. They said she could have accidentally knocked the vase over or some bullshit along those lines." She gave a heavy sigh.

I nodded, unsurprised. "Your mother's name?"

"Mazida. Mazida Quadir."

"And your father?"

"Carter Colton. Like I mentioned last night, he's been dead a few years now."

I pushed away from the counter and walked to the refrigerator, pulling out the orange juice. I poured two glasses and set them on the table, then retrieved the food I'd made.

"If you don't eat pork, I might have some chicken." I put a plate down and she finally pulled out the chair and sat.

"This is fine. Dad loved his bacon. Probably why he had a heart attack."

I took my own seat across from her. "Tell me about your mother. Who'd want to hurt her?"

"She's quiet. Keeps to herself. She married my dad when she was nineteen. He brought her here from Egypt. After he died, it was just the two of us."

"She work?" I'd found people didn't typically disappear at random. Although, some just had rotten luck. It was possible someone had taken notice of her and decided they had to own her. But most of the people I tracked down had gotten mixed up with someone they shouldn't have. A lot of young girls didn't understand a handsome guy with a nice smile could be hiding a black heart and a cruel streak.

"At a community center. Helping immigrant women adjust to life here. Teaching English, helping with paperwork. That kind of thing." She paused. "And she sometimes helped them escape from abusive situations."

I took a bite of food, letting the information settle. "Any strange calls? Men hanging around? Someone from her past show up unexpectedly?"

Zara's eyes widened slightly. "There was a man. About a month ago. I didn't see him, but Mom was upset after he visited. She wouldn't tell me who he was, just that it was someone from 'before.'"

"Before what?"

"Before America, I guess." Zara ran a hand through her hair. "She was raised in a strict household. Her father arranged a marriage for her when she was seventeen. That's why she ran -- to avoid being forced to marry some old man she'd never met. As I mentioned last night, her family is from Israel. I don't know why they moved to Egypt, or if they're even still there. I've never met any of them."

I rubbed my jaw. "You think this has something to do with her family? After all these years?"

"I don't know." Zara's voice cracked. "I just

know she's gone, and no one seems to care except me."

I studied her for a long moment. There was something she wasn't telling me -- I could see it in the way she wouldn't quite meet my eyes.

"How'd you hear about me, Zara? The truth."

She looked up then, her gaze steady despite the fear I could see behind it. "My mother told me about you. Not by name, but she said there was a man -- an avenging angel -- who sometimes helped women when they had nowhere else to turn. A few of the women at the center, they whispered about you too. How you've helped women escape abusive husbands, how you've punished men who hurt children. The fact you're one of us impressed them."

"Us?" I asked.

She nodded. "From the Middle East."

My jaw tightened. I hadn't expected that. Hadn't expected to be a story mothers told their daughters, a whispered legend among women who needed help.

"And what exactly do you think I can do that the police can't?" I asked, though I already knew the answer.

"Find her," Zara said simply. "And hurt whoever took her."

I finished my food and set the plate in the sink. Part of me wanted to send her away. This wasn't my usual game -- I dealt in certainties, in punishment for crimes I knew had been committed. Not in solving mysteries or finding missing persons. There had been a few exceptions over the years, but not many.

There was something about the desperation in her eyes that I recognized. I'd seen it before, in my own reflection.

"You have somewhere to stay?" I asked.

She shook her head. "I have to check out of the

motel today. I spent everything I had trying to find you."

I rubbed my eyes, already knowing this was going to blow up in my face. I'd let her stay here last night, but Charming had made it clear she couldn't remain.

"If we're going to help you, we need my President's approval."

"And will he approve?" Her voice was small.

I thought about Charming, about the unwritten rules of the Devil's Boneyard MC. We had a code -- protect women and children, always. But we also had boundaries. Lines we tried not to cross without good reason.

"I guess we'll find out," I said, then turned to wash my empty plate. As the water ran over my hands again, I found myself wondering if I was about to wash blood off them again soon. Some things were inevitable in my line of work.

I glanced back at Zara, at the way she sat ramrod straight in the chair, trying to look brave despite the fear that clung to her like a second skin. She'd come to me for a reason, tracked me down based on whispers and rumors. She'd put her trust in a man known for violence.

I just hoped I wouldn't end up letting her down. Or worse, dragging her into the kind of darkness that surrounded me like a shroud.

* * *

The Devil's Boneyard clubhouse was alive with the usual activity when I pulled up with Zara on the back of my bike. Brothers milled around outside, some smoking, others working on bikes in the fading light. A few of them straightened when they saw me, eyes narrowing at the unfamiliar woman. I killed the engine and turned to Zara, whose eyes had gone wide at the sight of so many patched members in one place.

"Stay close to me," I told her. "Don't make eye contact unless someone speaks to you directly."

She nodded, her shoulders tensing visibly. "They look... intimidating."

"That's the point." I climbed off the bike and waited for her to join me. "But they won't hurt you. At least, the men won't."

I placed my hand at the small of her back as we approached the clubhouse, a gesture that wouldn't be lost on my brothers. It was a clear signal -- this woman was under my protection, at least for now. Several nodded in acknowledgment as we passed, though I could feel their curious gazes following us.

The clubhouse doors swung open. Music played from speakers mounted in the corners, not loud enough to drown conversation but sufficient to provide privacy for those who wanted it.

"Azrael," a voice called from behind the bar. One of the Prospects, a young guy who'd been hanging around for about six months. Earnest, but green as hell. "President's waiting for you in Church. Said to bring your... guest."

I nodded and guided Zara through the room, aware of the conversations that quieted as we passed, the speculative glances that followed us. The women were more obvious in their scrutiny, several of them whispering behind their hands. Club women always knew when something was off -- when a new female entered their territory. And they sure as fuck didn't like the idea someone might snatch a patch from their hands. Not that any of them had a snowball's chance in hell of getting claimed by us.

At the back of the main room, a heavy wooden

door marked the entrance to our meeting room -- what we called Church. I stopped and turned to Zara.

"Wait here," I said, gesturing to a chair outside the door. "This meeting is members only, unless Charming says otherwise."

"But didn't he say to bring me?" she asked.

"Until I hear it from his lips that he wants you in the room, wait here. He may just want you close by."

Fear flickered across her face. "What if someone - _"

"No one will bother you." I caught the eye of the same Prospect who'd spoken to us earlier. "Hey. Make sure she's comfortable. Get her something to drink. Non-alcoholic."

The Prospect straightened. "Yes, sir."

I gave Zara's shoulder a reassuring squeeze, then pushed open the door to Church and stepped inside.

The room fell silent as I entered. Around the long wooden table sat the core members of the Devil's Boneyard MC. At the head, Charming watched me with measured eyes, his silver-streaked hair and face reflecting the decades he'd spent leading the club. To his right, Havoc -- our Sergeant-at-Arms -- sat with his massive arms crossed over his chest, his red hair now more white than copper, but his blue eyes as sharp as ever. Beside him was Renegade, our Road Captain, his expression unreadable beneath his graying beard.

Other brothers filled the remaining seats -- men I'd ridden with for years, men whose blood had mixed with mine on more than one occasion. They all watched me with varying degrees of curiosity and concern.

"Azrael," Charming said, gesturing to an empty chair. "Sit. Tell us what's so urgent it couldn't wait. I know you gave me the basics last night but get all of us up to speed. Depending on how this goes, we'll call in the others."

I took my seat but didn't relax into it. "There's a woman outside. Zara Colton. Her mother's been missing for several days. Signs of abduction. Police don't seem interested in pursuing it."

"And this concerns us how?" one of the brothers asked from farther down the table.

I fixed him with a hard stare. "Her mother helps at a community center for immigrant women. Helps them adjust to life here, navigate the system. She's spent years helping women escape bad situations. Sound fucking familiar?"

"One of ours?" Havoc asked, leaning forward.

I shook my head. "No. But she knows about us -- about what we do for women in trouble. Or at least, she knows about me. She's told her daughter stories about the 'avenging angel' who helps women when they have nowhere else to turn. Seems the other ladies at the center know about me too."

A murmur ran around the table. Our reputation in certain circles was something we cultivated carefully -- we wanted the right people to know they could come to us for help, but we kept a low profile with law enforcement and rival organizations.

"The cops?" Renegade asked, his voice rumbling from deep in his chest. "You said they aren't doing anything?"

"Took a report. Suggested she might have run off with a man or be on a bender." I snorted. "Standard bullshit. They're not looking."

Havoc's fist came down hard on the table, making several brothers jump. "Fucking typical," he growled. "Woman goes missing, they don't give a shit unless she's rich or connected."

His rage wasn't surprising. Havoc had a special hatred for men who harmed women -- we all did.

"What else do we know?" Charming asked, seemingly unaffected by Havoc's outburst.

I leaned forward, resting my forearms on the table. "Mother's name is Mazida Quadir. Middle Eastern origin, came to the States when she was nineteen. She married an American named Carter Colton when she was seventeen in order to escape an arranged marriage. Colton died a few years ago. Zara says there's been a man around recently -- someone from Mazida's past, from 'before America.' She thinks it might be connected."

Renegade uncrossed his arms and scratched at his beard. "Family honor shit, maybe? Those cultures, they don't forget when a woman dishonors them. Even after decades. Hell, if anyone knows about that, it's you."

"That's what I'm thinking," I agreed. "But there could be more to it. The community center -- it's the kind of place that helps women escape abusive situations. Could have made enemies."

"Or somebody took a liking to her," another brother suggested. "Decided to take what wasn't offered."

The thought made my jaw clench, but I nodded. "Possible."

Charming hadn't moved, his eyes steady on me. "And the girl? This Zara? What's her situation?"

"She's been sleeping at a motel, but says she has to check out today. Spent everything she had trying to find me based on rumors and whispers." I met his gaze evenly. "I let her sleep in my spare room last night. I can't exactly toss her out on the street today."

That raised a few eyebrows around the table.

"Since when do you bring strays home, Angel Boy?" someone asked from the far end.

I didn't bother looking at whoever had spoken. My eyes stayed on Charming. "She's desperate. Scared. And she came to us for help."

"To you," Charming corrected. "She came to you."

"Same thing," I said, a slight edge entering my voice.

Havoc leaned forward, forearms on the table. "I say we help. If her mother's been helping women get out of bad situations, she's doing the same work we do. Just in a different way."

Renegade nodded slowly, his eyes scanning the room. "Could be a trap. Someone using this girl to get close to us."

"It's not," I said firmly. "You didn't see her face. Girl is tough as hell, and didn't back down when she was attacked last night, but she's scared. That kind of fear can't be faked."

The room fell quiet as everyone looked to Charming. As President, his word was final. If he decided the club wouldn't get involved, that would be it -- officially, at least.

"What's your plan?" he asked finally.

I straightened in my chair. "Start with the mother's house. Look for anything the cops might have missed. Talk to the women at the community center, see if they know anything. Track down this man from her past."

"And if you find whoever took her?" Charming's voice was measured, careful.

The room seemed to hold its breath, waiting for my answer. They all knew what I was capable of. What I'd done in the name of justice -- or vengeance, depending on who you asked.

"I'll find Mazida," I said simply.

Charming's eyes narrowed slightly. "Even if I tell you to stand down?"

A tension crept into the room, electric and uncomfortable. Challenging the President wasn't something done lightly, not even by a brother with my standing in the club. I chose my next words carefully.

"We've never walked away from a situation like this before," I said, my voice low but firm. "A woman in danger, a daughter pleading for help. We've built our reputation on being different from other MCs -- on protecting women and children when no one else will. Are we going to throw that away now?"

Havoc grunted in agreement, while Renegade's gaze shifted between Charming and me, assessing the building tension.

"This isn't about disobeying orders," I continued. "It's about who we are as a club. As brothers." I leaned forward slightly. "And you know as well as I do, Charming, that if it was your woman missing, you'd want every brother out there looking, rules be damned."

A heavy silence fell over the room. Some of the brothers looked down at the table, others exchanged glances. What I'd said wasn't wrong, and they all knew it. Our code -- both written and unwritten -- put the protection of women and children above almost everything else.

Charming held my gaze for a long moment, his expression unreadable. Then, almost imperceptibly, he nodded.

"You've got club resources," he said finally. "But you take Havoc and Renegade with you when you start digging. No lone wolf shit, understand? This is club business now."

Relief washed through me, though I kept my face neutral. "Understood."

"What about the girl?" Renegade asked. "She gonna stay at your place while we handle this?"

And there it was -- the question I'd been expecting since I walked in. Club rules were clear about women staying at the compound. They either belonged to a member, or they didn't stay. Period.

Charming's eyebrow raised slightly, waiting for my answer. I could feel the weight of every brother's gaze on me, the unspoken question hanging in the air.

What exactly was Zara Colton to me?

Chapter Five

Azrael

Charming leaned back in his chair, gaze fixed on me with the kind of intensity that had made grown men squirm since before he became President. "So, Azrael," he said, his voice deceptively casual, "what exactly do you plan to do with Zara while we look for her mother?"

I knew what he was really asking. Every man at that table did.

"She's got nowhere to go," I said, keeping my voice even. "If she wants to remain close to the club, she'd be living out of her car. I can't exactly throw her out."

Havoc shifted in his seat. "She staying in your bed?"

I shot him a look that would have made a lesser man flinch. "Like I said, the guest room. This isn't about that."

"Maybe it should be," someone muttered from down the table. I didn't bother to see who.

Charming raised a hand, silencing the room. "You know the rules, Azrael. A woman stays at the compound, she belongs to someone. Period. Unless she's club pussy." His eyes didn't waver from mine. "No exceptions, not even for you."

The rules weren't arbitrary. They existed for a reason -- to protect the club, to maintain order, to avoid the kind of jealousy and infighting that had torn other MCs apart. Women who weren't claimed were free game for everyone, or they couldn't stay. It was simple, brutal math.

"She's not looking to join the life," I said. "She just needs a safe place to stay while we find her mother."

"Doesn't matter," Renegade said, his voice rumbling through the tension. "Rules are rules. Either she's your woman, or she's not staying."

I felt a tightness in my chest at the thought. It had been a long time since I'd been with anyone. A very long time. The last woman who'd been mine had ended up in a body bag, and I'd made a promise to myself after that -- no more innocents dragged into my world, no more blood on my hands that didn't belong to those who deserved it.

But Zara was already in danger. She'd be sleeping in her car, vulnerable to anyone who might come looking for her. And if the people who took her mother decided to tie up loose ends...

"I'm not making that decision for her," I said finally. "She didn't come here looking for a man. She came looking for help."

"Then help her pay for a motel," one of the brothers suggested.

I shook my head. "And leave her unprotected? If the people who took her mother decide she knows too much, or if they're looking to grab her too, she's dead."

"So protect her," Charming said simply. "Make her yours."

The way he said it made it sound so easy, so straightforward. Like claiming a woman was as simple as picking up a new shirt or buying a drink. For some of the brothers, maybe it was. But not for me. Not anymore.

"You know what that means," Havoc said, leaning forward. "She wears your patch, she's your responsibility. Your property, as far as the outside world is concerned."

"I know what it means," I said, my voice

hardening slightly. "I've been around long enough."

Charming studied me for a moment, then smiled. It wasn't a warm expression -- more like a predator sizing up its prey. "You afraid, Angel Boy? Afraid you might actually come to feel something for this girl?"

A few chuckles rippled around the table. I ignored them.

"I'm concerned about her safety," I said. "And about her consent. This isn't some club hang-around looking to be claimed. She's a civilian with a missing mother who came to us -- to me -- for help."

"So explain it to her," Renegade suggested. "Tell her how it works. Let her decide."

I nodded slowly. That was fair. Let Zara make her own choice, with all the information. If she decided the protection of the club -- of me -- wasn't worth the strings attached, I'd help her find somewhere else to stay.

"I'll talk to her," I agreed. "Explain the situation."

Charming nodded, apparently satisfied. "Good. In the meantime, I want you and Havoc to check out the mother's house tomorrow. Renegade, talk to your contacts in law enforcement, see if there's anything on the woman's disappearance they're not sharing publicly."

"What about the community center?" I asked.

"Day after," Charming decided. "We don't want to spook whoever's behind this by showing up everywhere at once. Start with the primary scene, then branch out."

The others nodded in agreement. It was a solid plan -- methodical, careful. The kind of approach that had kept the Devil's Boneyard one step ahead of rivals and law enforcement for decades.

"One more thing," Charming added, his eyes finding mine again. "If the girl decides to stay -- if she becomes yours -- you keep her out of club business. She doesn't need to know details, doesn't need to see things that might complicate matters down the road."

I knew what he meant. If we found the people responsible for Mazida's disappearance, what happened next wouldn't be pretty. Wouldn't be legal. And while Zara might want justice for her mother, witnessing club justice firsthand was different from imagining it.

"Understood," I said quietly.

Charming's gaze lingered on me for a moment longer, then he turned to address the rest of the table. "Anything else?" When no one spoke, he nodded. "Then we're done here. Keep this quiet for now -- no discussing it with your women or Prospects until we know more. I'll fill the others in after Azrael makes a decision about Zara."

The meeting broke up, brothers rising from their seats and filing out of the room. A few clapped me on the shoulder as they passed -- a silent show of support. Havoc lingered, waiting until most of the others had left before speaking.

"You sure about this?" he asked, his voice low.

I gave him a sideways look. "Who said I was taking responsibility for anything yet? She might tell me to go to hell when I explain the rules."

He snorted. "Doubt it. I might have gotten to my seat before you, but I saw the way she looked at you when you two came in. Girl's already halfway to being yours whether she knows it or not. Maybe she fell in love with the legend before she ever met you."

Before I could respond, Renegade joined us. "Just so we're clear," he said, "if we find whoever took her mother, they're not walking away, right?"

My jaw tightened. "No. They're not."

Both men nodded, satisfied with my answer. It was one of the things I respected most about the club -- when it came to protecting women and children, there were no half measures, no compromises.

"See you in the morning," Havoc said, clapping me on the back before heading out. "Meet at the gate by seven o'clock."

Renegade gave me a measuring look. "Been a long time since you had a steady woman in your life, brother. Might do you some good."

I didn't respond to that, just watched as he followed Havoc out the door, leaving me alone in the now-empty Church. I took a deep breath, trying to clear my head.

The choice ahead of me wasn't simple. If Zara agreed to be "mine," it would mean pulling her further into a world she probably couldn't imagine. A world of violence, loyalty, and rigid codes. A world where women were protected, yes, but also possessed. Well, with some exceptions. There were always those like Havoc's woman, Jordan. But they were few and far between.

If she refused, I'd have to find somewhere else for her to stay -- somewhere beyond the compound's protection, beyond my ability to keep her safe every minute of every day.

I rubbed my hand across my face. Then I stood, straightened my cut, and headed for the door. Time to have a conversation with Zara Colton about exactly what she'd gotten herself into.

I stepped out of Church and noticed the seat by the door was vacant. I moved to the main room, scanning the area. I found Zara sitting at a corner table, a can of soda in front of her. The Prospect I'd assigned to watch her was seated across from her, looking bored but attentive. A few of the club women cast curious glances her way, but none had approached her yet. That would change if she stayed -- they'd want to size up any new female in their territory, especially one connected to me. Thankfully, she'd have the old ladies to back her.

Zara straightened when she saw me approach, relief visible in the softening of her shoulders. The Prospect stood immediately.

"Everything good, sir?" he asked, trying to sound casual but unable to hide his curiosity.

"Fine," I said. "You can go."

He hesitated only a moment before nodding and retreating to the bar, where I knew he'd be pressed for information by his fellow Prospects. I slid into the chair he'd vacated, taking in Zara's appearance. She looked tired, the kind of bone-deep exhaustion that came from days of worry and nights without proper sleep.

"Are they going to help?" she asked, leaning forward and keeping her voice low. "Will they help find my mother?"

I nodded. "Yes. We start tomorrow. Havoc and I will check out your mother's house, see if there's anything the police missed. Another brother is going to make some calls, see if there's any information law enforcement isn't sharing."

Zara's eyes widened slightly. "You have contacts in the police?"

"We have contacts everywhere," I said simply. "That's how the club operates. We maintain relationships with people who can provide information when needed."

She nodded slowly, taking a sip of her soda.

"Thank you. I didn't know if... I wasn't sure they'd agree to help."

"The Devil's Boneyard has a code," I told her. "Protecting women and children is part of that code. Your mother's work -- helping women escape bad situations -- aligns with what we do, just in a different way."

Relief flooded her face, and for a moment I thought she might cry. Instead, she took a deep breath and composed herself.

"So what happens now? Do I go back to your place?" she asked.

This was the moment. The conversation I'd been dreading since Charming laid out the club's position. I leaned forward, resting my forearms on the table, trying to find the right words.

"There's something we need to discuss first," I said carefully. "About you staying here at the compound."

She tilted her head slightly. "Is that a problem?"

"The club has rules," I began. "Strict ones, about who can stay here and under what circumstances."

Zara's brow furrowed. "I don't understand."

I took a breath. "Women who stay at the compound need to belong to the club in some way. Either they... entertain the club members, or they belong to just one of us."

"Belong?" Her voice had gone quiet, and I could see her processing what I was saying. "You mean like... property?"

"That's how the outside world would see it," I acknowledged. "In reality, it's more complicated. A woman who belongs to a member is under his protection. She wears his patch, follows certain rules, and in return, she gets the security of the entire club standing behind her. Think of it like a marriage but without the legal crap."

Zara was silent for a long moment, her fingers tapping against her soda can. "And if I don't agree to... belong to someone?"

"Then you can't stay at the compound," I said simply. "I'd help you find somewhere safe to stay while we look for your mother, but it wouldn't be here."

She looked around the room, taking in the club members scattered throughout, the women by their sides. Across the room, I spotted Janessa with Irish. Looked like she was giving him hell in hushed tones, probably because of the club girl eyeing him like a steak.

"These women," she said quietly. "They've agreed to this? To being someone's property?"

"The one in the property cut has. The others are free game for anyone," I corrected. "Many of them came from bad situations -- abusive relationships, dangerous family dynamics. The club offers them safety, stability. In return, they accept certain roles and rules."

Zara's gaze found mine again. "And who would I belong to? Just... anyone who wants me?"

I shook my head firmly. "No. That's not how it works. You'd have a choice in who claims you, if anyone. No woman is forced into a relationship she doesn't want."

"But I'd have to choose someone, or leave."

"Yes."

She fell silent again, her gaze dropping to the table. I could see her weighing her options, thinking through the implications of what I was telling her. Part of me wanted to make it easier for her -- to tell her she didn't have to decide right away, that we could figure something out. But that would be a lie, and I'd promised myself I wouldn't lie to her.

"What about you?" she asked suddenly, her eyes lifting to meet mine.

The question caught me off guard. "What about me?"

"Could I..." She hesitated, a slight flush coloring her cheeks. "Could I be yours? Would you claim me?"

Something tightened in my chest at her words. It had been a long time since anyone had asked to be mine -- a long time since I'd considered allowing it. When I'd lost the only woman I'd cared about, aside from my mother, I'd sworn to never let anyone that close again.

But Zara was already in danger. Already connected to me through her search for help. And if I was honest with myself, there was something about her that pulled at me -- a strength beneath her vulnerability that I found myself drawn to.

"Is that what you want?" I asked, keeping my voice neutral. "To be mine?"

She didn't answer immediately, which I respected. This wasn't a decision to be made lightly.

"I came to you for help," she said finally. "When I heard about you, about what you do for women in trouble, I knew I had to find you. And now you're offering to help find my mother, to protect me. If the choice is between belonging to you or leaving the compound, then yes, I choose you."

"If it's because you want to be close and can't afford a motel..." I trailed off, not really sure what I was offering. Money? Or just making sure this was what she really wanted.

"While it's true I don't want to go home and

wish to remain close, it's more than that. I wasn't in your town long before I was attacked. If you hadn't happened by at the right moment, I might very well be dead right now. Or wishing I was."

"Plenty of people walk around this place without getting into trouble. But if someone really did snatch your mom, and they know about you, it's possible they could be waiting to grab you as well. Just speculation since there's shit we don't know about the situation yet."

"I feel safe when I'm with you," she said softly.

I studied her face, looking for any sign of hesitation or fear. I saw uncertainty, yes, but also determination. She'd made her decision with eyes open.

"You understand what it means?" I pressed. "In the eyes of the club, you'd be my woman. My responsibility. The outside world would see you as my property. And it wouldn't be a temporary thing. Like I said, it's similar to a marriage. There's no backing out once it's done."

"I understand." She lifted her chin slightly. "Would I have to… share your bed?"

Another complicated question. The relationship usually included physical intimacy. But there were exceptions -- arrangements of convenience or protection that didn't involve sex. Maybe not in my club, but I'd heard of others doing something similar. Although, most ended up falling in love at some point.

"Not if you don't want to," I said honestly. "We can take our time, get to know one another better. But let me just put this out there. The men in this club don't cheat on their women. So, if you never come to my bed, be prepared for a grumpy-ass old man because I'll have blue balls."

Something flickered in her eyes -- relief, perhaps, or maybe something else entirely. "And if I stay with you, I'll be safe while you look for my mother?"

"As safe as I can make you," I promised. "Which is safer than anywhere else you could be right now."

She nodded slowly, seeming to come to a final decision. "Then I want to be yours, Azrael."

I felt something shift inside me at her words -- a door opening that I'd kept firmly closed for years. It was unsettling, but not entirely unwelcome.

"If that's what you want," I said, giving her a slow smile, "then yeah, I can make that happen."

Zara returned my smile, tentative but genuine. "What happens now?"

"Now, I talk to Charming, make it official. You'll get a property cut -- something that shows you're under my protection." I leaned back in my chair. "And tomorrow, we start looking for your mother."

A shadow crossed her face at the mention of Mazida. "Do you really think we'll find her?"

"Yes," I said, with more certainty than I perhaps felt. "The club has resources most people can't imagine. If your mother is out there, we'll find her."

I didn't add the darker possibility -- that we might find her too late. Zara didn't need to hear that, not when hope was the only thing keeping her going.

She reached across the table, her hand hesitantly covering mine. "Thank you. For everything."

I turned my hand over, clasping hers briefly before releasing it. Public displays of affection weren't my style, especially in the clubhouse where every interaction was noted and discussed later.

"Don't thank me yet," I said, rising from my chair. "This is just the beginning. Wait here. I need to speak with Charming, make our arrangement official."

Zara Colton was now my responsibility -- my woman, in the eyes of the club. I'd sworn I wouldn't let anyone get that close again, wouldn't risk another innocent life because of my lifestyle, my enemies.

But sometimes life didn't give you the choices you wanted. Sometimes it only offered the least bad option, and you had to take it.

I glanced back at Zara, sitting alone at the table, her posture straight despite the exhaustion I knew she must be feeling. She'd come to me because she believed I could help her, believed in the stories she'd heard about the avenging angel who protected women in trouble.

Now I had to live up to that reputation -- had to find her mother and keep Zara safe in the process.

And I had to do it all without letting her get too close, without letting her become the kind of weakness my enemies could exploit.

It was going to be a delicate balance. But as I caught Charming's eye across the room and saw him nod in acknowledgment, I knew there was no turning back. Zara Colton was mine now, for better or worse.

And God help anyone who tried to hurt what was mine.

Chapter Six

Zara

The Prospect -- I hadn't bothered learning his name -- drove with one hand on the wheel, the other tapping an impatient rhythm against his thigh. I stared out the window, watching unfamiliar streets blur past, trying to process how quickly my life had careened off its predictable path. Twenty-four hours ago, I'd been a regular woman with a regular job and a regular apartment. Now I was riding in a club truck with a man who wore a leather cut that read "Prospect" on the back, heading to collect my belongings before moving in with a man people called the Angel of Death.

"You good?" the Prospect asked, shooting me a sidelong glance.

I nodded, not trusting my voice. What was there to say? That I was terrified? That a man named Azrael had declared I was under his protection -- and apparently that meant living under his roof for the rest of my life? In all fairness, he *had* given me a choice. Not much of one, but still...

The truck smelled like cigarettes and pine air freshener, an odd combination that made my nose twitch. The Prospect had a tattoo creeping up his neck -- some kind of twisted vine with thorns. His knuckles were scabbed over, evidence of a recent fight. These were the kinds of details I used to only notice in movies about dangerous men. Now they were my reality.

"Charming says you're important," he said, breaking the silence. "Says Azrael's claimed you."

I straightened in my seat. "It's not like I'm luggage or a stray puppy. He's protecting me."

The Prospect snorted. "Claim. Protect. Same thing in our world, sweetheart."

"I'm not your sweetheart," I snapped.

To his credit, he grinned rather than took offense. "Yep. You'll fit right in with the old ladies."

I bit back another retort. This wasn't the time to make enemies, especially not with someone who was apparently loyal to the man who now controlled my immediate future. I'd been clear with Azrael that I wasn't ready for a real relationship with someone I'd just met. He'd said we could take things slowly, but what if he changed his mind?

The Prospect pulled into the motel parking lot, a run-down place where I'd spent the night before Azrael had swooped in to save me.

"I'll wait here," he said, putting the truck in park. "Don't take forever."

I rolled my eyes and climbed out. The sun beat down mercilessly, making the faded asphalt shimmer with heat. My room was on the ground floor, second from the end. The key card took three swipes before the light blinked green.

Inside, the air conditioner rattled and wheezed, barely cooling the stuffy room. I hadn't unpacked much -- just enough for one night. My toothbrush on the bathroom counter. A change of clothes draped over the single chair. My phone charger plugged into the wall.

As I gathered my meager belongings, reality hit me like a slap. I was leaving my life behind. My apartment with its mismatched furniture and the balcony where I drank my morning coffee. My job at the accounting firm where I'd worked for three years. My book club that met every second Thursday. All of it suspended indefinitely. Probably forever.

"Fuck," I whispered, sitting heavily on the edge of the bed. The springs creaked beneath me.

I'd always thought of myself as strong, independent. The kind of woman who made her own choices and stood by them. Now I was being shuffled around like a chess piece by men with nicknames instead of real names, men who killed without hesitation and lived by a code I didn't understand.

But what choice did I have? Azrael was my only chance at finding my mother. Now that my father was gone, she was all I had left.

I shoved the last of my things into my overnight bag and did one final sweep of the room. Nothing left behind. I stared at my reflection in the bathroom mirror for a long moment. I looked the same -- dark hair pulled back in a ponytail, wary blue eyes, lips pressed into a tight line. But everything had changed.

The Prospect was leaning against the truck when I emerged, smoking a cigarette. He dropped it and crushed it under his boot when he saw me.

"That it?" he asked, eyeing my single bag.

"I travel light," I said. Most of my life was still in my apartment.

"You'll need to get the rest of your stuff soon. Or rather someone will most likely be sent to retrieve it. Azrael won't want you going back to your place alone."

I ignored that and walked to the motel office to check out. The clerk barely looked up from her phone as I slid the key card across the counter. One more tie severed.

Back in the parking lot, I headed for my car -- a modest sedan that had never seemed smaller or more vulnerable than it did parked next to the massive club truck.

"Follow me," the Prospect called. "Stay close."

I tossed my bag into the passenger seat and slid behind the wheel. My hands trembled slightly as I turned the key. The Prospect pulled out of the lot, and I fell in behind him, keeping a careful distance between us.

The route he took was circuitous, seeming to take twice as long as it had on the way to the motel. I wondered if he was taking a deliberately convoluted path to confuse me or to ensure we weren't being followed.

My mind drifted to Azrael. The intensity in his dark eyes when he'd told me I had a choice to make -- take my chances on my own or stay. I trusted him. Whether that was the right decision I couldn't be sure. What I did know is that I'd been half in love with him before we'd ever met. The stories I'd heard had given me a big case of hero worship. When I'd first met Azrael, he'd lived up to his name. But since then, I'd seen his softer side.

The Prospect's brake lights flashed, drawing me back to the present. We were approaching the front gate. I hadn't really taken the time to pay attention to it. The gate was set into a high fence. The fence extended in both directions, topped with razor wire. Very welcoming. Of course, it also meant whoever was inside should be safe.

A man emerged from a small building beside the gate, hand resting casually on the gun at his hip. He nodded to the Prospect, then peered into my car. I met his gaze steadily, refusing to show fear. After a moment, he stepped back and pressed a button. The gate rolled open with a metallic groan.

Welcome to the Devil's Boneyard. My new home.

The compound sprawled across what looked to

be twenty or more acres. A large clubhouse dominated the center -- a low, sprawling building with motorcycles parked in neat rows outside. Smaller structures were scattered around it -- houses, garages, what looked like a workshop. Men in cuts moved purposefully between buildings. A few women lounged outside the clubhouse, wearing clothes that left little to the imagination.

The Prospect led me past the main cluster of buildings to a section that seemed more residential. Here, the houses were well-maintained, with actual yards and carports instead of dirt patches. He turned down a narrow drive and pulled up in front of a single-story house painted a deep blue with white trim. The same one Azrael had brought me to the night before.

I parked in the driveway and took a breath, trying to steady my nerves. The Prospect turned and drove back toward the clubhouse, leaving me alone. Well, not entirely. I'd parked next to Azrael's bike, which meant he was inside waiting for me.

I took a deep breath and walked to the front door. It wasn't locked. I pushed it open slowly and followed the sound of movement to the kitchen. And there he was.

Azrael leaned against the counter, a mug of coffee in his hand. He wore faded jeans and a black T-shirt that stretched across his broad shoulders. His dark hair was damp, like he'd recently showered, and his equally dark eyes watched me with an intensity that made my skin prickle.

I wondered what job he'd been sent on, but he'd made it clear I wasn't supposed to ask. He'd intended to go with me to the motel. Then at the last minute, he'd said he was sending someone to watch over me.

He'd had weapons strapped to him and looked like he was about to go on a mission. But now he was back, and freshly showered.

The Angel of Death in his natural habitat, drinking coffee like a normal person. It reminded me of the breakfast he'd made that morning. For someone who killed people like it was just another day, he was oddly domesticated.

He flashed me a smile that transformed his face from intimidating to devastatingly handsome. "Welcome home," he said, the words simple but holding meaning.

Home. This place wasn't my home. My home was a third-floor apartment with a leaky faucet and a fire escape where I grew basil plants. This was a stranger's house where I'd slept one night because said stranger had decided I needed protection. Yet something about the way he said it -- like he meant it -- made my stomach flip in a way I refused to examine too closely.

"Is it?" I asked, setting my bag down by the kitchen island. "Home, I mean."

Azrael's smile faded slightly, replaced by something more considering. He took a slow sip of his coffee before answering. "For better or worse."

I nodded, not trusting myself to respond. The kitchen was clean and surprisingly well-equipped. I hadn't allowed myself time to really take anything in last night or this morning. So now, I did. A professional-grade range against one wall. Clean yet worn countertops. A knife block with handles worn from use. Homey and masculine at once.

"Coffee?" he asked, indicating the full pot behind him.

"Please." My voice came out steadier than I felt.

"Although, if this is truly my home now, we're going to need some creamer. Preferably hazelnut flavor."

He reached for a mug in the cabinet above his head, the movement causing his shirt to ride up and reveal a strip of tanned skin and the edge of what looked like a tattoo. I averted gaze eyes, suddenly fascinated by the grain of the hardwood floor.

The heat from the ceramic seeped into my palms as I clutched it like a lifeline. "I should put my things away."

"Same room as last night," he said, pushing off from the counter. "Come on."

I followed him down the hallway, noticing the door at the end of the hall, half-open, revealing a king-sized bed with rumpled dark sheets. We stopped at the room where I'd spent the previous night.

It wasn't large, but it was comfortable. A double bed with a navy comforter. A dresser with a mirror. A small closet. A window that overlooked the side yard with its scrubby grass and lone oak tree. The sheets had been changed, I noticed. The ones I'd slept on had been white. These were a soft gray.

"I'm sure you remember the bathroom's across the hall," Azrael said, leaning against the doorframe. "Use whatever you need and make a list of anything you're missing."

"Thank you." I set my coffee on the dresser and placed my bag on the bed. "For all of this. I know you didn't have to --"

"Yes, I did." His voice was firm, allowing no argument. "But the choice was yours. I wasn't going to force any of this on you."

I wanted to tell him I could take care of myself, but the memory of the men in the alley last night was still too fresh. If Azrael hadn't stepped in, they'd have raped me. Possibly killed me.

"I need to get the rest of my stuff from my apartment," I said. "And I need to figure out what to do about my rent. And my job. I can't just disappear."

"We'll handle it," Azrael said. "Once things cool down, we'll get your stuff. As for the rest..." He shrugged. "You won't have to work unless you want to."

"Just like that?" I raised an eyebrow. "I'm now the property of Azrael so everything is magically taken care of?"

A ghost of a smile touched his lips. "Something like that. Get settled. We'll talk more when you're ready."

He turned to leave, but I called after him. "Azrael."

He paused, looking back at me over his shoulder.

"Thanks. Really."

He nodded once, then disappeared down the hall, leaving me alone in the spare room that was now, apparently, mine.

I sank onto the edge of the bed, my fingers tracing the soft fabric of the comforter. The events of the past twenty-four hours crashed over me in waves. And now I was here, in his house, drinking his coffee, sleeping in his spare room. And apparently his woman.

I unzipped my bag and began unpacking the few items I'd brought. A change of clothes. My toiletry bag. My phone charger. Pathetic, really. My entire life was still in my apartment -- clothes, books, photos, the quilt my dad's mother had made, my laptop with all my work files.

My mind raced with logistics. How would I pay my rent without access to my apartment? Would my landlord think I'd abandoned the place? Would my boss fire me for not showing up? I had a deadline for the Henshaw account, and no way to access the files remotely. I may have taken a few days off, but I should have been back in my office by now. Since my job was a few hours away, it looked like I wouldn't ever be returning. I knew others worked remotely. Maybe they could set up something for me as well.

I pulled out my phone and checked for messages. One from my coworker asking if I was sick. None from friends. Not that I really had any. More like acquaintances.

What would I tell them? How could I explain any of this?

My breathing quickened, my chest tightening with panic. I'd taken the leap and agreed to be Azrael's, but now that I had more time to think about it, had I made the right choice? Was this a decision I could live with?

I stood abruptly, needing to move, to do something. I put my clothes in the dresser, arranged my toiletries on top, plugged in my phone. Normal actions that felt absurdly inadequate in the face of the chaos my life had become.

When everything was put away -- which took all of five minutes given how little I had -- I stood in the center of the room, at a loss. On the nightstand was a lamp, a clock, and a book. I picked it up. Hemingway. *The Old Man and the Sea.* Not what I would have expected from someone like Azrael. The pages were worn, the spine creased from multiple readings. I didn't remember it being here last night. I wondered if he'd left it for me.

I set it back down carefully and took a deep breath. Self-pity wouldn't help me now. I needed information. I needed a plan. Most of all, I needed to understand the world I'd stumbled into and the man whose protection I'd accepted.

I picked up my cooling coffee and headed back to the kitchen. Azrael was still there, now sitting at the small table by the window, scrolling through his phone. He looked up when I entered, those dark eyes unreadable.

"Better?" he asked.

"Not really," I admitted, sliding into the chair across from him. "But I'm dealing with it."

He nodded, setting his phone down. "You're stronger than you think."

"You don't know me well enough to say that."

"I know enough." He leaned back, studying me. "I know you didn't cry or faint when you were faced with those assholes. You screamed for help. I know you've handled this whole situation without falling apart."

I took a sip of coffee to hide my surprise. I didn't feel strong. I felt terrified and out of my depth.

"What happens now?" I asked, setting the mug down. "I need to know what to expect going forward."

Azrael's expression shifted to something more serious as he leaned forward, forearms resting on the table. His massive hands capable of such violence -- I'd seen it firsthand -- cupped his coffee mug almost delicately. "There are rules," he said, his voice dropping to that low timbre that seemed to vibrate through my chest. "For your safety as much as the club's. When I say something is club business, that means it's off-limits to you. No questions, no arguments, no trying to find out on your own. That's non-negotiable."

I matched his posture, leaning in. "Define 'club

business.'"

"Anything that happens behind closed doors at the clubhouse. Our dealings with other clubs. Our income streams. The decisions made by the officers." He held my gaze, unwavering. "You don't want to know most of it anyway."

"Maybe I do," I countered. "Maybe not knowing makes me more nervous than knowing."

A muscle in his jaw twitched. "It's for your protection, Zara. What you don't know, you can't tell -- willingly or otherwise."

The implication sent a chill through me. I'd already seen enough to understand that the Devil's Boneyard existed in a world parallel to normal society, with its own laws and consequences.

"So I'm just supposed to, what, sit here in your house while you go off and do God knows what, and never ask questions?" My voice rose slightly.

"I'm not asking you to be blind or stupid," Azrael said, his tone still measured. "You'll learn how things work. But there are boundaries. Church, for example -- that's when we meet around the table to vote on club matters. No one is allowed in unless they're patched in, or unless Charming specifically invites them."

"And that would include me."

He nodded. "Unless Charming asks for you, which he might if it concerns you directly. Otherwise, you keep out."

I took a sip of coffee, using the moment to gather my thoughts. "So I'm essentially being kept in the dark about most of what you do."

"About some of what I do," he corrected. "Most of my life is right here, in the open. I'm not some mystery man with a secret identity, Zara. I'm just a man who's part of a brotherhood that values privacy and loyalty above all else."

I studied him, searching for a hint of deception. His dark gaze met mine steadily, giving away nothing but sincerity.

"What happens when the people who took my mother are... dealt with?" I asked carefully.

A shadow crossed his face. "If you're hoping I'll say you can return to your old life, that's not going to happen. I gave you a choice. Now you get to live with the consequences of your decision."

He stood abruptly, moving to refill his coffee. I watched the fluid movement of his body, the controlled power in his shoulders and back. There was nothing superfluous about Azrael -- no wasted motion, no unnecessary words.

"There are other old ladies in the club," he continued, his back to me. "Women who belong to patched members. They're good people, for the most part. Some of them are a little... extra. Clarity is married to Scratch. He was our VP for years. She's solid. Then there's Jordan, she's with our Sergeant-at-Arms, Havoc. Quite a few others. They'll help you get oriented."

"Old ladies," I repeated, tasting the unfamiliar term. "That's what you call your... girlfriends?"

He turned back to me, leaning against the counter. "Wives, girlfriends, significant others. It's just the term we use. Has been since before my time."

"And is that what I am? Your 'old lady'?" I raised an eyebrow, trying to keep my tone neutral despite the flutter in my stomach.

Azrael's gaze was steady. "You're under my protection. You'll wear my patch. So, yeah."

I nodded slowly, filing that information away to

examine later when I wasn't sitting across from him.

"I'll introduce you to a few of the ladies tonight or tomorrow," he continued. "It might help to have women to talk to who understand this life."

"I appreciate that." And I did. The thought of navigating this strange new world alone was daunting.

Azrael hesitated, then added, "Most of the women you saw at the clubhouse this morning are club girls. Remember when I said the women here had one of two roles? They entertain the men in the club. They're not forced to be there -- they choose it. Some are looking to become old ladies. Others just like the lifestyle."

"Entertain," I repeated, the euphemism not lost on me. "When you said it before, I assumed you meant they had sex with the club members. Is that right?"

He didn't flinch. "Yes."

"And that's... normal? Expected?"

"It's how it's been for a long time," he said simply. "Not every member participates. It's a personal choice."

I took a deep breath, wrestling with my reaction. On one hand, I wanted to be judgmental. On the other, I couldn't ignore that these women had apparently made their own decisions.

"And you?" I asked, the question burning in my throat. "Do you... participate?"

His expression remained impassive. "I haven't been with any of them in over a year."

The relief that flooded me was as unwelcome as it was immediate. I had no claim on this man. No right to care who he slept with. Yet something possessive curled in my chest at the thought of him with one of those women.

"Why not?" I pressed, unable to stop myself.

A shadow crossed his face. "Doesn't interest me anymore."

There was more to it -- I could see it in the way his gaze shifted slightly, the minute tightening of his jaw. But I sensed it was one of those boundaries he'd just established. Club business, perhaps, or something personal he wasn't ready to share.

"I'm not judging," I said softly. "I'm just trying to understand this world I've landed in."

He nodded, some of the tension leaving his shoulders. "It's a lot to take in. And it probably seems barbaric to someone on the outside."

"A little," I admitted. "But I'm reserving judgment."

"Smart woman." A hint of a smile touched his lips.

"So what does an old lady do around here?" I asked. "If I'm not privy to club business and I'm not... entertaining the masses?"

The smile grew. "Live your life. Some work outside the club. Some help with legitimate club businesses. Some take care of their homes and families." He shrugged. "There's no rulebook, Zara. Just boundaries that keep everyone safe."

"And these boundaries -- they're for my protection? Or to keep me in line?"

His expression hardened slightly. "Do you think I brought you here to control you? To keep you 'in line'?"

I matched his stare. "I don't know why you brought me here, not really. Protection, yes. But there are other ways to protect someone."

He pushed off from the counter and came back to the table, lowering himself into the chair opposite me. "Listen carefully. If your mother was abducted, and it's by someone who knows about you, then it means you could also be in danger. I don't want you to leave the compound by yourself. They could know exactly where you are and be waiting for a chance to grab you."

"So why didn't they before now?"

"Maybe the timing wasn't right," he said. "You're safe here, Zara. I'll make sure of it."

I wanted to argue, to point out that being forced to live with a stranger and follow his rules didn't feel particularly freeing, but something in his expression stopped me. Concern, genuine and unmasked, filled his dark eyes.

"Look," he said, his voice softening. "I know this isn't ideal. But you're worth protecting."

I nodded slowly, absorbing this. "Okay. So I stay here, I avoid asking about 'club business,' I meet some other women in similar situations, and I wait until it's safe for me to... what? You said I couldn't go back to my old life."

Azrael didn't look away, didn't soften his response. "No, you can't. Before you decided to accept my property patch, I made sure you understood this would be like a marriage. This is your life now, Zara. Whether you like it or not. There's no walking away. Not now. As for the waiting, you'll eventually be free to go where you'd like without having someone glued to your side for protection. The ladies here typically go out for lunch, shopping, and whatever else they want to do. As long as we know where they're going, so we can get to them quickly if trouble pops up, then they have the freedom to do as they please."

I digested his words and hoped I hadn't made a really big mistake. Only time would tell.

Chapter Seven

Zara

The rumble of Azrael's Harley sent vibrations through the ground beneath my feet long before he appeared around the bend. I'd been waiting in the driveway, nervously adjusting my clothes and wondering if I'd dressed appropriately for meeting what he'd casually referred to as "some family." But he'd been called away before we could leave. Something about club business.

Azrael slowed as he approached, the powerful engine growling beneath him like a predator ready to pounce. The sleek black machine gleamed in the afternoon sun, polished to perfection like everything else about him. His intense gaze swept over me.

He brought the bike to a stop and killed the engine, the sudden silence almost deafening. With practiced ease, he swung his leg over and gave me a smile that made my stomach flip. He had to be the sexiest man I'd ever met -- all hard angles and swarthy skin, his dark beard neatly trimmed along his strong jaw.

"You ready?" he asked, his voice low and smooth as he approached.

"As I'll ever be," I replied, trying to sound more confident than I felt. "So we're going to Scratch's place?"

Azrael nodded. "We can ride or walk."

I eyed the bike. "Ride."

He flashed me another smile and got back on the motorcycle before holding out his hand to me. I climbed on and wrapped my arms around his waist. He started the engine again, and we were off. It really wasn't far, and we arrived in no time.

We pulled to a stop in front of a well-kept Victorian house. "He's been with the club for decades. In fact, he was patched in before we had a compound with homes. This one was custom-built after he moved his family here. Before, they had a place in town."

I took in the property -- the large yard, the detached garage that looked big enough to house several motorcycles and possibly an SUV, and the wide porch that wrapped around the front of the house. It wasn't what I'd expected when I thought of an outlaw biker's home. It looked... normal. Almost inviting.

Azrael's hand came to rest at the small of my back as we walked up the driveway, the heat of his palm seeping through my thin shirt. It was a possessive gesture, one I was still getting used to.

"Remember," he said as we approached the porch steps, "these people are my family. Scratch especially."

I nodded, understanding the importance of this introduction. Azrael wasn't just bringing me to meet friends. This was something more significant. We climbed the steps together, and I couldn't help but notice how the wood had been worn smooth from years of boots crossing its surface.

Azrael didn't wait for an answer after his sharp knock. He simply opened the door and guided me inside, his hand never leaving my back.

The interior was cooler than the spring heat outside, and the sudden change in temperature sent a small shiver through me. Or maybe it was the two women who stood in what appeared to be the living room, both turning to assess me with calculated gazes.

"Clarity, Janessa." Azrael nodded to them in turn. "This is Zara."

The older of the two women approached first.

She was perhaps in her late forties or early fifties, with streaks of silver woven through her dark hair and laugh lines that spoke of a life fully lived. Her eyes, however, were sharp and missing nothing as she looked me over.

"Nice to meet you," she said, her voice warm but measured. "I'm Clarity. Scratch's old lady."

Old lady. The term still jarred me a bit, though Azrael had explained it was a term of respect within the club, not the insult it might sound like to outsiders.

"It's good to meet you too," I said, extending my hand, which she took in a firm grip.

The younger woman, Janessa, stayed where she was, her posture casual but somehow still alert. She couldn't have been much older than thirty, with her hair pulled back in a practical ponytail and eyes that seemed permanently narrowed in suspicion.

"Janessa," she said simply, with a slight nod in my direction. No handshake offered. No smile. Just that assessing look that made me feel like I was being measured and possibly found wanting.

"Janessa is married to Irish," Azrael explained, and I recalled him mentioning Irish before.

I looked around the room, taking in every detail. It wasn't what I'd expected. Instead of the dark, smoke-filled den I'd imagined, the space was open and airy. Large windows let in plenty of natural light, illuminating the comfortable, if slightly worn, furniture. A massive leather sectional dominated one side of the room, positioned perfectly for viewing the large flat-screen TV mounted on the wall.

What caught my attention most, though, were the photos. One entire wall was dedicated to framed pictures -- some old and yellowed, others more recent. In many of them, men in leather cuts bearing the

Devil's Boneyard patch stood proudly beside their bikes or with arms slung around each other's shoulders. Women appeared in some too, looking fierce and beautiful beside their men. And children -- there were photos of children at various ages, growing up within the embrace of this unusual family.

"Scratch has been asking when Azrael would bring you around," Clarity said, drawing my attention back to her. "He's out back with some of the boys. Should be in soon."

I nodded, not quite sure what to say. This wasn't just meeting a boyfriend's friends. This was something else entirely -- an introduction to a way of life I still didn't fully understand.

"Can I get you something to drink?" Janessa asked, her tone more obligatory than hospitable.

"Water would be great," I replied, and she disappeared through a doorway I assumed led to the kitchen.

"Zara isn't used to all this," Azrael said. "I was hoping you could help ease her into this way of life."

Janessa returned with a glass of water and handed it to me without ceremony. I took a sip, noticing how the two women exchanged a quick glance when they thought I wasn't looking.

"I'm going to find Scratch," Azrael said. "You good here for a minute?"

The thought of being left alone with these women sent a flutter of anxiety through me, but I nodded anyway. "Of course."

Azrael's dark eyes held mine for a moment longer than necessary, a silent reassurance, before he leaned in and pressed a brief kiss to my temple. It was a deliberate gesture, I realized -- marking me as his in front of these women whose approval clearly mattered.

"Back in a minute," he said, then disappeared through a sliding glass door at the far end of the room.

As soon as he was gone, I felt the women's gazes even more intensely. I took another sip of water, using the moment to gather myself.

"So," Clarity said, settling onto one of the leather couches and gesturing for me to take a seat across from her, "how long have you known Azrael? We didn't get much in the way of details."

The question seemed innocent enough, but I sensed layers beneath it. "A few days," I admitted, perching on the edge of the couch.

Janessa made a small sound that might have been a scoff or a laugh -- it was hard to tell.

"Not long," Clarity observed, her expression neutral but her eyes sharp.

"No," I agreed. "But it's been… intense."

That earned me the first genuine smile from Clarity. "It usually is with these men. Especially Azrael. He doesn't do anything halfway."

I thought about how quickly things had progressed between us -- from our first meeting in the dark alley to him claiming me as his woman.

"I've noticed," I said, unable to stop the small smile that curved my lips.

"He's never brought a woman to meet the family before," Janessa said abruptly, leaning against the wall with her arms crossed. "Not in all the years I've been around."

The statement hung in the air between us, heavy with implication. I wasn't sure if it was meant as a compliment or a warning.

"I'm not trying to rush anything," I said carefully, setting my water glass on a coaster on the coffee table. "We're still getting to know each other.

But from what I've been told, when I agreed to be his, it was a permanent choice."

"Honey," Clarity said, her voice gentler now, "the moment he brought you here, things got serious. Azrael doesn't introduce women to the club. Ever. The moment I heard he was bringing you here, I knew he'd claimed you."

Claimed. The word sent a shiver down my spine -- part thrill, part uncertainty. What exactly had I stepped into by coming here today?

I looked back at the wall of photos, at the faces of the men and women who made up this unusual family. Their expressions ranged from fierce to joyful, but all of them shared a look of belonging that was unmistakable. They knew exactly who they were and where they fit.

I wasn't sure I could say the same for myself.

I shifted on the leather couch, the material creaking softly beneath me, and decided that if I was going to be part of this world -- part of Azrael's life -- I needed to understand it. I couldn't sit here like some timid mouse waiting for him to return and speak for me. These women, with their knowing glances and measured words, held answers I needed.

"So," I began, leaning forward slightly, "how long have you been with the club?"

Clarity settled back into her seat, a small smile playing at the corners of her mouth. "Been Scratch's old lady for over twenty years. Long enough to see this club grow from a handful of men with a dream to what it is now. At that time, there was only one other old lady."

"Twenty years," I repeated, trying to imagine the life she'd lived. "And you, Janessa?"

The younger woman pushed away from the wall

and took a seat beside Clarity, her movements fluid and confident. "I got here a few years after Clarity. But I grew up around MCs. My father rides with another club in Alabama."

I nodded, filing away this information. "And what exactly... I mean, I know the basics of what an MC is, but what does the Devil's Boneyard actually do?"

The two women exchanged a quick glance before Clarity answered.

"The club has legitimate businesses," she said carefully. "Auto shop, security firm, real estate investments. But I suspect that's not what you're really asking."

She was right. It wasn't.

"Azrael told me he handles problems for the club," I said, keeping my voice even. "He didn't elaborate much beyond that. But I came here looking for the Angel of Death, so I'm going to assume it's work along those lines."

Janessa let out a short laugh that held little humor. "Of course he didn't. But I'm surprised you know about the Angel of Death."

I felt a chill run through me despite the warmth of the room. I'd known Azrael -- or Samir, as his ID stated -- was dangerous. It was evident in the way he moved, the respect others showed him, the intensity that sometimes darkened his eyes. Not to mention the stories I'd heard from my mom and the ladies at the community center. But hearing it stated so bluntly made it more real somehow.

"The club protects what's theirs," Clarity said, her voice gentle but firm. "Territory, businesses, family. Sometimes that protection requires... decisive action."

"And Azrael is the one who takes that action," I finished for her.

Clarity nodded once, her eyes never leaving mine, gauging my reaction. "Although, he's not alone. The Sergeant-at-Arms handles the bulk of that sort of thing. His name is Havoc."

"Yeah, but he's getting older. I bet he steps down before too long," Janessa said. "If he does, it wouldn't surprise me at all if the torch gets passed to Azrael."

I took a deep breath, my hands gesturing as I tried to put my thoughts in order. "Okay. So there's the legitimate side of things, and then there's... the other stuff. What about day-to-day? How does the club work? Who's in charge? Where do the women fit in?"

My questions came in a rush, fueled by both curiosity and a growing need to understand the world I was peering into. Mostly I wanted to know where *I* would fit.

Clarity leaned forward, her elbows on her knees. "The club has a strict hierarchy. Charming is the President. Scratch was the VP, but now it's Ashes. Then there are the other officers: Secretary, Treasurer, Road Captain, Sergeant-at-Arms. Full patch members below that. Prospects at the bottom, working to earn their way in."

"And the women?"

"We're not members," Janessa said flatly. "Not officially. But make no mistake -- an old lady holds her own kind of power. The men run the club, but behind closed doors..."

"We have our say," Clarity finished with a knowing smile. "The politics can get complicated. A smart woman learns how to navigate them."

I nodded, trying to absorb it all. "And where does Azrael fit in this hierarchy?"

"He's one of the patched members," Clarity explained. "Not an officer, but he's respected -- feared, even. He reports directly to Charming most times."

My fingers tapped restlessly against my knee as I processed this. "I knew he handled certain situations, but I don't... I guess I only somewhat understand what it means."

"He eliminates threats to women and kids," Janessa cut in bluntly. "Anyone who crosses the old ladies or our kids, threatens the women in town, or poses a potential threat -- Azrael is who gets sent to deal with it."

The matter-of-fact way she said it made my stomach tighten. This wasn't talk of roughing someone up or scaring them off. This was something much darker. Then again, I'd seen what he'd done to the men in that alley, and I'd heard the stories about him before coming here. So, I expected it to some extent. But the way they talked about it, like they were discussing something as common as the weather, made me wonder what the hell kind of life I'd signed up for.

"And that doesn't bother you?" I asked quietly, looking between them. "Knowing what your men do?"

Clarity's expression softened slightly. "The world isn't black-and-white, honey. These men... They've chosen a life outside society's rules, yes. But they have their own code, their own justice. I've seen Scratch and the others protect women and children who had nowhere else to turn and stand up for people when the law failed them."

"Evil exists," Janessa added, her voice hardening. "Real evil. Men who prey on the weak, who hurt women and children. Our men make sure those people pay. Can you say that's wrong?"

I thought about it for a moment, about what

Azrael had told me of his childhood -- raised by a single mother who'd been gang-raped as a teen, never knowing which of her attackers might have been his father. How that had shaped him, given him an unshakable need to protect women at all costs.

"No," I finally said. "I can't say that's wrong."

Something in Janessa's posture relaxed slightly, as if I'd passed a test I hadn't known I was taking.

"Has Azrael taken you to the clubhouse yet?" Clarity asked, reaching for her glass of iced tea on the coffee table. "Someone mentioned you'd already been. Or was I misinformed?"

I nodded. "Yes, but we didn't stay. It was my second day here, when he told Charming about me."

Another significant look passed between the women.

"I saw you there that day, but I wasn't sure how much you knew about the women present. Some of the guys are up front of about it. Azrael seems like the type who would tell you everything up front, but I could be wrong. It's smart to take it slow," Janessa murmured. "Clubhouse has its own... challenges."

I raised an eyebrow. "What kind of challenges?"

Clarity sighed. "Every MC has what we call club girls -- or sweetbutts, club pussy, hang-arounds. Different names but same idea. Women who aren't attached to any particular member, who are... available to the brothers."

"Well, not *all* clubs," Janessa said. "The Dixie Reapers, my dad's club, tossed them all out on their asses."

"But this club didn't?" I asked.

"They were gone for a short while. Now they're back. Just consider them a part of club life," Clarity said. "They're useful in their way. Keep the single men happy, help out around the clubhouse. Some are just passing through, looking for a good time. Others have been around for years, hoping to catch themselves an old lady position."

"And that's where the trouble can come in," Janessa added, her eyes narrowing. "Club girls have a way of laying claim. Don't let them overstep."

The warning in her tone was unmistakable. I sat up straighter, suddenly understanding what they were telling me.

"You mean they might see me as competition?"

"Or as fresh meat," Janessa said bluntly. "Especially if you're with Azrael. He's never taken an old lady, never even brought a woman around more than once or twice. You showing up changes things."

"If he'd taken one and was able to claim Zara, then the other one would have to be dead," Clarity said with a pointed look.

I frowned, processing this new information. "So what exactly should I expect?"

Clarity leaned forward, her expression serious. "Some will test you. Try to make you feel like you don't belong, like you're temporary. They might flirt with Azrael right in front of you, act like they have history with him."

"Do they?" I asked, the question out before I could stop it. "Have history with him, I mean. He said he hadn't done anything with them in a year or more, but does that mean there could be some he *has* been with?"

Janessa snorted. "Azrael's not a monk. But he's always kept relationships separate from club business. Doesn't shit where he eats, if you get my meaning. If he was with any of those girls, I doubt anyone knows about it other than him."

"If one tries to get too close, let them know you're no pushover," Clarity added, her voice firm. "You don't have to be cruel -- that'll just make you enemies. But be clear about your boundaries. And never let them see you're rattled."

I nodded slowly, imagining what this might look like in practice. I wasn't naturally confrontational, but I wasn't a doormat either. Still, the thought of women actively trying to undermine me or stake a claim on Azrael made my stomach knot.

"The brothers will follow Azrael's lead," Janessa continued. "If he makes it clear you're his, they'll respect that. But the club girls..." She trailed off with a meaningful look.

"They play by different rules," I finished.

"Exactly," Clarity confirmed. "And remember -- respect is everything in this life. How you handle yourself, especially in those first visits to the clubhouse, will set the tone for how everyone treats you going forward."

I took a deep breath, smoothing my palms over my jeans. "I appreciate the warning."

"It's not meant to scare you off," Clarity said, her expression softening. "Just prepare you. This life... it's not always easy. But it has its rewards."

"Family," Janessa said simply. "Real family. The kind that would die for you without hesitation."

I thought about Azrael, about the intensity in his dark eyes when he looked at me, the way his hands moved with such careful precision, whether he was touching me, cooking a meal, or cleaning one of his guns. The man contained multitudes -- capable of both violence and tenderness in equal measure.

"Can I ask you something else?" I said, looking between them. "How do you deal with knowing what they sometimes have to do? The violence, I mean."

Clarity's eyes grew distant for a moment. "You learn to separate the man from his actions. Scratch has done things that would horrify most people. But he's also the man who held my hand through seventeen hours of labor, who read to our children, who still looks at me like I'm the most beautiful woman he's ever seen after all these years."

"The violence isn't who they are," Janessa added quietly. "It's what they do when necessary. There's a difference."

I nodded, understanding dawning. "Like soldiers."

"Something like that," Clarity agreed. "They fight so others don't have to. They carry that weight."

"And as their women, we help them carry it," Janessa finished. "We don't judge. We don't flinch. We just... love them through it."

The simple truth of her words resonated within me. Wasn't that what Azrael had shown me already? A man capable of compartmentalizing, of being both ruthless and gentle?

I wondered if Azrael had recognized something in me from the beginning -- some quality that told him I could handle this life, could handle him in all his complexity. Would he have even offered to claim me if he'd thought I couldn't handle it?

As if summoned by my thoughts, Azrael stepped back into the room, his dark eyes immediately seeking me out. The conversation abruptly halted as all three of us turned toward him.

"Everything okay in here?" he asked, his gaze moving between us, no doubt picking up on the serious atmosphere.

"Just girl talk," Clarity said smoothly, rising from

her seat. "Getting to know each other a bit."

Azrael's gaze found mine, questioning, and I gave him a small nod to indicate I was fine. The protective posture of his body relaxed almost imperceptibly.

"Scratch will be in shortly," he said. "Just finishing up some business with the boys."

The encumbrance of what "business" might mean hung in the air, but I didn't flinch. Something had shifted in me during this conversation -- a new understanding, perhaps, or the beginning of one.

I met Azrael's eyes steadily, and for the first time, I felt like I was seeing all of him.

And I wasn't afraid.

Chapter Eight

Zara

Clarity clapped her hands together once, the sound cutting through the lingering tension in the room. "We should have a family night soon," she announced, her eyes bright with an enthusiasm that felt slightly forced. "Get everyone together properly, make it official." The words "make it official" hung in the air between us, heavy with meaning I wasn't sure I fully grasped yet. Beside me, I felt Azrael stiffen almost imperceptibly.

"Family night?" I echoed, trying to keep my voice steady despite the sudden flutter of anxiety in my chest.

Clarity nodded, her eyes flicking briefly to Azrael before returning to me. "Nothing formal. Just dinner, drinks. A chance for everyone to meet you all at once instead of in bits and pieces."

"Which means kicking the club girls out for the night," Janessa said. "I'm always down for that."

Everyone. The word expanded in my mind, filling it with images of leather-clad men with hard eyes and guarded expressions, women watching me with calculating gazes, all of them measuring whether I was worthy of their Angel of Death.

"Everyone meaning…" I let the question trail off.

"The officers and their old ladies, patched members," Clarity explained. "Maybe the Prospects and kids. Depends on who's around. We try to do these gatherings every few months anyway, so it's about time."

Azrael moved closer to me, his arm sliding around my waist in a gesture that felt both possessive and protective. "We can discuss it later," he said, his deep voice resonating through me where our bodies touched. "Zara's still getting used to all this."

I shot him a grateful look, though part of me bristled slightly at being spoken for. I wasn't some fragile flower that needed sheltering. But another part - - the part still reeling from everything I'd learned in the past hour -- was thankful for the reprieve.

"Of course," Clarity agreed easily, though her knowing eyes missed nothing. "Just putting it out there. No rush."

Janessa snorted softly, apparently finding something amusing in the exchange. When I glanced her way, she merely raised an eyebrow as if to say, "See what I mean?"

The sliding glass door opened again, and a man stepped into the room. Even if Azrael hadn't mentioned his name, I would have known this was Scratch. Despite his age -- he had to be in his seventies -- he carried himself with the unmistakable authority of someone accustomed to command. His long gray hair and beard gave him an almost wizardly appearance, but there was nothing gentle or mystical in his sharp eyes as they assessed me.

"So this is her," he said, his voice gruff but not unkind. "The woman who's got our Azrael acting like a lovesick fool."

I felt heat rush to my face but refused to look away from his scrutiny. Exactly what had they discussed? There was no way Azrael was in love with me. Had he given them that impression on purpose?

"I'm Zara," I said, stepping forward slightly but not breaking contact with Azrael. "It's good to meet you, sir."

Scratch's face broke into a sudden grin. "Sir? Hear that, Clarity? The girl's got manners." He approached, and for a moment I thought he might offer his hand to shake, but instead, he pulled me into a brief, strong hug that smelled of motor oil and tobacco. "Welcome to the family, girl. About time this one found someone to keep him grounded."

When he released me, I stepped back into the comfort of Azrael's presence, slightly overwhelmed by Scratch's immediate acceptance.

"We won't keep you long today," Scratch continued, addressing both of us now. "Just wanted to get a look at the woman who's managed what half the females in the county couldn't." His eyes crinkled with amusement. "She's a pretty one, Az. Good taste."

"She's standing right here," Azrael reminded him, though I could hear the subtle note of pride in his voice.

"That she is," Scratch agreed, unrepentant. "You coming to the meeting tomorrow night? I know Charming didn't officially call Church, but it would be good if you showed up."

The question was directed at Azrael, who nodded once. "Unless something comes up."

"Good. Got some business to discuss." Scratch's tone shifted slightly, becoming more serious. "Trouble brewing over on the eastside. Nothing we can't handle, but we need to get ahead of it."

I felt Azrael's body tense beside me, though his expression remained neutral. "I'll be there."

Something wordless passed between the two men, an understanding that went beyond the simple exchange.

"We should probably get going," Azrael said after a moment, his hand still firm at my waist. "Long day tomorrow. We were supposed to go to her mom's house today to check things out, but I asked for an extra day. Wanted her to know a few people before I ran off and left her for a bit."

Clarity smiled knowingly. "Of course. It was lovely meeting you, Zara. Don't be a stranger."

"She needs to meet everyone," Scratch said.

"We already discussed holding a family night," Charity replied.

Scratch nodded. "No pressure, but it'd be good to get it done sooner rather than later. Let everyone know where things stand."

Goodbyes were exchanged, with Janessa giving me a small nod that felt more meaningful than her earlier reception. As we stepped out onto the porch, the late afternoon sun momentarily blinded me, and I lifted a hand to shield my eyes.

"You okay?" Azrael asked quietly as we walked toward his bike.

"Yeah," I said automatically, then reconsidered. "No. I don't know. It's a lot to take in."

He stopped, turning to face me fully. His dark eyes searched mine, concern evident in the slight furrow of his brow. "Too much?"

The question hung between us, heavy with implications. Was this life too much? Was he too much? For a moment, I considered the simplicity of my existence before Azrael -- my job, my small circle of... well not friends, but acquaintances, the predictable rhythms of my days. It had been comfortable. Safe.

But it had never made me feel the way I did when I was with him -- alive, seen, breathless with possibility.

"No," I said finally, meeting his gaze steadily. "Not too much. Just... intense."

Something in his expression relaxed, though the concern remained. "We don't have to do the family night thing right away. Scratch and the others will understand."

"But it's important, isn't it?" I pressed.

Azrael nodded slowly. "In this life... yeah. It matters. Tells everyone you're under my protection. That you're mine." He paused, his jaw tightening slightly. "But that doesn't mean we have to rush it if you're not ready."

The ride back to Azrael's house was silent. I clung to his back, my cheek pressed against the leather of his cut, the embroidered Devil's Boneyard patch rough against my skin. The wind whipped around us, carrying away my jumbled thoughts almost as quickly as they formed.

By the time we pulled into his driveway, the sun cast long shadows across the house. Azrael killed the engine and helped me off the bike before dismounting himself. Neither of us spoke as we walked to the front door.

Inside, the familiar scent of leather, sandalwood, and something uniquely Azrael enveloped me. The house was sparsely but thoughtfully furnished -- comfortable couch, solid wood coffee table, bookshelves filled with an eclectic mix of titles that had surprised me when I first saw them. This was a home, not just a place to sleep.

Without thinking, I made my way to the couch and sank down onto it, suddenly aware of how tense my body had been. Azrael moved to the kitchen, returning moments later with two glasses of water. He handed one to me before taking a seat close enough for our knees to touch.

"Talk to me," he said simply.

I took a sip of water, organizing my thoughts. "They were... Not unfriendly, exactly, but..."

"Cautious," Azrael supplied. "They're protective of the club. Of me."

"They warned me about club girls," I said, watching his face carefully. "Said they might try to stake a claim on you when I'm around."

Something darkened in his expression.

"Should they be a problem?" I asked, the question that had been nagging at me finally surfacing. "Do you have history there I should know about? You said you hadn't been with any of them in the last year, but that doesn't mean you never have. I guess what I'm really asking is... are these the same women who were at the clubhouse when you did sleep with some of them?"

"They won't be a problem. I'll make that clear." Azrael set his glass down and took mine from my hands, placing it beside his on the coffee table. Then he took my hands in his, his touch gentle despite the calluses that roughened his palms. "I've never brought a woman to meet the club before. Never introduced anyone as mine. There've been women, yes. I'm not going to lie about that. But nothing serious, nothing that mattered. Not in a long-ass time."

I noticed he didn't exactly answer my question. Which made me think at least one of those women had been with him before. It was silly to worry about it. Like he said, he hadn't touched them in a year. He was with me now. That's all that should matter but...

"How long?" I asked before I could stop myself.

"When I was just a Prospect for this club, I'd been dating someone seriously. Even back then, I wouldn't walk away from a woman in trouble. It came back to bite me in the ass. My girlfriend ended up dead because of me."

I reached up and placed my hand on his cheek,

wishing I could take away his pain. Even now, all this time later, I could see the anguish in his eyes. "I doubt she blamed you."

"Doesn't matter. I blame myself." His dark eyes held mine, unwavering. "You matter, Zara. That's why I took you there today. That's why Scratch and Clarity are talking about family night."

The intensity of his gaze made it hard to breathe. "We've only known each other a few days," I reminded him, though even to my own ears it sounded weak.

A small smile tugged at the corner of his mouth. "Time works differently in this life. When you know, you know."

"And you know?" I whispered.

His hand came up to cup my cheek, thumb tracing the curve of my bottom lip. "I knew the moment you looked at me in that alley and met my gaze without flinching. When most people look at me, they see what they're afraid of. You saw me."

I leaned into his touch, remembering that moment. I'd realized who he was, known I'd be safe.

"I'm still learning what all this means," I admitted. "The club, your role in it, what it means to be with you."

"I know," he said. "And I'll give you all the time you need. But I want you to understand something." His voice dropped lower, an edge of steel beneath the velvet. "I've done things that would horrify most people, and I'll likely do them again. That's who I am, Zara. That's part of what you're accepting by choosing this life with me."

I thought about what Clarity had said, about separating the man from his actions. About loving someone through the darkness they carried.

"The women said the violence isn't who you are, it's what you do when necessary."

Azrael's expression softened slightly. "Smart women. Maybe smarter than me. They've been in this life a long time. They probably see things differently than most."

"They also said that as your woman, I'd help you carry that weight. That I wouldn't judge or flinch." I met his gaze steadily. "I don't think I will. Flinch, I mean. Not from the truth of who you are. Even before we officially met, I saw you as a hero. A legend. That hasn't changed."

Something shifted in his eyes -- relief, perhaps, or hope. "That's all I can ask."

Later, after Azrael had gone to shower, I curled up on the couch alone, pulling the soft throw blanket over my legs as I stared out the window at the deepening twilight. The events of the day replayed in my mind -- the introduction to Clarity and Janessa, their warnings and advice, Scratch's immediate acceptance, the talk of a family night to meet everyone.

It was all happening so fast, this integration into a world I'd barely known existed. A world with its own rules and hierarchies, its own justice system, its own definitions of family and loyalty. A world where violence wasn't just possible but expected, where the man who'd claimed me as his own was known as the Angel of Death.

And yet, despite everything I'd learned today, I couldn't bring myself to be afraid. Not of Azrael, not of the life he represented. There was something almost liberating in the stark honesty of it all -- no pretense, no hiding behind social niceties. The club, for all its darkness, seemed to operate on a simple principle: protect what's yours, at any cost.

Wasn't that what Azrael had been doing all along? Protecting what was his? And now, somehow, that included me.

I pulled the blanket tighter around me, settling deeper into the couch as I listened to the sound of the shower running down the hall. This wasn't the life I had imagined for myself, not by a long shot. It was dangerous, complex, bound by codes I was only beginning to understand.

But as I sat there in the growing darkness, I realized with sudden clarity that I wasn't running from it. If anything, I was running toward it -- toward him -- with my eyes wide open.

Whatever came next, whatever this new life held, I would face it alongside the man who had seen something in me worth claiming as his own. The man I was beginning to believe might be worth claiming in return.

* * *

Azrael

The hot water hit my skin and I closed my eyes. I hadn't known what to expect when I'd taken Zara to meet Clarity and Janessa. Could have been worse. I had no idea how Jordan would have reacted. Maybe it would be a good idea to have her meet Alora and Grey. They were less intense. Mostly.

For a while there, Grey had managed to clear the girls out of the clubhouse. It hadn't lasted long. The single brothers had eventually told Charming it wasn't right to let the old ladies run things. But something was different. Now all the women were vetted, and we made sure they were there willingly and not as a way to run away from their problems. If they needed help, we offered it.

She'd made good points, ones we hadn't been able to ignore. Although, back then, I'd only been a Prospect. I'd only patched in four years ago. Since then, two others who had been Prospects with me had also been patched in. Hunter, who now went by Chaos, and Nick, who was now called Java. Since then, we'd gained some new Prospects.

I tipped my head back under the hot spray and contemplated what I'd do next. In the morning, I'd check out my mother-in-law's house. But after that? I'd told Zara she could have all the time she needed before we took the next step. Didn't mean my dick got any less hard around her. Even now, the damn thing was hard as a fucking rock.

Then again, not my first case of blue balls, or having to take care of the issue myself. Been doing that for over a year. Did it suck I had to do that after claiming a woman? Of course. At the same time, I wasn't going to press her for more than she was willing to give. Hell, she'd been through so much, and even now, I knew she was stressed over the disappearance of her mother.

I needed to be able to tell her at least something. I'd focus on finding my mother-in-law and getting to know Zara day by day. Eventually, we'd grow closer. It was inevitable.

She'd given up a life to stay here. A job, her apartment... It didn't feel right keeping her locked up in the house with nothing to do, no friends or family. Clarity and Scratch had made a good point about the family night. It was the best way for Zara to get close to the others. The times I was gone, she'd need people to rely on, ones she felt comfortable with. Right now, all she had was me.

Grabbing the soap, I washed quickly. Standing in

the shower wasn't going to solve anything. Not even the small stuff, like food. We hadn't discussed dinner yet, and I was running out of options in the fridge and pantry. Maybe I'd have Zara make an online grocery order for tomorrow and ask a Prospect to pick it up. If she got a few things for the house, items that would help make it feel more like her home and not just mine, it would keep her occupied while I was gone in the morning.

Why did I get the feeling it would only end up causing an issue? We hadn't talked about much of anything. Would she balk at me handing her my credit card to grocery shop or get the things we needed? I knew some of the old ladies hadn't liked being taken care of, while others had gratefully accepted what their men gave them. Which category would Zara fall into? I had a feeling she'd be in the first group.

I finished my shower and got out. I towel-dried my hair, pulled on a pair of sweats, and went in search of Zara.

* * *

Zara

The shower cut off and I settled deeper into the couch, waiting for Azrael to emerge. The silence of the house wrapped around me, broken only by the occasional distant rumble of motorcycles passing by on the road. I pulled my knees up to my chest, thinking about everything I'd learned today.

When Azrael finally appeared, wearing only a pair of low-slung sweatpants, I couldn't help but stare. Water droplets still clung to his broad shoulders, and his damp hair curled slightly at the ends. The tattoos that covered his chest and arms seemed to shift with each movement, telling stories I hadn't yet learned to read.

"You look deep in thought," he said, his voice a low rumble as he approached.

I smiled up at him. "Just processing everything from today. It was... educational."

He settled beside me on the couch, close enough that I could feel the heat radiating from his freshly showered skin. "I'm sure it was. Clarity and Janessa don't hold back."

"No, they don't," I agreed. "But I appreciate that. I'd rather know what I'm walking into than be blindsided."

Azrael nodded, his dark eyes studying my face. "Any second thoughts?"

The question hung between us, heavy with meaning. I considered it seriously, knowing he deserved honesty.

"Not second thoughts exactly," I said carefully. "But questions. Concerns. The usual stuff when your life takes a completely unexpected turn."

His mouth quirked up at one corner. "Fair enough."

I shifted to face him more directly. "Tomorrow you said we're going to my mom's house?"

"Actually, I said I was going. I want to look around, see if there's anything that might give us a lead on where she went or what happened. I'll take two of my brothers with me. But you are going to remain here, just in case someone is watching her house."

I narrowed my eyes, wanting to argue, but something told me to hold back. "And then you have that meeting at the club?"

He nodded. "I'll try to let you know I'm back before the meeting, but I can't promise I'll have the time."

Fine. It looked like that was all I would get from him on the matter. I'd just have to learn to live with it. Something told me this would happen again in the future. Not the exact same scenario, but him going off and me left wondering what the hell was going on.

Chapter Nine

Azrael

The side door of Mazida's modest home wasn't locked. Not a good sign. I pushed it open with my gloved hand, the hinges complaining quietly as I stepped over the threshold. Havoc moved in behind me, his bulk filling the narrow entrance while Gator brought up the rear. The air inside felt wrong -- stuffy and tinged with something metallic that settled in the back of my throat. Club business had taken me to plenty of disturbed homes over the years, but something about this one had my senses on high alert before I'd even seen the damage.

"Clear the rooms," I muttered, my voice barely audible. This wasn't my first rodeo with the Devil's Boneyard, and certainly not my first time walking into the aftermath of violence. The fact the police had been here meant the place should have been secured. Had someone come back after they'd left?

Mazida's neighborhood was quiet -- a collection of aging single-story homes with chain-link fences and patchy lawns that had seen better days. Nothing about the outside of her home had suggested trouble. No broken windows. No kicked-in doors. Just a garden gnome tipped on its side near a withered bush.

The hallway stretched before us, narrow and dim with late morning light filtering through closed blinds. Family photos hung crooked on the walls -- Mazida and her daughter, Zara, at various ages. A high school graduation. A birthday. Normal life moments now tilted at unnatural angles. I saw a few with a man who had to be Zara's father. The home in the background didn't match this one, which made me think Mazida had moved here after losing her husband.

"Someone didn't want any attention from the neighbors," Havoc said, his voice gruff as he pointed to the intact front door lock. But the issue was that it *wasn't* locked. I knew Zara wouldn't have left this place open. Someone had definitely been here. But why? If they already had Mazida, what else could they have wanted?

I nodded. "Whoever came in knew what they were doing."

We moved deeper into the house, our boots making little sound on the worn carpet. The layout was simple -- living room and kitchen to the right, bedrooms down the hall to the left. I signaled toward the bedrooms, taking point while Gator positioned himself to watch our backs.

The first bedroom door stood half-open. Mazida's room.

The scene inside told the story we'd feared. Clothes scattered across the floor like fallen leaves. An overturned end table lay on its side, a vase shattered beside it, ceramic shards mingling with a paperback novel and a pair of reading glasses. The bed was unmade, sheets twisted and halfway to the floor.

"Someone got dragged outta that bed," Gator observed from the doorway, his Cajun accent more pronounced in the tense moment. "How the fuck did the police not see this as a crime scene?"

"They didn't want to," Havoc said.

I moved to the dresser, where Mazida's purse sat untouched, her phone beside it, screen cracked but otherwise undisturbed. Cash still in the wallet. Credit cards present. This wasn't a robbery.

"Whoever did this wasn't after money," I said, taking mental inventory as I carefully picked through the items.

Havoc moved to the closet, sliding hangers across the rod with practiced efficiency. "Doesn't look like she packed anything. If she left, it wasn't willingly."

I nodded, still examining the dresser top. A bottle of prescription medication. A framed photo of Zara. A hairbrush with strands of dark hair caught in the bristles. Normal, everyday items that suddenly felt heavy with significance.

"Check the drawers," I instructed, moving toward the bathroom.

Havoc flipped open the top drawer of the dresser, rifling through folded clothes with the efficiency of a man who'd searched more homes than he could count. "Nothing unusual here."

The bathroom told the same story -- toothbrush in its holder, makeup scattered across the counter, a towel hung haphazardly over the shower curtain rod. Everything looked normal except for a small smear of something dark on the edge of the sink. I leaned closer. Could be makeup. Could be blood. Too small to tell for sure.

Back in the hallway, I gestured toward the kitchen. "Let's check the rest."

The kitchen was small but tidy, save for a coffee mug on its side near the sink, dark liquid staining the countertop. The dining area consisted of a rough-hewn wooden table with four mismatched chairs. One chair lay on its back.

That's when I saw it. A single drop of blood on the linoleum floor, near the fallen chair. Dark. Dried. But unmistakable.

I crouched down, pulling my phone from my pocket to snap a picture. The flash illuminated the small red-brown spot, no bigger than a dime. "Blood,"

I confirmed, glancing up at Havoc.

He nodded grimly, his face set in hard lines that emphasized every one of his sixty-eight years. Despite the gray threading through his once-red hair, Havoc's eyes remained sharp, missing nothing.

"Recent?" he asked, moving closer to examine the spot.

"Probably happened when she went missing," I replied, standing back up and surveying the kitchen. "Whoever took her knew what they were doing. Clean. Professional. No signs of forced entry means she knew them, they had a key, or they knew how to pick a lock without leaving evidence behind."

"So what? You think she let them in, went to bed, and then they betrayed her trust?" Havoc asked.

Before I got a chance to answer, Gator appeared in the doorway, his usual easy charm replaced by business-like efficiency. "Checked the back door and windows. No sign of forced entry there either."

"Any indication of where Zara might be?" I asked. "If anyone comes back here again, I want to make sure they can't find her."

Gator shook his head. "Other than the pictures we saw, there's nothing."

"Small mercies," Havoc muttered, running a hand over his short-cropped hair.

I moved back to the living room, scanning for anything we might have missed. A stack of mail on the coffee table caught my attention. Bills. Advertisements. And a postcard from the Florida Keys with a picture of palm trees and white sand. I flipped it over, reading the brief message: "Thinking of you both. Stay safe. - C."

"C could be Carter," Havoc suggested, reading over my shoulder. "Wasn't that her husband's name?"

"Carter's been dead for years," I replied, tucking the postcard into my pocket. "This is recent."

We stood in silence for a moment, absorbing the scene and its implications. Mazida Quadir -- a quiet, reserved widow who kept to herself -- was gone. Not by choice. And someone had sent her a warning to "stay safe" that she clearly hadn't been able to heed.

"We split up," I decided, tucking my phone away. "Havoc, check for any hidden spots -- false bottoms in drawers, loose floorboards, anything. Gator, go through her desk for any letters, cards, anything unusual. I'll check the garage."

They nodded and moved off to their assigned tasks. The garage was attached to the house through a utility room filled with laundry supplies and cleaning products. Nothing unusual there. In the garage itself, Mazida's modest sedan sat undisturbed, dust collecting on its hood suggesting it hadn't been moved in days.

I circled the car, checking under it, inside it, and around it. Nothing seemed out of place except for a small cardboard box tucked behind some gardening supplies in the corner. Inside, I found photos -- older ones, yellowed with age. A young Mazida without her hijab, smiling beside a handsome man I assumed was Carter. Some documents in Arabic that I couldn't read. A small journal with entries dating back decades.

I tucked the journal into my cut on the off chance we needed it. The rest I left as found. Whatever had happened to Mazida, these memories wouldn't help us find her now.

Back in the living room, Havoc and Gator had finished their searches.

"Nothing else of note," Havoc reported, his voice grim. "No hidden money, no secret messages."

Gator shook his head too. "Found her planner book. Mostly doctor appointments and emergency contacts. Her daughter's cell number is in there."

"Take it," I instructed. "I don't want them having a way to reach Zara, or track her."

"You think she's a target too?" Gator asked, tucking the small book into his pocket.

I shrugged, taking one last look around the disturbed home. "Don't know. But whoever took Mazida did it clean and quiet. Professional job. Might be connected to her past, maybe something from the Middle East. Either way, her daughter could be next."

"Or leverage," Havoc added darkly.

I nodded, this new problem settling between my shoulder blades like a familiar burden. "Let's bag any other evidence we're taking. Blood sample and her phone mainly. I have the postcard and a journal."

As we gathered what little evidence there was, my mind was already spinning forward to the next steps. Mazida's disappearance wasn't just another missing person case. The care taken, the precision -- it had the hallmarks of something deeper, something with tendrils that might reach all the way back to her life before America. If this place hadn't looked like this when the police came, then it meant someone came back. I couldn't think of a reason why unless they thought she had something important. Right now, I just had more questions than answers.

"Time to report to Charming," I said finally, heading for the side door we'd entered through. "He'll want to know what we found."

And what we didn't find -- like Mazida herself, alive and well. That particular absence hung in the air around us, unspoken but impossible to ignore as we stepped back out into the late morning light, locking the door behind us as if it mattered anymore.

* * *

The Devil's Boneyard compound loomed ahead of us. Security cameras tracked our approach, though the brothers manning the gate waved us through without hesitation, recognizing our cuts and bikes. I led our small procession, Havoc and Gator flanking me as we parked outside the clubhouse.

The main building stood solid against the afternoon sun, its weathered exterior hiding the fortified structure beneath. Years of club life -- celebrations, fights, deaths, and victories -- had seeped into the very walls. Our boots crunched against the gravel as we dismounted and made our way toward the entrance.

Inside, the familiar scent of leather, cigarettes, and whiskey greeted us. A few Prospects hustled around, cleaning and restocking the bar area. They nodded respectfully as we passed, their eyes curious but knowing better than to ask questions.

"Church in session?" I asked one of them, a skinny kid with tattoos crawling up his neck.

"Yes, sir," he replied, gesturing toward the closed double doors at the far end of the hall. "President and VP been waiting for you three."

We made our way across the room, passing the well-worn pool table and leather couches. Havoc stepped ahead and knocked once on the heavy wooden doors before pushing them open.

Charming and Ashes rose from their seats as we entered. Neither said anything right away and waited until we were closer.

"You found something," Charming stated rather than asked, gesturing for us to take seats.

I nodded, pulling the bag from inside my cut and

placing it on the table between us. The plastic crinkled as I spread out the contents -- Mazida's cracked phone, the postcard, and a small plastic baggie containing a scrape of the blood we'd found.

"The purse, the phone, and a few of the scattered clothes -- nothing was cleaned up," I reported, meeting Charming's gaze directly. "There was a drop of blood in the kitchen, which confirms a struggle took place."

Charming picked up the postcard, examining both sides before setting it back down. His face gave nothing away, but the tension in his shoulders told me he recognized the significance.

Havoc leaned forward, his massive forearms resting on the table. "The overturned furniture suggests she was desperate to escape and knocked it over herself. I don't think the type of men who'd enter the house so quietly would make a mess of the place."

"No sign of a break-in?" Ashes asked, his voice tight with controlled concern.

I shook my head. "That's what's strange. Locks intact. No broken windows. Either she knew them and let them in --"

"Or they had a key, or picked the fucking locks," Charming finished, sitting back in his chair. "Professional job."

"That's how it reads," I confirmed. "Nothing of value was taken. Cash and credit cards still in her purse. This wasn't a robbery gone wrong."

Gator shifted in his seat. "If the police determined this wasn't a kidnapping after seeing the state of her bedroom, they're idiots. Or someone came back, searching for something. Maybe she wasn't dragged from the bed. They could have tossed it during their search."

"Or looking for some*one*," Ashes added grimly.

Charming's fingers drummed once on the table, a rare tell that indicated his concern. "Zara?"

"That's what I'm thinking," I replied. "Once they had Mazida, they probably thought Zara would turn up and they could snatch her too. But that depends on why her mom was taken in the first place."

"That postcard," Charming finally said, tapping it with one finger. "Message is clear enough."

I nodded. "'Stay safe.' Signed only with a C."

"Her dad has been dead for years," Ashes noted, his brow furrowed.

"Exactly," I responded. "Which means it's from someone else. Someone who felt Mazida needed warning."

Charming exchanged a look with Ashes that spoke volumes about conversations I hadn't been privy to. Something deeper was happening here, something they'd seen coming.

"When was the last confirmed sighting of Mazida?" Charming asked, turning back to us.

"Zara didn't say, but I can ask." Although, I'd hoped I would have some answers for her today. Instead I just had questions.

"What about the blood?" Ashes asked, picking up the small baggie and holding it to the light.

"Not much of it," I replied. "Single drop in the kitchen. We'll need to get it tested to confirm it's hers. I'm sure Doc could help us out, or a contact in the police department."

"And how will you know it's hers?" Ashes asked.

"Compare it to Zara's? If there's roughly a fifty percent match, then we know it belongs to a parent, right?" I asked.

Charming leaned forward, placing both hands

flat on the table. "Here's what we know: Mazida Quadir is missing. Signs of struggle but minimal blood. No forced entry. Nothing of value taken. A warning postcard received recently." He looked at each of us in turn. "What we don't know is who took her, why, or where Zara fits into this."

"The phone might tell us something," I suggested, gesturing to the cracked device on the table. "Text messages, calls, emails."

Ashes nodded. "I'll get it to Shade immediately. If there's anything on it, he'll find it."

"Locked?" Charming asked, eyeing the phone.

"Password protected," I confirmed. "But that won't stop Shade for more than a few minutes."

Ashes collected the phone, tucking it into his pocket before standing. "I'll take this to him now. Want me to bring him back when he's got something?"

Charming nodded. "We need to move quickly on this. If they've had her for three days already, time isn't on our side."

"Longer," I said. "Zara has been with me for three days now. Her mom has been gone since before then. Not sure exactly what day she went missing. Could have been closer to a week by now. I think Zara said it had been a few days since her mom had disappeared."

As Ashes left, Charming turned back to us. "Gator, I want you to reach out to your contacts in south Florida. That postcard origin might not be coincidence."

Gator nodded, already pulling out his phone. "On it, Prez."

"Havoc," Charming continued, "get some of the brothers together. Start canvassing hospitals and morgues. Discreetly. We need to know if Mazida has turned up elsewhere."

"Will do," Havoc responded, his face grim with determination.

Charming's gaze finally landed on me. "Azrael, I want you to stick with Zara. Until we know who took her mom and why, she could very well be a target."

I nodded, already planning to do exactly that.

"Good." Charming sat back, his fingers steepled beneath his chin. "One more thing -- this stays close. Club business only for now. We don't know who we're dealing with or what their reach might be."

"You thinking this might connect back to Mazida's past?" I asked, voicing the question that had been nagging me since we'd found the postcard.

Charming's expression darkened. "Mazida left the Middle East for a reason. Fled, more accurately. She's kept a low profile for decades, but some enemies have long memories."

"And they have a longer reach," Havoc added ominously.

"How do you know she was laying low?" I asked, genuinely curious.

"Because those types of men would have gone looking, and I doubt her being married would have stopped them from retaliating."

The door opened, and Ashes returned with Shade trailing behind him. The club's hacker looked as he always did -- slightly disheveled, his hazel eyes sharp behind his glasses. At sixty-four, Shade remained the best technical mind in the club.

"Got something already?" Charming asked, surprised.

Shade nodded, adjusting his glasses. "Phone wasn't as locked down as it could have been. Simple six-digit code. Took less than two minutes to crack."

He sat at the table, placing a small notebook in front of him. "Last received call was over a week ago, duration four minutes, twelve seconds. Caller ID listed as 'Unknown.'"

"Any texts?" Gator asked.

Shade flipped a page in his notebook. "Several, most mundane. Shopping lists, reminders for appointments. But there's a thread with an unknown number that's interesting." He looked up, meeting Charming's gaze. "Your time is up."

A heavy silence settled over the room as the implications sank in. Did that mean Mazida was possibly dead? Or had they meant something else?

"What about law enforcement?" Ashes asked, voicing the question we'd all been avoiding.

Charming shook his head. "Not yet. If this connects back to Mazida's past, official channels might create more problems than solutions. We handle this ourselves first, see what we're dealing with."

I pushed through the Church doors, my mind already focused on Zara. Behind me, I heard Charming giving final instructions to Shade about digital surveillance. Ahead lay hours, maybe days, of searching, questioning, and piecing together the puzzle of the Quadir woman's disappearance. I didn't envy him.

For now, I had the honor of telling Zara we still didn't know who had her mom.

Chapter Ten

Azrael

I felt the tension before I even entered the clubhouse. It hung in the air, invisible but unmistakable. The usual pre-meeting bullshit had been replaced with hushed conversations and hardened expressions. Whatever Stripes had called us together for, it wasn't going to be good news. I caught Charming's eye as I walked in, and the slight shake of his head confirmed it. This was going to be one of those meetings that ended with bloodshed -- the only question was whose.

The main room of the clubhouse was uncharacteristically quiet. A Prospect was wiping down the bar with mechanical precision, his eyes darting toward the meeting room door every few seconds. Two of the younger members stood near the pool table, cues in hand but no game in progress. Even the fucking music had been cut, and I didn't see club pussy anywhere.

"Azrael." Charming nodded at me, his voice kept low. "They're waiting."

I followed him into Church. I took my seat, noting how Phantom kept checking his phone, how Doc's fingers drummed an irregular beat on his thigh, how Ripper stared at a water stain on the ceiling as if it held the secrets of the universe.

Stripes entered last, a manila folder clutched in his hands. At seventy-one, he moved with the deliberate grace of a man who'd survived too much to be rushed by anything. His white beard and hair gave him the look of a biker Santa, but the steel in his eyes would make any naughty-lister shit themselves.

"Brothers," he began, his Russian accent thick

despite decades in the States. "We have a situation." He didn't sit, instead remaining standing by the table. That alone told me this was worse than I'd thought. Stripes preferred to sit, to lean back in his chair with his boots crossed at the ankles, spinning tales of the old days to anyone who'd listen, or doing his best to make us laugh.

The folder slapped onto the wooden surface, and he spread out several documents -- surveillance photos, what looked like transaction records, and a map marked with red lines crossing continents.

"Mazida's family has taken her back to the Middle East," he announced, his voice filling the room with a heaviness that seemed to press the air from my lungs.

I felt my jaw tighten. This was really fucking bad. Getting her back while on US soil was one thing. But overseas?

"We traced Balal Quadir to Tel Aviv," Stripes continued, pointing to a grainy surveillance photo of a well-dressed man in his late fifties exiting what appeared to be a private jet. "Mazida's brother. He has ties to the top Israeli crime family there."

"Kidnapping," Phantom muttered. "So, your woman was right, Azrael. Her mother was definitely taken, and by her own damn family."

Stripes nodded. "*Da*. It's looking that way. Balal never approved of Mazida marrying an American. Even less of her having a half-American daughter. When Mazida's husband died, Balal saw an opportunity. From what my contacts could find, he's been working on a deal the last few years, and Mazida is the prize on offer."

"How solid is this intel?" I asked, leaning forward to examine the documents. The photos were date-stamped just yesterday.

"Solid as a Russian winter," Stripes replied, tapping a finger on a document covered in Cyrillic script. "My contact in FSB owes me a big favor. This is the flight manifest, security footage, hotel reservations. Balal arrived in Tel Aviv with a female companion matching Mazida's description. Woman appeared... not willing."

Charming picked up one of the photos, squinting at it before passing it to me. The image showed a woman being guided -- or forced -- into a luxury sedan, a man's hand gripping her upper arm tightly. She wore a hijab, but even from the side angle, the resemblance to Zara was unmistakable. I passed the photo on, trying to ignore the sick feeling in my gut.

"Why now?" Doc asked, adjusting his glasses as he studied the map. "Mazida's been on her own for what, three years? And married for probably twenty or thirty? I have no idea how old she is."

"Zara," I said before I could stop myself. All eyes turned to me. "Zara turned twenty-two. What if she's the one they're really after? They couldn't use her mother to broker any deals when she was younger, so now maybe they want Zara."

"Azrael's right," Stripes confirmed with a nod in my direction. "In a traditional family like the Quadirs, an unmarried daughter becomes the best way to leverage deals. Balal wants control of both women."

"So when you said they would use her for leverage, what type did you mean?" Ripper asked, finally looking away from the ceiling.

Stripes' expression darkened. "Many possibilities, none are good. Could be an arranged marriage for Zara to cement business ties. Could be punishment for Mazida's disrespect all these years.

Could be about money. Colton left a sizable estate to both his wife and daughter, despite the small home Mazida has now."

"Does Zara know her mother's been taken?" Charming directed this question at me. "Or is she still just assuming that's what happened?"

"She knows her mother is missing. I did tell her I believe she was kidnapped, but that we just had more questions than answers right now. So she doesn't have all the details." I gestured to the pile of evidence on the table. "I wanted all of you to review what I dug up first and see if we could narrow down what happened."

"She must be told what happened, and told who is responsible," Stripes said solemnly. "But first, we must decide what the club will do."

The tension in the room ratcheted up another notch. What Stripes was really asking was whether this was club business or my personal problem. If it was just my issue, I'd have the club's support but would be expected to handle it mostly on my own. If it was club business, the full resources of the Devil's Boneyard would be deployed -- and that meant blood would definitely flow.

"The Quadirs have deep connections," Charming mused, running a hand through his graying hair. "Getting to Mazida in Tel Aviv won't be easy."

"And what's our interest here?" asked Magnus, one of the quieter members who rarely spoke unless he had something important to say. "Why is this club business?"

I started to speak, but Stripes cut me off. "Zara is Azrael's woman. Isn't that enough reason?"

Several of the older members nodded. I could tell the thought of us going to the Middle East to retrieve Mazida bothered the younger ones. I couldn't blame them. It wasn't high on my list of places to visit. Despite how beautiful it looked in pictures online, I had a feeling we'd get into trouble fast.

"If Balal Quadir is working with the Tel Aviv crime families, we could be looking at a new pipeline for drugs and weapons coming into our territory. The fact they came to Florida for her means they had time to scope things out. Lots of ways for them to smuggle shit into this state. We're surrounded by water on three sides for fuck's sake. Getting Mazida back gives us leverage and information." Charming eyed each of us. "Makes you wonder what he noticed and what his future plans might be."

I sat back, letting them frame it as club business. Sure, Zara was mine. But, as far as they knew, I'd claimed her as a way to keep her safe. No one knew I'd started to feel something for her. They didn't need to know that somewhere along the way, the avenging angel had found something worth fighting for beyond vengeance.

"So what's the play?" Phantom asked, cracking his knuckles one by one, a habit that usually signaled his readiness for violence.

"We need more information," Charming said. "Contacts on the ground in Tel Aviv. Safe houses. Extraction routes."

"My contacts can provide this." Stripes nodded. "But it will take time. Few days, at least."

"And money," Doc pointed out.

"Club has money." Ripper shrugged. "What is it there for if not for times like this?"

I studied the map, tracing the marked route from the States to Tel Aviv with my finger. The distance felt insurmountable, not in miles but in influence. We were powerful here, on our turf. There, we'd be strangers walking into someone else's kingdom.

"We'll need more than money and information," I said finally. "We'll need allies over there. Local muscle that knows the territory. And sat phones. We need secure lines."

"Anatoly," Stripes said, a slight smile appearing beneath his white beard. "Our President's ex-best friend. He has connections with the Russian community in Israel. Many former FSB, military."

"Can we trust him?" Charming asked. "Sure, he helped us once before, but that's been a while."

Stripes laughed, a harsh sound that held little humor. "Trust? No. But family is family. He will help because you ask, and because between you and me, we know enough secrets to destroy him if he betrays us."

The old Russian's frankness drew a few grim chuckles around the table. In our world, such arrangements were often more reliable than friendship or even blood.

"Then it's settled," Charming declared, looking each of us in the eye. "We're going to get Mazida Quadir back. Stripes will coordinate with his contacts for intelligence. Havoc, you handle logistics -- transport, weapons, whatever we need. Doc, medical contingencies. Ripper, research on Balal Quadir and his associates. I want to know what we're walking into. And, Shade, pull me everything you've got about every aspect of this mission."

He turned to me last. "Azrael, you'll be point on this. It's your operation. Pick who you want to take."

I nodded, feeling the assignment settle on my shoulders like a heavy load. It wasn't just club business anymore -- it was officially my responsibility. As it should be.

"And Zara?" I asked.

Charming's expression softened slightly. "Tell her what she needs to know. But keep her here. Last thing we need is an emotional civilian in the mix."

I didn't argue, though I already knew that conversation would be the hardest part of this whole operation. Telling Zara to sit and wait while we went after her mother would be like telling a wildfire to stay put.

As the meeting continued, with details being hashed out and plans taking shape, I found my thoughts drifting to my house and the woman waiting there, unaware that her world was about to shift again. Unaware that the man she'd sought out for help was now officially committed to giving it -- with the full might of the Devil's Boneyard behind him.

The Russians hadn't offered their assistance for nothing, and neither would anyone else. I only hoped whatever price was asked was one I or the club would be willing to pay.

The meeting was winding down, the initial shock of Stripes' intel giving way to the cold calculation of men used to violence. I watched as Charming leaned forward in his seat, his hands splayed across the scattered documents. His eyes, still sharp despite the crow's feet framing them, scanned each of our faces before he spoke. "We reach out to the Russian Mafia, officially this time," he said, his voice conveying a decision already made. "I'll contact Anatoly personally."

No one objected. When Charming spoke like that, it wasn't a suggestion. It was the road we'd be taking, whether we liked the terrain or not.

Around the table, the brothers began shifting in their seats, the wooden chairs creaking beneath leather cuts and tensed muscles. Phantom cracked his knuckles one last time. Doc removed his glasses, polishing them methodically with the edge of his shirt -- a ritual he performed whenever he was processing something troubling. Normally, we wouldn't have brought him in on this type of discussion, which meant Charming was trusting him more and more. Havoc gathered the maps, folding them with military precision, while Ripper simply stared at his hands, his face a mask of contained violence.

"We move on this tomorrow," Charming continued, pushing back from the table. "Get some rest. Clear your heads. Once we're in motion, there won't be time for second thoughts. I want your asses in Tel Aviv within the next few days, before we lose Mazida for good."

As the men began to rise, collecting papers and exchanging quiet words, my attention caught on something half-hidden beneath one of Stripes' intel reports. I reached out, sliding the document aside to reveal a small photograph. It wasn't part of the intelligence packet -- it was personal. Zara smiled up at me, her blue eyes startling against her swarthy skin, a contradiction inherited from her mixed heritage. The photo must have fallen from my cut when I sat down. I'd swiped it from her mother's house, feeling the need to have Zara with me even in this small way.

I quickly picked it up, but not before Stripes noticed. His hand covered mine for a brief moment, his eyes meeting mine with an understanding that made my throat tighten.

"It's not a weakness to care for something worth protecting," he said quietly, his accent thicker with emotion. "Is a reason to fight better, yes?"

I didn't answer, just pressed my lips together and slipped the photo into my inner pocket. The weight of it against my chest felt suddenly significant, like armor over my heart. I glanced away, not wanting the others to read whatever might be showing on my face. The brotherhood understood revenge, understood loyalty, understood fighting for the club. What they might not understand was the uncomfortable truth I was barely admitting to myself -- that somewhere along the line, Zara Colton had become more than just a woman who needed help. She'd become something I couldn't define but couldn't ignore.

We filed out of Church in near silence, boots heavy on the worn floorboards. This hallway had seen generations of Devil's Boneyard business, the walls themselves soaked in secrets and blood oaths. Tonight, they'd witnessed another.

The heavy door thudded shut behind us with a finality that sent a chill down my spine. That sound marked the official beginning of whatever was coming next. It would end with another sound: either the celebration of victory or the silence of men who wouldn't be coming home.

"You good with this?" Phantom asked, falling into step beside me as we moved toward the main room of the clubhouse. His frame blocked most of the hallway, forcing others to slide past him along the wall.

"With what part?" I asked, knowing exactly what he meant but playing for time.

He gave me a sideways look that said he wasn't buying it. "With bringing the club into your personal shit. With going halfway around the world for a woman you don't know and another you seem to know better than you're letting on. I'd thought you'd claimed her out of a sense of duty. Now I'm thinking I was wrong."

I stopped walking, turned to face him. "You questioning the President's decision?"

"Fuck no," he replied without hesitation. "I'm asking my brother if his head's on straight before we roll into something that could get us all killed."

The rest of the men continued past us, giving us space for what they recognized as a necessary conversation. In the dim light, Phantom's face was all hard angles and shadow, but his eyes held genuine concern beneath the challenge.

"My head's straight," I told him, meeting his gaze steadily. "This is club business with personal stakes. No different than when we protected Grey, Meg, or any of the other women here."

He considered this, then nodded slowly. "Just making sure. Because the way you looked at that picture just now... that's the look of a man with something to lose."

I didn't confirm or deny it. Instead, I clapped him on the shoulder and moved past him. "We all have something to lose, brother. That's why we win."

The main room had transformed in the time we'd been meeting. The Prospect had set out bottles of whiskey and glasses on the bar, anticipating the need for liquid courage or comfort. A few of the old ladies had arrived, sensing something was happening. They hovered at the edges of the room, exchanging worried glances but knowing better than to ask questions until they were brought into the circle of knowledge. Still no club pussy in sight, although that was a good thing right now. Couldn't always trust them, no matter how many checks we ran.

I grabbed a bottle and a glass, avoiding the concerned looks. I needed to get back to my place, needed to figure out what I was going to tell Zara. The thought of facing her made my stomach twist in a way that had nothing to do with fear of danger and everything to do with fear of her reaction.

What would I say? *Your mother has been kidnapped by her controlling brother and taken to the Middle East. I'm going to get her back with a bunch of bikers and Russian mobsters. Wait here and don't worry.* Yeah, that would go over well.

"Keep your dick in your pants and your head in the game," Ripper muttered as he passed, reading me too easily for comfort. "Save the domestic drama for after we get back."

I flipped him off without looking, but he had a point. Whatever was happening between Zara and me -- or not happening -- had to take a back seat to the mission. Getting Mazida back safe was the priority, not sorting out my inconvenient feelings for her daughter.

I downed my whiskey in one swallow, letting the burn center me. As I set the glass down, I caught Charming watching me from across the room. He beckoned me over with a slight tilt of his head.

"You'll need to tell her tonight," he said without preamble when I reached him. "We're moving fast on this. Stripes is already on the phone with his contacts. We'll have transport arranged by day after tomorrow."

"I know," I replied, glancing toward the door. "I'm heading back now."

He studied me for a moment. "She's not coming, Azrael. Not negotiable. I need your word on that."

"You have it," I said automatically, though I already knew it wouldn't be that simple. "But she's not going to like it."

"She doesn't have to like it. She just has to accept it." His tone softened slightly. "This isn't her fight."

"It's her mother," I pointed out.

"And it's my club I'm risking," he countered. "My brothers I'm sending into unknown territory. If she came along and something happened to her, how would that affect the mission or you?"

The question hit too close to home, and I didn't have an answer that wouldn't reveal more than I wanted to. Instead, I just nodded my understanding.

"I'll handle it," I assured him. "She stays here."

Charming seemed satisfied with that, clasping my shoulder briefly before moving away to speak with Doc. I took it as my dismissal and headed for the door, pausing only to exchange a few words with Stripes, who was barking orders in Russian into his phone.

"You will need a passport," he told me, covering the mouthpiece briefly. "And patience. Tel Aviv is not like here. We cannot just shoot our way in and out."

"I've never been to the Middle East," I admitted.

He gave me a grim smile. "Then you are in for an education. Anatoly will meet us at airport in Tel Aviv. After that" -- he shrugged expressively --"we improvise."

Improvisation with Stripes usually meant blood and fire, but I kept that observation to myself. I still remembered what happened when he swooped in to rescue his woman. "I'll be ready," I promised instead.

Outside, the night air hit me like a splash of cold water. The clubhouse was set back from the main road, surrounded by enough land to give us privacy and security. The parking lot was filled with motorcycles and a few trucks, chrome gleaming under the security lights. My Harley sat waiting, a black shadow among its brothers.

I swung my leg over the seat, feeling the familiar comfort of the machine beneath me. For a moment, I sat there without starting the engine, letting the consequence of what was coming settle over me. Israel. A foreign crime family. A rescue mission with too many unknowns. And waiting for me at home, a woman whose reaction I couldn't predict but whose trust I couldn't bear to lose.

The photo of Zara pressed against my chest, tucked safely in my inner pocket. I reached up and touched the spot. A reminder of what was at stake -- not just Mazida's life, but whatever fragile thing had been growing between her daughter and me.

I kicked the bike to life, the roar drowning out my thoughts momentarily. The road stretched before me, a ribbon of asphalt leading home to Zara and the conversation I didn't want to have. Beyond that lay another road -- one that would take us across oceans to face an enemy we barely understood, in a land where our reputation and strength meant nothing.

I opened the throttle, letting the speed clear my head. One challenge at a time. First, I had to tell Zara what had happened to her mother. Then I had to convince her to let me handle it.

And then I had to make damn sure I came back alive. Because despite all my efforts not to, I'd given her something dangerous: a promise. And in my world, promises were kept, or you died trying.

The wind whipped past as I leaned into a curve, the bike responding to my body's slightest shift. In that moment of perfect control, I found a sliver of peace. Whatever was coming -- whatever battles, whatever revelations, whatever pain -- I would face it. Not just because the club demanded it or because duty required it. But because somewhere along the way, the avenging angel had found someone special, someone who made the blood on my hands feel like a price worth paying, if it meant keeping her world intact.

Chapter Eleven

Azrael

I wasn't used to coming home to the smell of someone else's cooking. For nearly a decade, my house had been a place to crash between jobs for the club -- somewhere to wash blood off my hands and catch a few hours of sleep before the next call came in. But within a day, Zara Colton had turned my barren space into something that resembled a home, and I wasn't sure how I felt about it. Tonight, though, I had news about her mother, and that complicated everything.

As I walked through the door, the savory aroma of baked chicken hit me first. Then I saw her, moving with determined efficiency around my dining table, arranging silverware with precise movements of her slender fingers. The table -- a piece of furniture I'd used mainly as a place to clean my guns -- now had a tablecloth. Fucking tablecloth. Where had she even found that?

"You're just in time," Zara said, looking up. Those blue eyes of hers locked onto mine, a jarring contrast against her darker complexion. Half Middle Eastern like me, but where I was all hard edges, she was soft curves that my fingers itched to trace.

She was too young. Too innocent. Too fucking beautiful for a man with my history.

"I made dinner," she added unnecessarily, gesturing to the spread with a nervous flutter of her hand. "I hope that's okay."

I nodded, dropping my cut on the back of a chair before sinking into a seat at the table. Until she'd come into my life, it had been ages since I'd sat at a table for a meal.

"Eat while it's hot," she urged, placing a plate of

chicken, mashed potatoes, and green beans in front of me.

I stared at the meal. Who was the last person to cook for me? Probably my mother. Even my girlfriend hadn't bothered. Even though her mother was in trouble, Zara was standing in my kitchen, serving me dinner like we were just your average couple.

"You find anything?" Zara asked, her voice casual, but I caught the tremor underneath. She'd been asking the same question every day since she'd shown up, begging for my help.

I took a bite of chicken to buy myself time. It was good -- seasoned perfectly with herbs I didn't even know I had in my kitchen. "Eat first," I said after swallowing. "Then we'll talk."

Her eyes narrowed, and for a moment I thought she'd argue, but then she sat across from me with her own plate. Smart girl. She was learning when to push and when to stand down.

We ate in silence for a few minutes. I watched her covertly between bites. Twenty-two years old, yet she carried herself with a gravity beyond her years.

"Is my mother alive?" Zara finally asked, unable to maintain the silence any longer.

I set down my fork and met her gaze directly. "Yes."

The breath whooshed out of her, and her hand trembled as she reached for her water glass. "Where is she?"

"She's being held at a place in Tel Aviv. From what we dug up, her brother is the one who took her." I still didn't know who "C" was on the postcard, the one warning her to run. That had proven to be a dead end so far.

"Tel Aviv?"

"I have confirmation she's there."

"How did you --" She stopped herself, then squared her shoulders. "No, I don't need to know how you got the information. When are we going to get her?"

I took a long drink of water, then set the glass down with deliberate care. "I'm going day after tomorrow. You're staying here."

Her back stiffened. "The hell I am."

"You asked for my help. This is how it works."

"She's my mother."

"And that's exactly why you can't be anywhere near this operation." I leaned forward, resting my forearms on the table. "Your uncle has armed men at his beck and call. We have photographs of him with your mother, getting off a private jet and into a car. But he's in bed with some bad men. I can't risk you going."

Zara flinched but didn't look away. "I need to be there. I need to see her."

"You will. After I get her out." I pushed my plate away, appetite gone. "Listen carefully, Zara. I promise I'll bring her home safely. But that's only going to happen if I can focus entirely on the job without worrying about keeping you safe too."

She stood suddenly, plates clattering as she gathered them with jerky movements. "Then why can't I come with you? I could wait somewhere safe, away from the action. I could help when you get her out -- she might be scared, confused. She'd recognize me."

I shook my head, my jaw tight. "Not happening."

"I'm not some delicate flower, Azrael. I can handle myself."

"This isn't about whether or not you're tough enough." I rose to my feet, towering over her. "Your presence will jeopardize the mission. Period. These men -- they'll use anything they can against me. If they see you, if they even suspect you're connected to me or to your mother, they'll grab you too. And then I'd have to split my focus."

She turned away, but not before I caught the shimmer of tears in her eyes. She began aggressively washing dishes, her back rigid.

"Zara." My voice softened despite myself. "I understand wanting to be there. But this is what I do. The club is sending some of our best men with me. We'll get her out."

"And what if something goes wrong?" she asked, still not looking at me. "What if this is my only chance to see her again, and I miss it because I'm sitting here, waiting like a good little girl?"

I crossed the kitchen in three strides and gently turned her to face me, my hands on her shoulders. The contact sent an unwelcome spark of heat through my palms. "Nothing's going to go wrong. But if it does, it won't be because I was distracted trying to protect you too."

She looked up at me, those blue eyes swimming with tears she refused to let fall. This close, I could smell her shampoo -- something floral that had no business in my house but somehow seemed right on her. Her lips parted slightly, and for one insane moment, I thought about lowering my head to taste them.

Instead, I stepped back, dropping my hands from her shoulders. "I'll need to meet with the club tomorrow to work out the details. After that, I'll tell you everything I know about where she's been and what to expect when she comes home, or as much as Charming says I can."

Zara took a deep breath, then nodded once.

"Fine. But I want regular updates. And I want to know exactly who's going with you." She hesitated, then added quietly, "I may not know everyone yet, but I'll feel better having names. I need to know you'll come back too."

Something twisted in my gut. No one had worried about whether I'd come back from a job in... hell, maybe ever. The club expected results, not feelings.

"I always come back," I said, my voice rougher than I intended. "It's kind of my specialty."

She gave me a tremulous smile that hit me like a punch to the solar plexus. "Good. Because when you bring my mother home, I'm going to need you to explain to her why I've been staying in your house and am now considered your woman."

I almost smiled at that. Almost. "I'm sure she'll be thrilled to know her daughter's been shacking up with a forty-year-old biker nicknamed after the Angel of Death."

"Thirty-nine," she corrected, the ghost of mischief crossing her face. "And she'll be grateful to the man who saved her, no matter what his name is." She finished drying her hands and moved closer, resting her palm briefly against my chest. "Thank you, Azrael. For finding her."

I nodded, not trusting myself to speak with her hand burning an imprint through my shirt. After a moment, she withdrew it and turned back to finish the dishes.

I retreated to the living room, then to the hallway, needing space to think. Less than two days to plan the extraction, to figure out how to keep both Mazida and myself alive so we could come back to this woman who'd somehow carved out a place in my solitary life in less than a week.

I stood in the hallway with my back against the wall, the house quiet except for the occasional clink of dishes as Zara finished cleaning up. My phone had buzzed twice in the last hour -- messages from Samurai and Phantom letting me know they'd be there if I needed them. Good men. But even with them at my back, the mission would be dangerous. The kind where not everyone comes home. And that knowledge had me on edge, especially with Zara under my roof, her scent lingering in every room.

The dim light from the living room cast long shadows down the corridor. I'd never bothered replacing the hallway fixture when it burned out months ago. Never saw the point. Now the darkness felt appropriate -- a physical manifestation of the shadows I lived in, the ones I was about to drag Mazida Quadir out of, the ones I wanted to keep Zara from ever knowing.

I checked my messages again. I'd killed men before -- more than I cared to count -- but this operation was different. This one wasn't just club business. This one mattered to the woman who'd been sleeping in my spare bedroom.

"Azrael?" Her voice came softly from the end of the hallway.

I looked up, slipping my phone into my pocket. Zara stood at the juncture where the hallway met the living room, the light behind her turning her silhouette into something ethereal. The loose pajama pants and fitted tank top she wore revealed the curves I'd been trying not to notice.

"Everything okay?" I asked, my voice low.

She stepped closer, moving into the shadows with me. "I wanted to apologize."

"For what?"

"Pushing about coming with you." She stopped a few feet away. "I know you're doing this for me, and I'm grateful. I just..." She trailed off, wrapping her arms around herself.

"You just want your mother back."

She nodded, taking another step closer. "It's been hell not knowing if she was dead or alive."

"That's why you tracked me down. And now I'm going to do what I promised."

"Yes." She was close enough now that I could see her face in the dim light, could make out the determination etched in her features. "If anyone can find her, it's you."

I shifted my weight, uncomfortable with the reverence in her tone. "I'm not the hero you think I am, Zara."

"You found my mother when no one else could."

"I haven't rescued her yet."

"But you will." She reached out, her fingers brushing my forearm, light as a feather but searing as a brand. "I believe in you."

Her touch sent heat crawling up my arm and settling low in my gut. Days of careful distance, of maintaining boundaries, threatened to collapse from that simple contact. I'd kept space between us for good reasons -- she was too young, too innocent, too Goddamn important to get tangled up with a man like me. I may have claimed her, but we had all the time in the world. No sense in rushing into things.

But standing in this darkened hallway with her hand on my arm, those reasons felt far away.

"Zara," I said, her name a warning.

She didn't back off. Instead, she stepped closer, close enough that I could feel the warmth radiating from her body. "I've been your woman for more than a day, and you barely touch me. You watch me when you think I don't notice, but then you pull away." Her voice dropped lower. "Why?"

The question hung between us, filling the narrow space. "You know why," I finally said.

"Because I'm too young? Because my mother is missing? Because you're dangerous?" She tilted her head. "I don't think those are the real reasons."

My jaw tightened. "Then what are they?"

"I think you're afraid." Her hand slid up my arm to my shoulder, leaving fire in its wake. "Not of this mission. You're afraid of wanting something for yourself."

"You don't know what you're talking about." But I didn't move away. Couldn't move away.

"Don't I?" She leaned in, her face turned up to mine, her breath warm against my chin. "I've watched you too, you know. The way you make sure I have everything I need. The way you look at me when you think I'm asleep. The way you position yourself between me and any man who comes near, even when those men are just your brothers, people you know won't hurt me."

My hands hung uselessly at my sides, itching to grab her, to pull her against me or push her away -- I wasn't sure which. "I'm too old for you."

"Seventeen years isn't that much."

"It's a lifetime."

Her hand moved from my shoulder to my cheek, her palm cool against my stubbled skin. "I'm not asking for your heart, Azrael. I'm just asking for tonight, to be close to you just this once."

Before I could respond, she rose on her tiptoes and pressed her lips to mine. Soft. Tentative. A question in the form of a kiss.

For one heart-stopping moment, I stood frozen, every muscle rigid with shock and want. Then something broke loose inside me, some floodgate I'd been holding closed since she first walked into my life. My hands found her waist, gripping hard enough to leave marks as I backed her against the wall.

I deepened the kiss, taking control, telling myself this would be enough -- just this one taste before I pulled away and did the right thing. Her lips parted on a gasp, and I took ruthless advantage, my tongue sweeping into her mouth as if I could devour her from the inside out.

She made a small, broken sound against my lips, her hands clutching at my shoulders, pulling me closer. The heat that had been simmering in my blood erupted into an inferno. Her body molded against mine, soft where I was hard, yielding where I was unyielding.

It would be so easy to lift her, to carry her to my bedroom and lose myself in her for hours. To forget about Tel Aviv and Mazida and the Devil's Boneyard and everything else for just one night.

That thought was enough to make me pull back, breathing hard. Her lips were swollen from my kiss, her eyes half-lidded and dazed. Beautiful enough to make a man forget his own name, let alone his duty.

"We can't do this," I said, my voice rough.

Her fingers tangled in my hair, preventing me from moving farther away. "We just did."

"You don't know what you're asking for."

"I'm not asking for anything. I'm telling you what I want." She held my gaze, no trace of doubt in her eyes. "I want you, Azrael. I'm ready for a real relationship -- not just someone to rescue my mother, not just a protector, but a partner."

I closed my eyes, fighting for control. "You don't know who I am. What I've done."

"I know exactly who you are. You're the man who's going to save my mother. The man who's killed to protect women like her -- like me." Her voice was steady, sure. "The man I've been falling for since the day I walked into this house. Maybe even before that."

"I'm the man who's about to walk through fire to get your mom back, a man who is going to fight like hell to get back to you." The words tasted bitter on my tongue, as did my omission. The fact I might *not* make it back. "I can't give you what you deserve, Zara."

"I don't want what I deserve. I want what I choose." She pulled me closer, her body flush against mine again. "And I choose you. For however long we have. And if you don't come back, then that means all we have is tonight and tomorrow. I want to make it count."

Those words hit me like a bullet to the chest, piercing through the armor I'd built around myself over decades. Two days. That's all we might have. Two days before I entered a country I'd never been to before. Two days before I added more names to the long list of men I'd killed, before I either brought Mazida Quadir home to her daughter or died trying.

Two days seemed so short measured against the time I wanted with her.

"If we do this," I said, my hands sliding from her waist to her hips, "there's no going back. No pretending it didn't happen."

"I don't want to go back." She pressed a kiss to my jaw, then my throat. "I want to move forward. With you."

My resolve crumbled like ash. I captured her lips

again, kissing her with all the pent-up need I'd been denying for days. My hands roamed her body, memorizing the curve of her hips, the dip of her waist, the swell of her breasts pressed against my chest.

She responded with equal fervor, her fingers digging into my shoulders as if she could anchor herself to me. One of my hands slid beneath her tank top, finding the warm, smooth skin of her lower back. She arched into the touch, a soft moan escaping her lips.

"Azrael," she whispered against my mouth, my name a prayer and a demand all at once.

I broke the kiss, my forehead resting against hers as we both fought for breath. "This changes everything," I warned her.

"Good." Her smile was small but sure. "It was about time something did."

I huffed out a laugh despite myself. "You're going to be trouble, aren't you?"

"Probably." She traced the line of my jaw with her fingertip. "Is that going to be a problem?"

I caught her hand and pressed a kiss to her palm, watching her eyes darken. "No. But it might get in the way of my focus for this mission."

"Then let me make a deal with you." She wrapped her arms around my neck. "For the next two days, I won't ask to come along. I won't argue about staying behind. I'll let you plan and prepare however you need to." Her gaze held mine, unwavering. "But in return, tonight is ours. No holding back, no second-guessing, no regrets."

The offer was tempting -- more than tempting. But I needed her to understand what she was getting into. "And what happens after? After I bring your mother home? After you have what you came for?"

Her expression softened. "I came looking for the Angel of Death to find my mother. I wasn't expecting to find something for myself too." She pressed a gentle kiss to my lips. "But now that I have, I'm not letting go easily."

Those words settled something inside me, some restless part that had never found peace. Two days until the mission. A lifetime of darkness behind me. And somehow, in this dimly lit hallway with Zara in my arms, the future didn't look quite so bleak.

I lifted her, her legs wrapping instinctively around my waist as I carried her toward my bedroom. Tomorrow would bring planning, preparation, the heaviness of the mission ahead. But tonight -- tonight belonged to us.

And God help anyone who tried to take her from me now.

Chapter Twelve

Zara

I hadn't expected Azrael to lift me like that, so suddenly yet so gently. One moment I was standing in the hallway. The next I was wrapped around him, my weight seemingly nothing to him. The hard planes of his body felt like a fortress against mine as he carried me down the hallway, his footsteps deliberate and unhurried.

"Az," I whispered, my fingers curling into the soft fabric of his shirt.

"Sam. Call me Sam when it's just us," he said.

"Sam." No, that didn't feel quite right. "Samir."

He didn't respond with words. Instead, his arms tightened around me. His scent enveloped me -- leather, musk, and something uniquely him that I couldn't name but had grown addicted to over these past days.

"You don't have to carry me," I said, though my body betrayed my words as I nestled closer to him.

"I know," he replied, his voice a low rumble I could feel vibrating through his chest. "I want to."

Two simple words, but coming from Azrael -- Samir Hamdi, Sam to his friends, and the Angel of Death to his enemies -- they carried power, like a vow. I'd learned quickly that he never said anything he didn't mean, and he never wanted anything he couldn't take.

The traffic outside created a distant hum, occasionally punctuated by the growl of a motorcycle that made me think of the club. Azrael's brothers. The men who called him when there was a problem that needed permanent solving. The thought made me shiver, not with fear of him but with the knowledge of what he was capable of. I'd seen it firsthand.

"Cold?" he asked, misinterpreting my reaction.

"No." I couldn't lie to him, not now. "Just thinking about what's coming."

His jaw tightened, the only indication that my words had affected him. "Don't."

"How can I not?" I challenged, keeping my voice soft despite the steel behind it. "A handful of you against how many of my uncle's men?"

"I told you --"

"I know what you told me. That the club has your back. That you'll get my mom out safely." I traced the line of his jaw with my finger, feeling the stubble that had grown throughout the day. He'd shaved off his beard yesterday, even though I didn't know why.

Azrael paused in the middle of the hallway, his dark eyes finding mine in the half-light. At thirty-nine, the lines around his eyes spoke of years of hard living, but it was the intensity behind them that always captured me. Half Middle Eastern from his mother's side, he had inherited her coloring -- swarthy skin, nearly black eyes, and dark hair that I'd wanted to run my fingers through countless times.

"Zara," he said, my name like a prayer on his lips. "I've been the boogeyman that keeps men like your uncle up at night since before you knew there was evil in the world."

He wasn't exaggerating. Azrael had earned his road name for a reason. The Angel of Death. Their cleaner. Their executioner.

And somehow, against all logic and self-preservation, he had become my protector and was about to become my lover.

I clung tighter to him as we continued down the hallway, feeling the muscle beneath his shirt shift with each step. The man was solid, built by years of fighting and riding and surviving. My fingers brushed against an old scar on his forearm -- a knife wound from years ago, he'd told me, from a time when he'd been less careful.

"What time will you leave?" I asked, needing to know how much time we had left.

"To meet the club or to get your mom?"

"I mean tomorrow. When you meet with the others," I clarified.

"Early," he replied. "Meeting the others at the clubhouse no later than eight."

The quiet rustle of my pajamas against his jeans filled the silence between us. We passed the spare bedroom, the one he kept ready but that no one ever seemed to use. Until I'd come here.

"You should sleep in my room tonight," he said, as if reading my thoughts as we passed the spare room. It wasn't a question.

"I wasn't planning on going anywhere else," I responded.

The thud of his boots against the hardwood floor created a steady rhythm, like a heartbeat. I matched my breathing to it instinctively, finding comfort in its regularity. Azrael was like that -- a force of nature you could set your watch by. I'd been watching him intently, wanting to know every little thing about him. And from what I'd observed, he was predictable in his routines, unpredictable in his actions. A contradiction wrapped in leather and danger.

The pictures on the walls were sparse -- a few black-and-white photos of motorcycles, one of the full club lined up on their bikes, and a single color photograph of a beautiful Middle Eastern woman with Azrael's eyes. His mother, who'd died of cancer when he was young. The woman who'd been gang-raped at fifteen and had raised her son alone, never knowing which of her attackers had fathered him.

As we approached the bedroom, I felt the tension in the air shift from something heavy with words unsaid to something charged with promise. The dangerous mission loomed over us, but it had created an urgency that made every touch, every moment, more significant.

Azrael paused at the threshold, looking down at me with an expression I'd come to recognize -- the look he got when he was memorizing my face, as if preparing for a time when I wouldn't be there. It was both flattering and terrifying.

"What?" I asked.

"Just making sure this is what you want," he said, his voice husky.

I almost laughed at the absurdity. As if I hadn't made it clear from the moment I'd kissed him. As if my body against his wasn't answer enough.

"Take me to bed, Samir," I said, meeting his gaze without flinching. "We've only got tonight and tomorrow."

His lips quirked into what might have been a smile on any other man. On Azrael, it was barely a softening of his usual intensity. But I'd learned to read it, to treasure those small breaks in his carefully maintained control.

"Then we better not waste time," he said, and carried me the final steps into his bedroom, where the shadows from the hallway gave way to deeper darkness broken only by the pale moonlight filtering through partially drawn blinds.

I felt a flutter in my stomach -- anticipation, fear for the mission ahead, and the undeniable pull I felt toward this dangerous man who held me like I was something precious in a world that had taught him nothing was.

The moment Azrael laid me down on his bed, I felt the worn mattress dip beneath my weight, the familiar scent of leather and bourbon rising from the sheets that had absorbed so much of him. His body followed mine down, his weight both comforting and demanding as he settled over me, his dark eyes never leaving mine even as his hand found the curve of my hip. I reached up to trace the hard line of his jaw, feeling the contrast between rough stubble and the unexpected softness of his lips as they descended to claim mine.

The kiss started slow, deliberate, like everything Azrael did. Nothing rushed, nothing wasted. His mouth moved against mine with a precision that spoke of experience, but there was something else there too -- a hunger that seemed specific to me. I'd never felt that before, the sense that a man like him -- who could have anyone -- wanted me with such singular focus.

"Zara," he murmured against my lips, my name becoming something sacred in his mouth. His hand slid up from my hip to my ribs, stopping just beneath my breast in a question that wasn't really a question at all.

I arched into his touch, answering without words. The danger heading his way soon hung over us, making each touch feel like it might be the last, making each sigh more precious.

His bedroom was sparse, like the rest of his house. No clutter, no unnecessary decoration. A heavy dresser against one wall, a chair, a nightstand with a lamp, a gun, and a book dog-eared halfway through. The blinds were partially drawn, allowing slivers of moonlight to cut across the bed, highlighting the planes of Azrael's face as he looked down at me.

"You're thinking too much," he said, his thumb brushing my lower lip, drawing my attention back to him.

"Pot, kettle," I replied, earning a rare half-smile that softened his features and made him look younger than his thirty-nine years.

"Fair enough." His hand moved to cup my breast, his thumb circling the nipple through the fabric of my tank top until it hardened beneath his touch. "But I'm thinking about you. Only you."

I believed him. In that moment, with his eyes fixed on mine and his body warm and solid above me, I believed that the Angel of Death, the man whose name made hardened criminals tremble, was thinking only of me. It was a heady power that I never asked for but couldn't deny wanting.

He lowered his head again, this time to trace the line of my jaw with his lips, working his way down to the sensitive spot where my neck met my shoulder. His teeth scraped gently against my skin, drawing a gasp from me that seemed to echo in the quiet room.

"I like that sound," he murmured against my throat, and did it again, harder this time, bringing his teeth down in a gentle bite that had me clutching at his shoulders.

The material of his shirt was smooth beneath my fingers. I tugged at it, wanting to pull it off, needing to feel more of him, needing the barrier gone. He helped, yanking it over his head and tossing it onto the chair across the room. It landed perfectly, as if even in the midst of passion, Azrael couldn't allow disorder.

His chest and abdomen were a terrain of scars and tattoos that mapped his life. Bullet wounds, knife marks, the Devil's Boneyard insignia over his heart, and above that, in Arabic script that flowed like calligraphy, a woman's name. "Your mom?"

He nodded. I traced her name with my fingertips, feeling him shudder beneath my touch.

"Cold?" I echoed his earlier question, knowing full well he wasn't.

"No," he admitted, his voice rougher now, less controlled. "Just... you."

I smiled, pulling him back down to me, my hands exploring the muscled expanse of his back, feeling the ridges of old scars. Each one a reminder of close calls, of violence survived, of the dangerous world he inhabited and that I had stepped into willingly.

He slowly removed my tank top and tugged down my pajama pants. When he tugged the fabric away, exposing my skin to the cool air and his heated gaze, I felt vulnerable in a way that had nothing to do with nudity and everything to do with the intensity with which he looked at me.

"Beautiful," he said, the word simple but heavy with meaning coming from a man so economical with praise.

My breath caught as his mouth descended again, this time to the newly exposed skin of my collarbone, my chest, the curve of my breast. His stubble scraped deliciously against my sensitive skin, leaving a trail of fire in its wake. I arched up, seeking more contact, more friction, more of him.

Azrael's hand slid beneath me, large and warm against the small of my back, supporting me as his mouth closed around my nipple. The wet heat of it tore a moan from my throat, loud in the otherwise quiet room. The only other sounds were our breathing, increasingly ragged, and the occasional distant rumble of traffic.

"Samir," I gasped as his teeth grazed sensitive flesh, sending sparks of pleasure-pain radiating through me. "Please."

He raised his head, his dark eyes finding mine, pupils dilated with desire. "Please what?"

"More," I managed, my hands moving to the buttons of his jeans. "Everything."

A ghost of a smile touched his lips before he bent to capture my mouth again, this kiss deeper, hungrier than before. His tongue swept against mine in a rhythm that promised other, more intimate invasions to come. I fumbled with his button fly, my usually deft fingers clumsy with want.

He pulled back, just enough to help me, pushing his jeans down his hips and kicking them off with an efficiency that spoke of practice. When he returned to me, there was only the thin barrier of his boxer briefs between us, doing little to hide his arousal.

My hands skimmed down his sides, feeling the subtle shift of muscle beneath taut skin, the occasional ridge of scar tissue, the sharp jut of his hipbones. When I reached the waistband of his underwear, he sucked in a breath, his control slipping just enough for me to notice.

"Keep that up," he warned, voice like gravel, "and this'll be over too quickly."

"We have all night," I reminded him, hooking my fingers beneath the elastic and tugging down. "And I want you. Now."

Need flashed in his eyes -- hunger, possession, and something darker I couldn't name -- and then he was moving, helping me remove that last barrier, then reaching for the drawer in his nightstand. I stopped his hand.

"I'm on the pill," I said. "And I'm clean. You?"

"Clean," he confirmed. "Get tested regularly."

A necessary precaution in his world, though I didn't ask and he didn't elaborate. There was enough trust between us now that I believed him without question. And enough desire that I didn't want anything between us, not tonight.

He settled back between my thighs, the weight of him both comforting and thrilling. I felt the hard length of him against me, hot and insistent. His eyes held mine as he positioned himself, one hand braced beside my head, the other guiding him to my entrance.

"Tell me you want this," he demanded, his voice strained with the effort of holding back.

"I want this," I said, my hands sliding up his arms to his shoulders, feeling the tension coiled there. "I want you, Azrael."

He pushed forward slowly, filling me inch by deliberate inch, his eyes never leaving mine. I watched his face, fascinated by the play of emotion across features usually so controlled -- pleasure, concentration, and something that might have been awe.

When he was fully seated within me, he paused, both of us adjusting to the sensation. I felt stretched, completed, connected to him in the most primal way possible. My legs came up to wrap around his waist, changing the angle and drawing him even deeper.

"Fuck," he groaned, the curse sounding like a prayer on his lips.

"Yes," I agreed, rocking my hips against his in invitation. "Please."

He chuckled softly, then began to move. Long, measured strokes that spoke of his iron control even in the midst of passion. His eyes remained locked on mine, watching each reaction, learning what I liked, what made me gasp and clutch at his shoulders.

I'd been with men before, but never like this. Never with this level of intensity, of focus. Azrael made love the way he did everything else -- with complete commitment and deadly precision. Each thrust was calculated for maximum effect, each touch designed to elicit the strongest response.

Our bodies moved together in the muted light, finding a rhythm that felt both new and familiar. I ran my hands down his back, feeling the shift of muscle as he moved above me, the light sheen of sweat that made his skin glow in the darkness.

"You feel so good," I whispered, needing him to know, needing to break the silence that had fallen between us, punctuated only by the sounds of our breathing and the subtle creak of the mattress.

His response was to angle his hips differently, hitting a spot inside me that made stars explode behind my eyelids. I cried out, my nails digging into his shoulders hard enough to leave marks. He did it again, and again, relentless in his pursuit of my pleasure.

"Look at me," he commanded as I felt the tension building, my body tightening around his. "I want to see you."

I forced my eyes open, meeting his gaze as the wave crashed over me. The orgasm rippled through me with an intensity that bordered on pain, my body arching beneath his, my inner muscles clenching around him. Through it all, he watched me, his eyes burning with something that went beyond desire.

Only when the last tremor had passed did he allow himself to chase his own release, his rhythm becoming more urgent, less controlled. I held him tightly, my lips at his ear, whispering encouragement, wanting to give him even a fraction of what he'd given me.

When he came, it was with a groan that seemed torn from deep within him, his body tensing above mine, his face momentarily unguarded in a way I rarely saw. For those few seconds, he wasn't Azrael, the Angel of Death. He was just a man, vulnerable and human.

He collapsed beside me, careful not to crush me with his weight, one arm thrown across my waist in a gesture that felt both possessive and protective. Our breathing gradually slowed, our heartbeats returned to normal as we lay together in the quiet aftermath.

I turned my head to look at him, finding his gaze already on me, watching with that intensity that never seemed to dim. He traced idle patterns on my stomach, raising goose bumps despite the warmth of the room.

"What are you thinking?" I asked, my voice sounding loud in the silence.

He considered the question, taking his time as he always did. "That I'd like to keep you here. In my bed."

The simple admission hit harder than a flowery declaration might have. From Azrael, it was probably the highest form of love, the most precious gift he could offer.

"I can take care of myself," I reminded him gently. "If that's why you want me here..."

"I know." His fingers continued their path across my skin, dipping into the hollow of my hip, tracing the curve of my waist. "Doesn't mean I don't want to keep you safe anyway. And it's not entirely why I want you in my bed."

I understood then what he wasn't saying -- that

this mission was about more than club business. It was about removing a threat, about making the world safer for those he cared about. About me.

"Come back to me," I said, turning to face him fully, my hand coming up to cup his cheek. "After this task is completed. Come back to me."

Something flickered in his eyes -- a promise, a determination. "I always finish what I start, Zara."

It wasn't quite an "I love you." It wasn't quite a promise to return. But from Azrael, it was enough. For now, it was enough.

I nestled against him, my head finding the perfect spot on his chest, just above his heart where I could hear its steady beat. His arm tightened around me, his lips pressing a kiss to the top of my head. Outside, the world continued to turn, oblivious to the bubble we'd created in this room, on this bed.

Tonight, in the arms of a man who dealt in death but held me with surprising gentleness, I found a peace I hadn't known I was seeking. And as sleep began to claim me, I realized that somewhere along the way, without intending to, I had fallen in love with the Devil's Boneyard's Angel of Death.

Chapter Thirteen

Azrael

The Tel Aviv market churned with bodies as I weaved through the evening crowd, my senses on high alert. Sunset painted the sky in shades of orange and purple, casting long shadows across the stalls of spices, electronics, and cheap souvenirs that lined the narrow passageways. Stripes and Samurai flanked me, their vigilant eyes scanning each face we passed. None of us spoke. We didn't need to. After years of handling the Devil's Boneyard MC's most delicate problems, we had developed an understanding that went beyond words. Tonight's meeting wasn't one I looked forward to, but then again, being the Angel of Death rarely involved pleasant social calls.

"Three o'clock," Samurai murmured, his chin barely moving as he indicated a man watching us from behind a display of knockoff designer sunglasses.

I gave a slight nod, acknowledging without looking directly. "Probably one of the Russian's people. Let him watch."

The weight of my SIG pressed against my lower back, a constant, comforting presence. I didn't plan on using it -- gunfire in a crowded market would be messy and complicate our already delicate situation -- but I'd learned long ago that peaceful negotiations often required the quiet promise of violence.

Stripes' thick accent cut through the din of haggling vendors. "I do not like this place for our meeting. Too many people. Too many variables."

Despite his age, the old Russian moved with the agility of a man decades younger.

"That's exactly why Viktor chose it," I replied. "Hard to set up an ambush when you can't tell which random tourist might be working for the other side."

We'd been in Tel Aviv for three days now, setting up the groundwork for a negotiation that, if successful, would secure the release of my mother-in-law.

"There," Samurai said, nodding toward a stall displaying imported electronics -- everything from counterfeit AirPods to tablets of questionable origin.

Behind the counter stood Viktor, his pale eyes scanning the crowd with the dispassionate interest of a predator assessing which prey was worth the energy to hunt. His fingers tapped an irregular rhythm on the folding table in front of him, the only outward sign of impatience.

"Azrael," he said as we approached, my road name falling from his lips with practiced precision. He didn't offer his hand, and I didn't expect him to. "You're late."

"Market was crowded," I replied, not bothering to point out that we were exactly on time. Power plays were part of the dance.

Viktor's gaze flicked to Stripes, recognition dawning in his eyes. "Mikhail Petrov. I'd heard you were dead. Your call was unexpected."

Stripes shrugged. "I left that life behind."

A smile that never reached Viktor's eyes briefly touched his lips. His attention returned to me. "You've made quite the name for yourself, Samir -- or do you prefer Azrael now? The Angel of Death. Very dramatic."

The use of my birth name was another power play. I let it slide. "Just business. Are we here to reminisce or to finalize details?"

Around us, the market continued its evening dance. Tourists bargained for souvenirs they didn't need, locals purchased dinner ingredients, and everyone pretended not to notice our tense little gathering. The vendor to our left, a heavyset woman selling scarves, deliberately turned her back on us, recognizing trouble when she saw it.

Viktor gestured to a young man standing nearby, who brought over a tablet. "The terms are set. You'll meet him in an hour," Viktor said, handing the tablet to me. His fingers lingered on the edge for a moment before he added, with steel in his voice, "Don't disappoint."

I took the tablet, scanning the information displayed. GPS coordinates for a warehouse, security details, and a grainy photo of Mazida. The sight of her face hardened something inside me.

"Your mother was Middle Eastern, wasn't she?" Viktor asked, watching me too closely. "This must feel… personal."

My jaw tightened. I didn't ask how he knew about my mother. Information was currency in this world, and Viktor had always been rich. "Every trafficked woman is personal. How many guards?"

"Eight visible. Possibly more inside. Their leader, Darwish, expects payment, not trouble."

"And he'll get what he expects," I said, passing the tablet to Samurai, who memorized the details with a quick glance before passing it to Stripes.

Viktor leaned in slightly. "Darwish is not a patient man. He's also not stupid. He'll be looking for a double-cross."

"We're not in the business of deception," I replied. "We pay, she walks, everyone goes home happy."

"And if complications arise?" Viktor asked, one eyebrow raised.

I met his gaze steadily. "Then he'll understand why they call me the Angel of Death."

A tense silence stretched between us, broken only when Stripes handed the tablet back to Viktor's assistant.

"Your reputation precedes you," Viktor acknowledged with a small nod. "There's one more thing you should know. Darwish recently aligned himself with the Kazarian network."

The name sent a ripple of tension through our small group. The Kazarians were notorious for their brutality and reach. What had been a straightforward exchange had just become significantly more complicated.

"That changes things," Samurai said quietly.

Viktor shrugged. "Perhaps. Perhaps not. They're still businessmen. The question is whether you're prepared to pay the higher price they'll demand when they recognize who they're dealing with."

"Money isn't an issue," I said.

"I wasn't talking about money." Viktor's eyes narrowed. "The Kazarians collect debts in blood and favors. Be prepared to offer both."

With that, he inclined his head slightly and stepped back, signaling the end of our meeting. His assistant disappeared into the crowd, and a moment later, Viktor followed, leaving us standing at the now-empty electronics stall.

"This is fucked," Samurai muttered once Viktor was out of earshot. "If Darwish is tied to the Kazarians, this isn't just about retrieving the woman anymore."

I nodded, already calculating the new variables. "Call Charming. He needs to know the situation's changed."

Samurai stepped away, phone in hand, while

Stripes moved closer to me.

"Kazarians have a long memory," he said gravely. "If they recognize me, this complicates things further."

"Your Bratva days catching up with you, old man?" I asked, though there was no humor in my voice.

Stripes' face remained impassive. "Over forty years ago, I killed a Kazarian's younger brother in Moscow. Some things are not forgiven."

"Fuck." I ran a hand over my face, feeling the day's stubble rasp against my palm. "Can you sit this one out?"

His expression hardened. "*Nyet*. I don't hide from my past. Besides, you need me. My Russian will be useful."

Before I could argue, Samurai returned, his expression grim. "Charming says to proceed. Whatever it takes. Since Zara is your woman, that makes Mazida family."

"And you specifically told him about the Kazarian connection?" I had to make sure. It felt like Charming had agreed too easily.

Samurai nodded. "He's calling in some markers, seeing if there's any leverage we can use. But he was clear -- we get her out tonight, no matter what. And we get our asses home."

We were walking into a situation that had all the makings of a trap, dealing with people notorious for their sadistic creativity when crossed. But the image of Mazida's frightened eyes stayed with me. I thought of my mother, of the stories she told me about the men who had violated her when she was barely fifteen. I hoped like hell no one had touched my mother-in-law, but who knew what these men were capable of.

"An hour gives us just enough time to prepare," I said. "Samurai, get the cash from the hotel safe. Stripes, I want you to scout the perimeter of the meeting point before we arrive."

"And you?" Stripes asked.

I checked my watch, calculating the timing. "I'm going to make sure we have a backup plan if this goes sideways. Meet back at the hotel in thirty."

As we separated, blending into different streams of market-goers, I felt a familiar coldness settle over me -- the detachment that came before violence. It was the state of mind that had earned me my road name. Azrael. The Angel of Death. Tonight, I hoped that name would be enough to keep us alive and bring Mazida home.

But as I walked, I couldn't shake the feeling that this mission had just become something much more dangerous than a simple exchange. The Kazarians didn't deal in ransoms and releases. They dealt in blood and power. And by sundown, I had a feeling we'd be trading in both.

* * *

Zara

The rain tapped against the windows like impatient fingers, matching the rhythm of my pacing across the worn hardwood floor. Three days. Three days since Azrael had left for Tel Aviv with Stripes and Samurai, and the noticeable void from his absence added pressure with each passing hour. I clutched the photograph in my hands so tightly the edges had begun to crease -- Azrael and me taken the day before he'd left, his rare smile catching the sunlight while his arm wrapped possessively around my waist. The Devil's Boneyard compound sat quiet beyond my window, most members gone on various assignments or holed up against the unseasonable downpour. I checked my phone for the thousandth time. No messages. No calls. Just the endless, maddening silence that came with loving a man they called the Angel of Death.

I traced my finger over Azrael's face in the photograph. The man guarded his emotions like they were precious contraband, letting them out only in our most private moments. Sometimes I wondered if I was the only one who knew how deeply he felt things. Beneath the ruthless biker was a man haunted by his mother's suffering, determined to balance scales that would forever remain tipped.

The phone on the counter chirped, and I nearly tripped over my own feet rushing to grab it.

"Hello?" I answered, not bothering to check the caller ID.

"Just me." The disappointment must have been audible in my exhale because Clarity continued, "Still no word?"

"Nothing." I sank onto the sofa, the photograph still clutched in my other hand. "It's been three days."

"That's normal, though. Charming would know if something went wrong, and he'd send someone to tell you, or show up himself."

"I just wish I knew for sure he was still alive and well." I stared up at the ceiling.

"He's fine. I'm sure of it. I just wanted to check on you."

We talked for a few more minutes before hanging up. The conversation had done nothing to ease the knot in my stomach. I resumed my pacing.

A knock at my door jolted me from my memories. I froze, heart racing, before forcing myself to move. Club members rarely visited unless there was news -- good or bad. That's something Clarity had made sure I knew when Azrael had left.

I opened the door to find Dakota, Charming's wife, standing there with two steaming travel mugs and a paper bag that smelled of warm pastry.

"Thought you could use some company," she said, brushing past me into the house without waiting for an invitation. Dakota carried herself with the confidence of a woman who had seen the worst life could offer and decided to live anyway. Her hair was pulled into a messy bun, and she wore no makeup, but there was a natural beauty to her that time couldn't touch.

"Is there news?" I asked, unable to keep the desperation from my voice as I closed the door behind her.

Dakota set the mugs and bag on the kitchen table before turning to face me. "Not exactly, but Charming had a call from Samurai about an hour ago."

My heart jumped into my throat. "And?"

She tilted her head and studied me. "I'm going to tell you what I know, and then you decide for yourself what you'll do with the information. But first, sit down and drink this coffee before you wear a path in that floor."

I complied, though my hands shook slightly as I accepted the mug she pushed toward me. "That sounds ominous."

She shrugged. "It is what it is. Look, Charming had a meeting this morning with someone connected to our contacts in Israel. I also know that the mission parameters have changed. I'm just not sure of all the details. There are some things Charming won't tell me."

I set my mug down before I could drop it. "Are they in danger?"

"More than they expected to be," she admitted. "But less than they've handled before."

The photograph I'd been clutching all evening sat on the table between us now. Dakota glanced at it, a small smile touching her lips. "He's good at what he does, Zara. They all are."

"That's what scares me." I wrapped my hands around the warm mug, trying to absorb its heat into my suddenly cold fingers. "Being good at what he does means being the one they send in when death is the only language left to speak."

Dakota nodded, understanding in her eyes. "The first time Charming went on a run like this, I didn't sleep for days. Kept imagining every possible horrible outcome. By the time he got back, I was a wreck."

"How do you handle it now?" I asked.

"I still worry. That never stops." She reached across the table and placed her hand over mine. "But I've learned to trust. Not just in his abilities, but in the brotherhood. They protect each other as fiercely as they protect us."

Rain drummed against the windows. I picked at the pastry Dakota had brought -- some kind of cinnamon roll -- but couldn't muster much appetite.

"There's something else you should know," Dakota said after a moment of silence. "It seems they know quite a bit about Azrael, which means they've looked into him."

I closed my eyes briefly. "I'm sure he didn't like that."

"He didn't, and it's made things more dangerous. Complicated."

"The Angel of Death," I finished. "They know

who he is."

"Yes."

"But why would they care about someone from America?" I asked.

"Your man doesn't just rescue women. He has a tendency to save Middle Eastern women. I have a feeling he's saved some who were being trafficked by these assholes." She took another sip of her coffee. "Charming told me once that he's never seen anyone become so calm before unleashing hell. It's like he steps outside himself. I'm sure the same will happen over there, if that's what's needed."

I twisted the bracelet on my wrist -- a silver chain with a small angel wing and motorcycle charm Azrael had given me right before he left.

"When will they be back?" I asked.

"If things go as planned, they should be on a flight tomorrow morning. Back here by tomorrow night." She hesitated. "If things don't go as planned..."

"Let's not go there," I said quickly.

Dakota reached for her phone as it buzzed. She read the message, her expression giving nothing away. "Charming says they've made contact. The exchange is happening now."

My stomach clenched. "Now? As in right this minute?"

She nodded. "Midnight in Tel Aviv."

I glanced at the clock on my wall. Somewhere across the world, Azrael was walking into danger. I closed my eyes and sent a silent prayer to whatever deity might be listening.

Dakota watched me with knowing eyes. "The first time is the hardest. Eventually, you develop a sense for when to truly worry and when to trust that they've got it handled."

"And which is this?" I asked.

She considered the question. "Honestly? A little of both. The situation is volatile, but they've got good intel and backup plans."

"What happens after?" I asked. "When they get Mom, I mean."

"They'll bring her here, to the compound." Dakota's expression hardened slightly. "And the men who took her will no longer be in a position to hurt anyone else."

The implication was clear. Those men would be dead, if they weren't already. There was a time when that knowledge would have disturbed me, but that time had passed. Loving Azrael meant accepting certain truths about the world -- some people deserved the violence they received. Just like the men in the alley the first night we met.

"Will they call when it's done?" I asked.

Dakota shook her head. "Probably not. But Charming will know, and he'll tell us."

We sat in companionable silence for a few minutes, the rain creating a soothing backdrop to our thoughts. Despite my anxiety, Dakota's presence had calmed me somewhat. There was strength in the shared experience of waiting, of loving men who walked willingly into darkness.

"You know," Dakota said finally, "you should be there when he gets back."

I looked up from my coffee. "At the clubhouse?"

She nodded. "These men -- they'd never admit it but seeing you waiting after a mission like this... it matters. It reminds them what they're fighting to come home to."

I considered her words, remembering the rare vulnerability I sometimes glimpsed in Azrael's eyes when he thought I wasn't looking. The way he held me a little tighter after our first night together.

"I'll be there," I decided.

Dakota smiled, satisfied. "Good. Now finish that pastry. You need your strength."

As we continued talking, the knot in my stomach slowly began to unravel. The fear didn't disappear -- it never would as long as I loved a man like Azrael -- but it became manageable. I could breathe again.

Later, after Dakota had left, I stood at the window watching the rain slowly taper off. The sky had darkened, stars beginning to peek through breaks in the clouds. Somewhere under those same stars, Azrael was fighting to save my mother and make it back to me.

I placed the photograph on the nightstand and began deciding what I'd wear to the clubhouse. Tomorrow night, I would be there when he walked through those doors. And whatever darkness he carried back with him, whatever weight rested on his shoulders, I would be ready to help him bear it.

Because loving the Angel of Death meant accepting all of him -- the protector and the destroyer, the man and the myth. And in the quiet moments between missions, when he laid his head in my lap and let me see the vulnerability behind his eyes, I knew I wouldn't trade this life for anything.

Chapter Fourteen

Azrael

The bar in Tel Aviv smelled like stale beer and bad decisions. I'd made plenty of those in my time, but sitting across from Eli in the dim back room, I knew this might be the worst one yet. The wooden table between us bore the scars of countless deals gone south, knife marks and cigarette burns telling their own stories. I kept my face neutral, waiting. In my world, the first one to speak usually lost.

Stripes' Russian contacts had set this meeting up. It was our best chance at extracting Mazida with the least possible resistance. While he might not be the very top guy, he was close enough.

Behind me, Samurai leaned against the wall, arms folded across his chest. Not a bodyguard -- I didn't need one -- but a reminder I wasn't alone. I had a brotherhood, ties to other men like myself, and those ties came with responsibilities. Stripes stood near the door, his gaze missing nothing.

Eli tapped his fingers on the table, the sound barely audible over the muted bass from the main room of the bar. He wasn't nervous. Men like him didn't get nervous. He was impatient.

"You're a hard man to find," he said finally, his voice carrying the slightest hint of an Israeli accent, telling me he spent most of his time elsewhere. "If your Russian friends hadn't requested this meeting, I may have missed this opportunity."

"Not if you know where to look." I kept my tone flat. "But then, I wasn't hiding from you."

Eli's lips twitched. Not quite a smile. "Let's not waste time. I have Mazida Quadir. You want her back."

I didn't flinch. We'd known her brother had kidnapped her and brought her here, to Tel Aviv, but until we got here, we hadn't realized he'd handed her off to someone else. Someone more powerful, and far more deadly.

"What I want is for you to tell me why I shouldn't kill you right now." I kept my hands visible on the table. It was a power move. I didn't need to reach for a weapon to be dangerous.

Eli actually smiled then. "Because I'm not the worst monster in this room, Azrael. And because Mazida is not here. Kill me, and she dies alone in a place you'll never find. After my men have had their fun, of course."

I felt rather than saw Samurai shift his weight behind me. A warning: *Don't make this personal.* I ignored it.

"What do you want?" I asked, already knowing I wouldn't like the answer.

Eli leaned forward, his expensive suit rustling softly. "Three men. Three problems that need to go away."

"Assassination isn't my specialty," I said, which wasn't exactly true. I'd killed before, but always for my own reasons. Never as a hired gun.

"No? The avenging angel who takes out trash humans? That's what they call you now, isn't it?" Eli's eyes narrowed. "Or is it only righteous when you decide who deserves to die?"

Stripes cleared his throat, a subtle warning in the sound. I'd known the old Russian long enough to recognize it. He was telling me to keep my temper in check.

"Mazida will be released if you eliminate three of my rivals," Eli continued, his voice cold and precise now, all business. "Each one is a cancer. Each one deals in human flesh, in children. The kind of men you hunt anyway."

"I do what I must," I replied, jaw tight. I didn't like being manipulated, even if the targets aligned with my personal code. "But I don't work blind. Names. Locations. Security details."

Samurai stepped forward then, his footfalls nearly silent on the grimy floor. "This will put the club at risk," he said, voice low and even. His dark eyes locked with Eli's. "We're not mercenaries."

"The club isn't involved," I said sharply, turning to look at him. "This is on me."

Samurai's eyes narrowed slightly. "You wear the Boneyard patch, Azrael. There is no 'just you' anymore."

I knew he was right, but I wasn't backing down. Not with Mazida's life on the line. Not with Zara counting on me.

"Details," I said to Eli, turning back to face him. "Or we walk."

Eli nodded once, then motioned to Stripes. "Your man already has what you need. I sent it when you entered the building."

Stripes pulled his phone from his pocket, his fingers tapping the screen. "*Da*, it's here," he confirmed. He moved to stand beside me, turning the phone so I could see.

Three photographs appeared on the screen. Three men, all middle-aged, all wealthy-looking. Below each photo was a name, an address, and a brief profile.

"First target is Javier Mendoza," Stripes said, enlarging the first photo. "Arms dealer who expanded into trafficking five years ago and moved into this country a year ago. Compound outside Jerusalem. Heavy security, twelve men minimum." He swiped to the next. "Second is Boris Kerensky. Russian national with diplomatic immunity. Operates from a hotel penthouse in Jerusalem." Another swipe. "Third is Hassan Al-Bahir. Saudi businessman. Currently on his yacht in the Mediterranean. Moves every few days, never docks for long. But it looks like he'll be attending meetings over the next three days in Gaza."

I studied each face, memorizing details. "Timeline?"

"One week," Eli replied. "All three, confirmed dead, or Mazida joins them."

"And the proof she's alive?" I wasn't making deals without verification.

Eli removed a phone from his jacket, tapped the screen, and slid it across the table. A video played, showing a woman in a sparse but clean room. She looked tired but unharmed, reading aloud from today's newspaper. Mazida Quadir -- Zara's mother -- with her distinctive features she'd passed to her daughter.

I watched the video twice before sliding the phone back. "If she's harmed --"

"She won't be," Eli interrupted. "Not if you do your job. But understand this: these men have protection. Governments look the other way because they're useful. If you're caught, no one will claim you."

"I've been a ghost my whole life," I replied. "Being disavowed won't be anything new."

Samurai moved closer to the table. "We need assurances. Devil's Boneyard stays clear of this. No blowback."

Eli studied him. "Your club has its own reputation, Samurai. Don't pretend your hands are clean."

"We protect our own," Samurai replied, unflinching. "We don't assassinate for hire."

"Even to save an innocent woman?" Eli asked, raising an eyebrow.

I'd had enough. "The club stays out of it. This is between you and me." I leaned forward. "But I want daily proof of life, and when the job is done, you deliver Mazida to a location of my choosing, personally."

Eli considered this, then nodded slowly. "Acceptable. But understand this -- fail to eliminate even one target, and our deal is void."

"And understand this," I countered. "If Mazida isn't returned exactly as she appears in that video, I'll find you. No matter where you hide."

The threat hung in the air between us.

"Three men who deserve to die," Eli said finally. "For the life of one innocent woman. It seems a fair exchange."

I stood up, signaling the end of our meeting. "Nothing about this is fair."

As we prepared to leave, Stripes showed me more intel on his phone -- building layouts, security rotations, daily routines. The old Russian had mapped everything with military precision, his eyes hard as he pointed out potential entry points and escape routes.

"These men, they are careful," he said quietly. "They have many guards, many eyes. It won't be easy."

"Nothing worth doing ever is," I replied.

Samurai remained silent as we left, but I could feel his disapproval. Once we were outside in the warm Tel Aviv night, he finally spoke. "Phantom won't be happy about this," he said, referring to his cousin, another club member. "We hunt predators, yes, but not like this."

"I'm not asking the club to help," I repeated. "This is my mission. My responsibility."

"And what happens after?" Samurai asked. "When powerful men are killed and people start looking for who did it? You think it won't lead back to us?"

I had no answer for that. He was right to be concerned. But if it came down to it, I'd leave the club. I wouldn't let them pay for what I was about to do.

Stripes put a hand on my shoulder, his grip strong. "The club is your family, Azrael. Family stands together, even when the decisions are shit." He glanced at Samurai. "We'll help him. Quiet, *da*? No patches, no colors. We leave our cuts behind for this one."

Samurai stared at him for a long moment before giving a slight nod. "Three targets. If we help, you'll be able to get to them faster. Handle this safer." He fixed his gaze on me. "But after this, we decide as a club how we handle such matters. No more solo decisions. Charming should have been notified before you went off and agreed to this bullshit."

I nodded, knowing it was the best compromise I'd get. As we walked toward the bikes we'd rented, I thought of Zara, of the promise I'd made to her to bring her mother home. I'd cross lines I'd sworn never to cross, become little more than a mercenary. But for her, I'd do it. For her, I'd become whatever monster I needed to be.

The night air felt heavy with what was to come, but my resolve was set. Three men for one woman. A soul for a soul. And maybe, when it was done, I could look Zara in the eyes without any regrets.

* * *

I stood in the shadows of an alley, leaning against the wall. My sat phone felt heavy in my hand as I scrolled to Zara's number, but I had to be on a secure line for this conversation. She'd be waiting, probably pacing, chewing on her bottom lip the way she did when worried. I'd seen it often enough in our short time together. I hit dial, bracing myself for the conversation ahead.

She answered on the first ring. "Azrael?"

"It's me," I confirmed. "You're still up."

"Like I could sleep." The sound of her movements came through the line -- restless pacing, from the sound of it. "Did you find anything? About my mother?"

I closed my eyes, weighing my words carefully. Zara deserved the truth, but the whole truth would only put her in danger. "We've confirmed she's alive."

Her sharp intake of breath felt like it carried across the miles between us. "Where? Who has her?"

"Zara." Just her name, but firm enough to stop the flood of questions. "You need to trust me on this. I have a location, and I have a plan."

The silence stretched between us now, crackling with unspoken words.

"I found the man who has her," I said finally. "He's willing to release her, but there's a price."

"Money? I can get money."

"Not money." I cut her off. "A job. More than one, actually."

Silence followed, heavy with understanding. Zara wasn't naive. She knew what kind of man I was, what kind of work I did. "You're going to kill someone." Not a question. Her voice had gone flat, emotionless.

I saw no point in sugarcoating it. "You know I

can't discuss the details, but these are men who traffic women and children. The kind of men I'd hunt anyway."

"But not like this," she said softly. "Not because you're being forced to."

"Does it matter why, as long as your mother comes home safe?" I asked after a brief pause.

"It matters to me." The pacing had stopped. I pictured her sitting on the edge of the bed. "It matters because you're doing this for me, and that means I'm responsible for whatever happens to you."

"You're not responsible for my choices, Zara."

"Aren't I?" Her voice caught, just slightly. "You weren't for hire, but I asked for your help anyway. You were known as the Angel of Death, a man who sought justice. Not a mercenary. Not a hitman. But getting my mother back is going to force you into that position."

"I promise, I'll bring her home," I assured her, my voice low and steady despite the war raging inside me. The line between what I would and wouldn't do had been clear once. Now it was blurring, and all because of a woman I'd known for less than a month.

"At what cost?" she asked.

I had no answer for that.

"The club," she continued, "will they help you?"

"Samurai and Stripes will." I didn't mention Samurai's reluctance. "The rest of the club stays clear. This isn't their fight."

"But it's yours?" The question carried weight beyond its simple words.

Was it my fight? Yeah. Mazida was my mother-in-law, or the closest thing I had to one.

"Someone took your mother," I said finally. "That makes it my fight."

Her breath caught at that. "I need you to be safe.

Even if you're taking on more than you bargained for, I need you to keep your promise to come home to me."

The distant street noise faded as I focused on the faint static on the line and the sound of my own steady breaths as I listened intently to her words.

"I've never been safe a day in my life," I told her, in a rare moment of raw honesty. "That's not who I am."

"It could be," she countered softly. "After this is over. After my mother's home."

The possibility hung in the air between us -- a future I hadn't allowed myself to imagine. A life beyond the next target, the next monster to eliminate.

"One step at a time," I said, unwilling to make promises I couldn't keep. "First, we get your mother back."

"And then?" The question was loaded with possibilities.

I took a slow breath. "And then we figure out what comes next."

"When do you leave?" Her practical nature reasserted itself.

"Tomorrow. Early," I said. "The first target is outside Jerusalem."

"How long?"

"One week to complete all three jobs." I didn't tell her what would happen if I failed. She didn't need that burden.

"I wish I could be there with you." The stubbornness was back in her voice.

"I need you exactly where you are. Safe."

"One week," she repeated finally. "I'll be here when you get back. With my mother."

"Yes, you will."

"Azrael?" Her voice had gone soft again. "Thank

you. For doing this. For being who you are."

Something twisted in my chest. Gratitude wasn't what I wanted from her, but I wasn't sure what I did want. Or rather, I knew, but wasn't ready to admit it.

"Get some sleep, Zara," I said instead. "I'll check in when I can."

"Be careful," she whispered. "Please."

"Always am." It was a lie, and we both knew it.

After we hung up, I straightened, waiting, motionless, staring at the phone in my hand. The mission ahead was clear. Three targets, one week, one woman to save. Simple on paper. But nothing about this was simple. Not the job, not the stakes, and certainly not my feelings for Zara Colton. Somewhere out there, Samurai and Stripes would be preparing, gathering intel, checking weapons. Good men crossing lines they shouldn't have to cross, because I'd dragged them into my mess. And somewhere, Mazida Quadir waited for rescue, not knowing that her daughter had set an avenging angel on her trail. In one week, I'd either be bringing Mazida home to her daughter, or I'd be dead. There was no middle ground in deals like this.

And if I survived? That question haunted me most. I had no answer. Only the mission ahead, and the nagging feeling that when this was over, I'd be changed in ways I couldn't yet imagine.

Chapter Fifteen

Azrael

I settled into position on the worn rooftop, the crumbling brick rough against my elbows as I positioned the rifle. Below me, the café buzzed with life -- tourists laughing, locals reading newspapers, waiters balancing trays of colorful drinks. None of them were aware of the death I was about to deliver. I took a slow breath, while adjusting the scope's focus on my target. Some men deserved to die in the middle of their coffee. This one certainly did.

The wind picked up, carrying with it the scent of grilled seafood from the café's kitchen. I made a slight adjustment to compensate, my fingertips tingling against the cold metal of my rifle. Three stories up gave me the perfect vantage point and a clean exit route. A fire escape on the north side of the building would take me down to the alley where my motorcycle waited.

Through my scope, I watched the target laugh at something on his phone. This piece of shit had been trafficking girls through the port for years. His connections had kept him protected until now.

The crosshairs settled on his temple. I could see the beads of sweat on his forehead, the way his fingers nervously tapped the side of his coffee cup. Did he sense something? Some men seemed to develop a sixth sense for danger after living on borrowed time. If so, his instincts were right, just not quick enough.

I slowed my breathing, finding the perfect rhythm where my body became absolutely still between heartbeats. The café was busy -- maybe twenty civilians within fifteen feet of my target. Not ideal, but unavoidable given his patterns.

"Nothing personal," I whispered, though it was a

lie. Everything about this job was personal for me, and for the women he'd hurt.

I'd been given this assignment three days ago. I'd intended to start immediately but it had taken longer to plan than I'd anticipated. Especially after one of my targets had changed their schedule. After this asshole, I had less than four days to make the other two targets and haul ass back to US soil. Which was why I'd decided to get all three done on the same day. Not to mention, there was less chance of the others getting the sense something was off and increasing their protection.

The target stood suddenly, nodding to a waiter. Shit. Was he leaving? I tracked him through the scope, finger tensing on the trigger. No -- just heading to the bathroom. I eased my grip slightly, waiting. A bathroom shot would be messy, confined. Better to let him return to his table.

Five minutes passed. I didn't move a muscle, barely blinked. Perfect stillness was a skill I'd mastered years ago. Finally, he emerged, stopping to chat with someone at another table. A business associate, maybe. Or just another scumbag. Not my concern today.

He sat back down, signaling for the check. Time was running out. I took one final breath, held it, and gently squeezed the trigger.

The rifle kicked against my shoulder. Through the scope, I watched as the bullet traveled the distance in a fraction of a second, then entered my target's skull. The impact jerked his head back, a spray of red misting the air behind him. His body slumped forward, face hitting the table with a finality that confirmed the job was done.

For a moment, the café continued as normal -- a strange pocket of time where death existed but hadn't yet been acknowledged. Then, a woman screamed. Chaos erupted as people realized what had happened, scrambling from their seats, diving for cover, pointing wildly in all directions.

I didn't linger to watch. Already, I was breaking down my rifle with practiced efficiency, each component sliding into its designated compartment in my case. Thirty seconds -- that's all it took. Nothing left behind, no shell casings, no fingerprints, no evidence I was ever here. It was a good thing I'd come prepared for anything. Using a borrowed rifle for this would have made things more difficult.

The adrenaline came now, after the job was done. My hands tingled as I secured the case, my senses hyperaware of every sound. Sirens in the distance. Shouts from the street below. I moved to the fire escape, descending quickly but controlled. No use surviving the hit just to break my neck falling down rusty stairs.

The alley was empty when I reached the bottom, my motorcycle exactly where I'd left it. I strapped my rifle to my back and pulled my helmet on, the dark visor concealing my face. By the time police would cordon off the area, I'd be miles away, my existence here nothing but a ghost story.

I eased into traffic, riding conservatively -- nothing to draw attention. Unless people knew what to look for, the rifle on my back could pass for the case to an instrument. I felt the familiar emptiness that always came after. Not guilt. Not exactly satisfaction either. Just a hollow space where emotion should be, like I'd pulled the trigger on myself in some way too. One name crossed off the list, two more to go before nightfall. I wanted this done.

My phone vibrated in my pocket at a red light. I

didn't need to check it to know it was Stripes, confirming the hit. The light turned green, and I accelerated through the intersection, leaving death and chaos in my wake. The sea breeze followed me for a while, carrying the salt and the memory of a single perfect shot.

Three more miles and I pulled into an abandoned gas station, exactly as planned. I dismounted, removed my helmet, and ran a hand through my sweat-dampened hair. My heartbeat had returned to normal, my breathing steady. Professional. Detached. The way I needed to be to do this job right.

I pulled out the phone, typed a single word. *Done.*

The reply came seconds later. *Second target confirmed for Club Vortex. Move now to have time to plan.*

Back on the bike, I plotted the fastest route to the nightclub. The day was still young, and I had more work to do. I needed to scope the place out, get an idea of when the target would be there, and figure out the best entry and exit for the job. Seeing things on paper wasn't the same as viewing them in person. The club wouldn't be in full swing for hours.

As I rode, I thought about the fact this was personal for me. If I didn't do this, I wouldn't get Mazida back. There was no way I could go home without her. Not and face Zara.

Family. That's what Mazida was to me now. The word still felt strange to me, even after all these years with the club. But I understood loyalty. I understood debt. And I understood sometimes justice came from the barrel of a gun or the edge of a knife rather than a courtroom.

The second target would be trickier -- close quarters, witnesses, security. But I needed this done today, all three targets eliminated before midnight.

I merged onto the highway, pushing the bike faster. The emptiness inside me began to fill with purpose again. By nightfall, three men would be dead by my hand, and maybe -- just maybe -- we'd be one step closer to bringing Mazida home.

* * *

Seven hours later

I stepped from the cool night air into a wall of sound, heat, and sweat. Club Vortex lived up to its name -- a whirlwind of bodies, lights, and pounding bass that hit my chest like physical blows. My ears adjusted slowly as I scanned the crowd, the knife tucked into my boot suddenly feeling inadequate compared to the rifle I'd left behind. This would be messy. Personal. I'd feel my target's last breath against my skin, watch the light fade from his eyes. Some might call it more honest that way. I just called it necessary.

The place was packed wall-to-wall with bodies, writhing and gyrating to music that seemed designed to scramble the brain. Lights pulsed in violent blues and reds, casting strange shadows across faces, making everyone look slightly demonic. I pushed through the crowd, keeping my movements casual but deliberate, another face in the sea of night crawlers looking for a good time. Except I was hunting.

Stripes had given me the intel on this one. "Real sadistic fuck. Likes to cut people up while they're still breathing, make examples out of them."

He'd said this was the place the man would be, and I'd watched and waited. He'd finally shown up an hour ago. I'd hoped it had given him enough time to get drunk and relax.

I scanned the VIP section, the raised platform where the self-important sat on velvet couches and drank overpriced bottles. There he was -- Boris, though everyone called him "The Surgeon." Not for any medical skills, but for his precision with a blade. Dark hair slicked back, designer clothes, surrounded by women who didn't know they were pressing their bodies against a monster. Or maybe they did but just didn't care.

Two bodyguards flanked him, thick-necked men with telltale bulges under their jackets. Guns, despite the club's metal detectors. Then again, I'd slipped in with my knife unnoticed. I'd need to deal with them first.

I made my way to the bar, ordered a whiskey I had no intention of drinking, and studied the layout. Three exits -- main entrance, side door by the bathrooms, service entrance behind the DJ booth. The bodyguards rotated positions every fifteen minutes, a standard security protocol. Boris himself seemed relaxed, hands wandering over a blonde in a silver dress, laughing at something she said.

I checked my watch. Almost eleven o'clock. The club would reach peak capacity soon, which meant more chaos to disappear into, but also more potential witnesses and collateral damage. Not ideal, but I'd make it work.

I abandoned my untouched drink and moved toward the bathrooms, timing my approach to intersect with the path of one of the bodyguards. As expected, the man made his rounds, heading for the hallway that led to the restrooms. I stumbled slightly, bumping into him.

"Watch it, asshole," he growled, hand instinctively moving toward his weapon.

I mumbled an apology, swaying as if drunk, and continued past him. In the dimly lit hallway, I pressed myself against the wall and waited. Three seconds later, he rounded the corner. His eyes widened in recognition -- not of me, but of the sudden danger -- a split second before I struck.

My palm slammed into his windpipe, crushing it instantly. As he gasped for air that wouldn't come, I dragged him into the men's room, kicked open a stall door, and finished him with a quick thrust of my knife just under his ribcage, angled upward into his heart. He twitched once, then went still. I lowered him onto the toilet, closed the stall door, and washed his blood from my hands.

One down.

Back in the club, the music had shifted to something with a harder edge, the bass so deep it seemed to rattle my teeth. The second bodyguard had noticed his partner's absence, his eyes scanning the crowd with increasing concern. He leaned down to say something to Boris, who frowned and checked his phone.

I wouldn't get a better chance. I moved through the dance floor, letting the surging crowd push me closer to the VIP section. A waitress with a tray of shots created the perfect opening -- I slipped past her just as she arrived at Boris's table, momentarily blocking the bodyguard's view.

By the time the bodyguard spotted me, I was already inside his reaction radius. His hand went for his gun, but I was faster. The knife I'd palmed slid between his ribs, the blow cushioned by our bodies pressed close together, looking to anyone watching like an embrace between friends. His eyes widened in shock as I twisted the blade.

"Nothing personal," I whispered in his ear as he slumped against me.

I eased him down onto one of the couches, arranging him to look passed out drunk. The music swallowed his dying gurgle, the lights concealed the spreading dark stain on his shirt. Boris, focused on the woman in his lap, hadn't even noticed.

When he finally looked up and saw me standing there, his face cycled through confusion, recognition, then fear. He shoved the woman aside roughly, reaching inside his jacket.

"You --" he started, but I was already moving.

I flipped the table between us, sending bottles and glasses crashing to the floor. The woman screamed, drawing attention our way. Boris pulled a small pistol from his jacket, but I was already too close. My hand clamped around his wrist, forcing the gun upward as it discharged into the ceiling. The shot was barely audible over the music, but people nearby began to notice something was wrong.

Boris was strong, his face contorted with rage as he wrestled against my grip. He head-butted me, stars exploding behind my eyes as pain lanced through my skull. I maintained my hold on his gun hand, but he slashed at me with a knife I hadn't seen, opening a cut across my cheek.

We crashed over the back of the couch, landing hard on the floor behind the VIP section. The gun skittered away across the floor. Now it was just man against man, blade against blade.

"You're dead," he snarled, slashing at me with practiced precision. "Fucking Angel of Death. Even here, we've heard of you."

I didn't waste breath on words, focusing instead on the dance of death between us. His knife caught the pulsing lights, leaving glowing trails in the air as he attempted to open my throat. I parried with my own blade, metal striking metal with sharp clangs drowned by the music.

Blood ran down my face from the cut on my cheek, warm and sticky. Around us, people began to realize this wasn't a standard club fight. Some screamed, others backed away, creating a clearing around us while bouncers pushed through the crowd.

Boris lunged, his technique revealing his reputation was well-earned. I barely twisted away, feeling his blade slice through my jacket and graze my ribs. The pain was distant, adrenaline keeping it at bay. I countered, my knife finding flesh at his shoulder.

He hissed but didn't slow, coming at me again with renewed fury. We crashed into a table, sending glasses shattering across the floor. I lost my footing on the wet surface, going down on one knee. Boris saw his opening and moved in for the kill, knife arcing toward my neck.

I threw a handful of broken glass into his face. He cursed, momentarily blinded, slashing wildly. I drove my knife upward, under his sternum, feeling the resistance of muscle and tissue before the blade found his heart.

Boris's eyes widened in shock, his own knife clattering to the floor. "How --" he gasped, blood bubbling at his lips.

"See you in hell." I thought of all the people this asshole had tormented and killed over the years. Now they would get justice.

I twisted the knife once, ensuring the job was done, then let him collapse to the floor. Around us, chaos had fully erupted. People screamed and pushed toward exits, the music still pounding relentlessly. A bouncer broke through the crowd, saw the blood and bodies, and reached for his radio.

Time to go.

I snatched up Boris's fallen pistol, fired two shots into the ceiling, and used the resulting panic to make my escape. Bodies pressed against me from all sides as people scrambled toward exits. I moved with the flow toward the service entrance, discarding the gun into a trash can as I passed.

The hallway behind the DJ booth was empty, staff having fled at the sound of gunshots. I pushed through the service door into the cool night air of an alleyway. Once the door shut behind me, the music became muted except for the thump of the bass. The quieter atmosphere was almost as disorienting as the club's noise had been.

Blood dripped down my face and side, but the wounds were superficial. I took a moment to catch my breath, wiping my knife clean on my pants before resheathing it. My motorcycle waited where I'd left it, hidden behind a dumpster halfway down the alley.

As I mounted the bike, police sirens wailed in the distance, growing closer. I kicked the engine to life and pulled into traffic just as the first patrol cars screeched to a halt in front of the club.

Two down. One to go.

I found a 24-hour convenience store, parked behind it, and used their bathroom to clean up. The cut on my face needed stitches, but it would have to wait. I pressed a wad of paper towels against it until the bleeding slowed, then applied some butterfly bandages I'd brought just in case. The gash along my ribs was shallow, more painful than dangerous.

Back outside, I checked my phone. A message from Stripes: *Target 3 confirmed at old Paz gas station.*

Alone.

Perfect. I still had time. Not a lot, but I could get this done. My blood was up, adrenaline flooding me. I didn't feel the emptiness this time, just a cold rage thinking about Mazida and what she must have been through all this time. Soon, I'd take her home to her daughter.

I revved the motorcycle's engine and headed east, toward my final target of the night.

Chapter Sixteen

Azrael

The industrial district loomed before me, all rust and broken windows under flickering streetlights. My body ached from the club fight, the cuts on my face and ribs throbbing in time with my heartbeat. I killed the motorcycle's engine two blocks from the old Paz station, opting to approach on foot. The night had grown colder, or maybe it was just blood loss making me shiver. Three hits in one night was pushing it, even for me, but Mazida's time was running out. The final target, Hassan, would be the easiest of the three. At least, that's what I told myself as I melted into the shadows between abandoned warehouses.

When Stripes had said the Paz station was old, he hadn't lied. It looked like a bomb had landed near this one at some point. The lights inside told me it was still somewhat operational, but the pumps out front looked like they hadn't been used in a long time. According to Stripes' intel, our target used the place to arrange drug drops and exchange information.

I crouched behind a dumpster across the street, watching. My ribs protested the position, the gash from Boris's knife sending sharp reminders with every breath. I pushed the pain aside, focusing on the task at hand. A high-end Mercedes sat out front -- my target's car, matching the description Stripes had given me.

From my vantage point, I could see a nervous-looking man pacing inside the store, periodically checking his watch and peering out the windows. This man wasn't any less dangerous than the others I'd dealt with today. But he didn't come across as being as ruthless. It made me wonder why he was so twitchy tonight. Did he know he was being hunted?

I checked my phone one last time. A message from Samurai: *After this one, meet at the hotel. We get Mazida at 0200.* I hoped that meant Eli had already come through and given up the information we needed. Roughly two hours from now. It would be tight, but I could finish this job and get to the hotel, maybe even have time to clean up.

The sound of an approaching car caught my attention. Headlights swept across the lot as a black SUV pulled in, parking beside the Mercedes. I pressed deeper into the shadows, watching as two men exited the vehicle and headed toward the store. Not part of the plan. This asshole was supposed to be alone.

"Shit," I muttered, reassessing. I could wait them out, but time was ticking. Or I could adapt. Three targets instead of one would be messy, but doable.

The men entered the store. Through the windows, I could see them talking with my target, gesturing animatedly. The conversation appeared heated. I couldn't afford to wait. Decision made, I moved.

I circled around the back of the service station, finding a rear entrance as expected. The lock was old and simple. It took only seconds to pick. I eased the door open, wincing at a slight creak. Inside was a storeroom filled with dusty boxes and the smell of stale cigarettes. Voices filtered through from the front of the store.

"-- tells me you fucked up. Some asshole is picking off high-end players one by one." The voice was deep, authoritative. And I had no doubt the asshole he'd mentioned was me.

"I don't know why anyone would be after us," he responded, his voice higher-pitched with fear. "I was careful --"

"Careful? Boris's dead. Gutted in that club he practically lived in. And Mendoza got his brains blown out at his favorite café. That's not careful, that's a fucking message."

Did that mean these three had some deal going? Maybe the targets had more in common than I'd thought. Didn't matter. The job was the same regardless.

I moved silently through the storeroom, positioning myself behind a shelf near the doorway to the main store. From here, I could see Hassan and one of the men -- a tall, broad-shouldered figure in an expensive suit. The second man was out of my line of sight, but judging by the shadow cast on the floor, he was standing near the front door.

"Did you get the informant to talk?" Hassan asked. Informant? Looked like maybe the man calling the shots, the one who gave me a hitlist, had more on his plate than he realized. A rat.

"Not a peep, even after we took fingers. Tough bastard."

The second man moved into view, heading for the refrigerated section. "We should just kill him, dump the body. Cut our losses."

"The boss wants information first," Suit replied. "He knows something about the Bratva shipments. Once he talks, then we'll dispose of him."

I'd heard enough. The element of surprise was my only advantage against three men, likely all armed. I reached into my jacket, retrieving the garrote wire I carried for situations requiring silence. Clean, effective. But not as quick as I'd have liked.

The second man had his back to me, examining beer options in the cooler. I moved, a shadow detaching from shadows, crossing the distance in three silent strides. The wire looped around his neck before he registered my presence, cutting off his startled cry before it could form. I yanked back hard, the thin metal biting deep into flesh.

His hands clawed at the wire, feet kicking as I dragged him backward toward the storeroom. I held my breath, straining to see if the others had heard him. Thankfully, the hum of the machines seemed to drown out his struggles. Ten seconds, fifteen, thirty -- his struggles weakened, then ceased altogether. I lowered him quietly to the floor and turned back toward the main store.

Hassan and Suit were still talking, unaware of what had happened mere feet away thanks to a display rack blocking their view. I drew my knife, calculating angles and distances. Two targets, at least one certainly armed. The door was fifteen feet from their position. No clean escape without being seen.

Suit checked his watch. "Let's wrap this up. You're coming with us. Boss wants to hear your explanation in person."

Boss? So Hassan wasn't the one in charge? Interesting. Not my problem, though.

Hassan paled visibly, sweat beading on his forehead. "Look, I can fix this --"

"Car. Now." Suit turned toward the door, then paused. "Where the hell did Marcus go?"

That was my cue. I moved swiftly from cover, knife in hand. Suit spotted me immediately, his hand diving inside his jacket. Fast, but not fast enough. My knife found his throat before he could clear his weapon, a precise thrust that severed his carotid artery. Blood sprayed in a crimson arc as he stumbled backward, gun clattering unfired to the floor.

Hassan stood frozen, eyes wide with terror as his

associate collapsed, drowning in his own blood. Recognition dawned on his face as he took in my appearance, the cuts and blood on my face.

"You -- you're..." he stammered, backing away, hands raised. "Listen, I don't know what I did, but I have no problem with you."

"Liar. If you know who I am, then you know men like you are my favorite types of prey. Much like the you enjoy hurting young women and children."

"I'll tell you where she is!" he blurted. "The woman. Mazida. That's why you're in this country, right? I heard they brought her here from the US, Florida. That's your territory, from what I hear. The warehouse on Harborside, old fishing plant. There's a basement level, that's where they're keeping her."

I paused. We already had arrangements to get her. It wasn't like I needed his intel. But just the same...

"How many guards?" I asked, letting him think his information might save him.

"Six, maybe seven. They rotate shifts. Heavier security at night." The words tumbled out desperately. "Look, I'm giving you everything. You can rescue her. Just let me walk away. I'll disappear. You'll never see me again."

I pretended to consider this, watching him relax slightly as hope flickered across his face. "One more question," I said quietly. "How many of the young girls you snatched did you personally sample?"

His expression was answer enough -- the flash of guilt, the unconscious swallow. "I wasn't -- I mean, I haven't --"

My knife entered his stomach, angled upward toward vital organs. His eyes widened in shock and pain.

"For all the innocents you've harmed," I whispered, twisting the blade.

He made a wet, gurgling sound, hands clutching weakly at my arms. I held him up as the life drained from him, watching the light fade from his eyes. When he was gone, I let him slump to the floor.

The store was silent now except for the humming of the refrigerators. Three bodies, a lot of blood. I moved quickly, wiping down surfaces I'd touched, retrieving my garrote wire from the first man's neck. Outside, a car drove past slowly, headlights sweeping across the front of the store. I froze in the shadows until it passed.

Then I heard it -- the faint wail of sirens in the distance, growing louder. Had someone spotted me? Was there another man with the two unexpected guests? I needed to move.

I exited through the back door, keeping to the shadows as I made my way to my motorcycle. The sirens were closer now, maybe six or seven blocks away. I started the engine just as flashing lights appeared at the far end of the industrial park.

I gunned the bike in the opposite direction, taking back streets and alleys until I was clear of the area. Only then did I pull over briefly to check my phone.

A message from Stripes: *All three confirmed. Return to hotel immediately. Extraction time.*

Confirmed with who? I hit send and waited.

One of Eli's men. Good enough for me. I just had to hope they actually told Eli I'd done my job.

I typed a quick response. *On my way. Target gave confirmation on location. Basement level.*

The night wasn't over. Killing the men responsible had been the easy part. Now came the real mission -- getting Mazida out alive. I accelerated onto the highway, heading for the hotel where Samurai and Stripes would be waiting. The clock was ticking. In less than two hours, we'd launch the rescue operation, and God help anyone who stood in our way.

* * *

I parked my bike next to Samurai's and made my way into the hotel and up to my room, my body running on fumes and adrenaline. The cuts on my face and side had stopped bleeding, but every movement sent fresh pain radiating through my ribs. It didn't matter. Nothing mattered except getting Mazida back. I found Stripes and Samurai waiting in the hall. They looked up as I approached, eyes taking in my bloodied appearance without comment. They'd expected nothing less.

"You good to continue?" Samurai asked, his voice betraying no emotion though his eyes lingered on the gash across my cheek.

"I'm fine," I replied, moving to unlock the door. We all stepped inside, letting it shut behind us. "What's the plan?"

Stripes straightened up, his face set in hard lines. His Russian accent thickened as it always did before violence. "We have confirmation Mazida is still alive. Security cameras show seven guards on rotation, three at entrance points, four patrolling interior. But if Eli keeps his word…"

"And if he doesn't?" I asked.

"Basement level, as your target confirmed. Single stairwell access, reinforced door. They are not expecting us to know location, but after tonight's activities, they will be on high alert."

"Breaching charges are ready," Samurai said. "I was hoping we wouldn't need them but prepared just in case. I only wish we had more men."

"Any word from Eli?"

"*Nyet.*"

"Extraction plan?" I asked. If Eli wasn't going to help us like he'd said, then we'd handle it on our own. Either way, we were getting her out of there, and all of us were going home. Now.

Stripes allowed himself a small, grim smile. "My old Bratva connections have arranged a private jet at the municipal airstrip. Once we have Mazida, we fly back to the US."

I raised an eyebrow. "The Bratva is helping us again? What's the catch?"

"No catch," Stripes replied. "More old debts being repaid. Plus, these men who took Mazida -- they stepped on Bratva toes too. Enemy of my enemy, *da*?"

Preparations moved quickly after that. I quickly tended my wounds, changed my clothes, and donned tactical gear, strapping on a Kevlar vest that pressed painfully against my injured ribs. Fresh magazines for my pistol, extra knife, flashlight, zip ties -- the tools of extraction rather than assassination.

Forty minutes later, we were in position. The warehouse loomed against the night sky, a hulking shadow punctuated by security lights around its perimeter. From our position, I could see two guards patrolling the fence line, automatic rifles slung over their shoulders.

Samurai's gaze held mine. "On my mark. Three. Two. One. Execute."

Our SUV lurched forward, accelerating toward the chain-link fence. The guards spotted us too late, raising their weapons as our vehicle crashed through the barrier with a metallic scream. We were inside the perimeter. Thank God for armored vehicles! Whoever had procured this one for us had saved our asses.

Everything moved with practiced precision after that. I was out of the vehicle before it fully stopped, dropping the first guard with a double-tap to the chest while Samurai took down the second. Stripes covered our flank as we approached the main entrance.

I pressed explosives against the door, then backed off. Samurai nodded, and I pressed the detonator. The door blew inward with a concussive blast that left my ears ringing.

We moved through the smoke and debris, weapons up, communicating with hand signals. The interior was industrial -- concrete floors, exposed pipes, the lingering smell of fish processing still detectable beneath the newer scents of gun oil and cigarettes. An alarm began to wail, red emergency lights casting everything in a bloody glow.

The first resistance came at the intersection of two corridors -- a guard emerging from a side room, eyes wide with surprise. I dropped him before he could raise his weapon, the suppressed shots making dull thwacking sounds that were nearly lost beneath the alarm.

"Stairwell, twenty meters ahead," Stripes murmured, gesturing with his weapon.

We moved forward, encountering two more guards who put up more of a fight. Bullets pinged off metal pipes above our heads as we took cover. Samurai signaled, and I laid down covering fire while he flanked their position. I heard rather than saw the resulting struggle -- grunts, a wet gurgling sound, then silence.

"Clear," Samurai's voice rang out.

The stairwell door was locked -- a heavy steel affair with a keypad.

"Allow me," Stripes said, kneeling to examine the lock. From his pack, he produced a small electronic device that he attached to the keypad. Numbers flickered across its display for several seconds before it beeped. The lock disengaged with an audible click. "Thank Shade for this one. He sent me prepared for anything."

"We have ten minutes, max. After that, we'll likely be dealing with police."

I took point down the stairs, sweeping each corner with my weapon. The basement level was cooler, the air heavy with moisture and the metallic scent of blood. A single corridor stretched before us, four doors visible -- two on each side.

A guard appeared at the far end, shouting into a radio. My shot took him in the throat, cutting off his warning mid-sentence. We moved quickly down the corridor, checking each room. The first contained supplies, the second empty. The third held a makeshift torture chamber -- a chair with restraints, a table of implements that made even my stomach turn. Blood spattered the floor and walls, some of it fresh.

The final door was reinforced steel with another electronic lock. Stripes went to work while Samurai and I covered the corridor.

"Got it," Stripes whispered as the lock disengaged.

Samurai took a deep breath, then nodded. I pushed the door open, weapon raised, and stepped inside.

The room was small, concrete on all sides, illuminated by a single bare bulb. In the center sat Mazida Quadir, bound to a metal chair. Her face was barely recognizable beneath the bruising and dried blood. Her clothes were torn and stained. Despite everything, her eyes remained defiant as she looked up at our entrance.

"Took you long enough," she rasped, her voice cracking a little.

Stripes moved past me, his face softening as he knelt before her. "Mazida. We've come to take you home." He spoke gently, as if to a child, while his hands worked quickly to free her from her restraints.

"How did you know we're here to rescue you?" I asked.

She snorted. "Three men: Russian, Japanese, and Middle Eastern. You're clearly not from here. Otherwise, the three of you wouldn't be working together, much less breaking into this room."

I stood watch at the door while Samurai assisted Stripes. Behind me, I could hear Mazida's sharp intake of breath as they helped her stand, the muffled sound of pain she tried to suppress.

"Can you walk?" Samurai asked.

"If it gets me out of here, I could fly," she answered, though her voice wavered with the effort.

I checked the corridor. "Clear for now, but we need to move fast."

Stripes supported Mazida on one side, Samurai on the other. Her legs threatened to buckle with each step, but determination kept her moving. I took point as we retraced our steps to the stairwell.

Sirens were closing in on our location, and I quickly altered course, moving toward an emergency exit. Behind us, the sound of boots on the stairwell announced the arrival of more guards. I dropped back, stepping behind a concrete pillar.

"Go," I told the others. "I'll cover."

The first guard appeared in the corridor, and I dropped him with a headshot. A second followed, more cautious, firing wildly in my direction. Bullets chipped concrete near my position, sending fragments stinging against my cheek. I waited for a pause in his fire, then leaned out and put two rounds center mass.

I caught up to the others at the emergency exit. Samurai was working on the alarm system, trying to prevent it from triggering when we opened the door. Mazida had slumped against Stripes, her strength failing.

"Almost got it," Samurai muttered, sweat beading on his forehead as he spliced wires. The door clicked. "Done."

Samurai pushed the door open carefully, scanning the exterior. "Clear. Vehicles in position fifty yards south."

We emerged into the cool night air, moving as quickly as Mazida's condition would allow. I could hear sirens in the distance, see flashing lights reflected against nearby buildings. The police perimeter was closing in.

"There!" Samurai pointed to where two motorcycles and a van waited in the shadows of a loading dock. "Looks like Eli at least somewhat came through for us."

I hoped like hell it was Eli. If not, I wasn't sure who would be helping us. Had Stripes told him where we'd be? I wasn't going to stop to ask questions. We needed to get the hell out of this country.

We were thirty yards from the vehicles when a spotlight caught us, the harsh beam momentarily blinding. A loudspeaker crackled to life, the man speaking in a language I barely remembered from my childhood.

"What the fuck did he say?" Samurai asked.

"Police. Stop where you are." My brow

furrowed. "At least I think that was it."

Instead, we ran. Bullets pinged off the concrete around us as officers opened fire. I returned fire, not aiming to hit but to force them to cover, buying precious seconds. We reached the vehicles, Samurai and Stripes carefully loading Mazida into the van.

"Go!" Samurai ordered. "We'll rendezvous at the airstrip."

I hesitated, not wanting to leave them.

"Now, Azrael," Stripes snapped, his accent thicker than ever. "We need all vehicles moving to split pursuit."

I nodded, jumping onto one of the motorcycles. Samurai took the other. We roared away in different directions as the van peeled out, drawing the majority of the police pursuit. I cut through back alleys and service roads, losing the single patrol car that attempted to follow me.

Twenty minutes later, I arrived at the small municipal airstrip on the outskirts of town. A sleek private jet sat on the tarmac, engines already running, stairs deployed. Samurai arrived shortly after me, his motorcycle skidding to a halt beside mine.

"Any sign of them?" he asked, voice tight with worry.

Before I could answer, headlights appeared on the access road. The van, moving at high speed, two police cruisers in pursuit. The van swerved through the gate, tires squealing as it made directly for the plane.

"Cover them!" I shouted, drawing my weapon and firing at the pursuing vehicles. One cruiser veered off, a tire blown. The second kept coming.

The van screeched to a halt beside the plane. The side door slid open, and Samurai emerged, supporting

Mazida. Stripes followed, firing back at the police cruiser. A bullet struck him in the shoulder, spinning him around, but he recovered and continued covering their retreat.

Samurai and I laid down suppressing fire as they made for the plane. The wounded Stripes moved with surprising speed despite his injury, his face set in grim determination. More police vehicles appeared at the gate, lights flashing.

"Go!" Samurai shouted to us as they reached the stairs. "Now!"

I sprinted for the plane as bullets whined past. I felt a sharp sting along my arm where one grazed me but kept moving. We reached the stairs, Samurai going up first. I turned to provide one last burst of covering fire, then scrambled aboard.

The stairs retracted immediately, the door sealing with a pressurized hiss. Inside, Mazida had been strapped into a seat, Stripes beside her, pressing a bandage to his bleeding shoulder. Samurai stood by the cockpit door, speaking rapidly to the pilot.

"We clear?" I asked.

"For now." Samurai nodded. "Bratva pilot says he has clearance to take off immediately. Claims his paperwork will check out if they try to ground us."

The engines roared louder as the jet began to move, taxiing swiftly toward the runway. Through the windows, I could see police vehicles giving chase across the tarmac, but they couldn't stop a plane already in motion.

I dropped into a seat opposite Mazida, finally allowing myself to feel the exhaustion and pain of the night's activities. She looked at me through her one unswollen eye, a ghost of a smile on her battered lips.

"Thank you," she whispered, her voice barely

audible over the engines. "Whoever you are."

I nodded, not trusting myself to speak. The plane accelerated down the runway, pressing us back into our seats. As we lifted off, banking sharply away from the pursuing lights below, Stripes reached over with his good arm and patted my knee.

"You did good tonight," he said. "Your woman will be pleased."

Outside the window, the city lights receded, the night sky opening up before us. Behind us lay three dead targets, countless wounded enemies, and a trail of destruction. Ahead lay uncertainty, but also the knowledge we'd done what family does -- protected our own, no matter the cost.

As the jet climbed into the clouds, I closed my eyes and let the adrenaline finally ebb from my system. The job wasn't finished -- Mazida needed medical attention, Stripes' wound required treatment, and Mazida's brother was still out there. But for now, in this moment, we had won. We had our family back.

And God help anyone who came after us again.

Chapter Seventeen

Azrael

The growl of our engines filled the air as Stripes, Samurai, and I rolled through the gates. Dust kicked up behind our wheels, settling on the leather of my cut as I eased my bike to a stop. The brothers gathered in a loose semicircle, their faces a mix of relief and wariness. I cut the engine and swung my leg over the seat, boots hitting the gravel with a crunch that seemed to underscore the weight of the moment.

Stripes pulled in beside me, his face showing the fatigue of our journey, and he'd paled from blood loss. Not that a bullet was going to keep him from getting home. Same for me. I'd been cut, shot, stabbed, and even burned more times than I could count. If it wasn't fatal, I wasn't slowing down. Samurai flanked my other side, his dark eyes scanning the compound with the alertness that never seemed to leave him.

"Home sweet fucking home," Stripes said.

I nodded but kept my attention on the Prospect driving the club truck through the gates behind us. The kid looked nervous, probably wondering if he'd fucked up the simple job of transporting our precious cargo. The truck rolled to a stop, and I watched the passenger door, waiting.

When it swung open, Mazida stepped out, her movements careful and deliberate. She wore a deep blue hijab that framed her face, highlighting the exhaustion in her eyes. But she was alive. She was whole. That's what mattered.

My gaze shifted to the clubhouse door where Zara stood frozen, her hands gripping the doorframe as if it was the only thing keeping her upright. For a moment, she didn't move, didn't seem to breathe. I'd seen that look before -- the fear that hope might be snatched away if you believed too quickly.

Then, like someone had cut invisible strings, she launched herself forward. Her dark hair streamed behind her as she ran, her voice breaking as she called out, "Mom! Mom!"

Mazida's head snapped up, her tired eyes suddenly alive with recognition. She stepped forward, arms opening just as Zara crashed into her. The impact nearly knocked both women over, but they clung to each other, becoming a single, swaying unit of relief and disbelief.

"Zara," Mazida whispered. "My Zara."

I stood back, giving them space. This was their moment -- the payoff for the blood spilled and risks taken. Zara's hands clutched at her mother's back, her fingers digging into the fabric as if afraid Mazida might disappear if she loosened her grip. Tears streamed down her face, unchecked and unashamed.

"I thought --" Zara's voice cracked. "I thought I'd never see you again."

Mazida pulled back just enough to cup her daughter's face, thumbs wiping away tears. "Allah brought you to me. He sent his angel." Her eyes flicked toward me, and I looked away, uncomfortable with the gratitude I saw there.

Around us, the brothers maintained a respectful distance. Havoc stood with his arms crossed, his face softened just enough to show he approved. Charming nodded once when I caught his eye -- the silent acknowledgment of a job completed. Gator leaned against a post, trying to look casual, but I caught the way he swallowed hard, his own eyes suspiciously bright as he watched the reunion.

These men had seen blood and death, had caused

both when necessary. But they understood family. It was why we existed as a club -- to protect our own when the world wouldn't.

Zara finally pulled back, though she kept one arm around her mother's waist. "Are you hurt? Did they --"

"I am fine," Mazida interrupted firmly. "Nothing that will not heal." She squared her shoulders, and I saw where Zara got her strength. Despite everything Mazida had endured, her dignity intact. "You should not have come looking for me. It was dangerous."

"I had to," Zara said simply. Then she looked at me, her blue eyes still swimming with tears but filled with something else now -- something that made my chest tighten. "And I found help."

All eyes turned to me. I didn't want their gratitude or their awe. I'd done what needed doing, nothing more. But I stood a little straighter under their collective gazes, acknowledging without words that this was my work. The avenging angel they called me -- Azrael, the Angel of Death -- and I'd earned the name with blood and bone.

Stripes clapped me on the shoulder, his gnarled hand heavy with approval. "Our brother brings back the lost," he said, his voice carrying across the compound. "As he has always done."

Samurai nodded, the gesture slight but meaningful coming from a man of few words.

I shrugged off their praise, uncomfortable with it. "Get Mazida inside," I directed one of the Prospects. "She needs food and rest."

The kid jumped to attention, eager to be useful. "Yes, sir. This way, ma'am."

Zara hesitated, looking between her mother and me. I nodded once, giving her permission. "Go. Be with your mother. We'll talk later."

Relief and gratitude washed over her face. She squeezed her mother's hand and led her toward the clubhouse, following the Prospect. But not before she threw me a look over her shoulder that promised more than thanks. It was a look that said she remembered every touch, every whispered word between us before I'd left to find her mother. A look that said she was counting the minutes until we were alone.

I watched them go, aware of the gazes on me. The club had questions -- they always did after an operation like this. No. There had never been a job like this one. None that had taken me outside the country before. They wanted to know what we'd found, who we'd killed, what threats might follow us home. But those conversations could wait.

"Charming," I said, turning to our President. "We need to talk. But first, I need a fucking shower and a drink."

He nodded, understanding the priority. "Clubhouse in an hour. Bring Stripes and Samurai."

With that settled, the brothers dispersed, some heading into the clubhouse while others moved toward the garage or their homes within the compound. The tension eased but didn't disappear. They'd wait for answers, but they wouldn't wait long.

Stripes lingered, lighting a cigarette with hands that betrayed a slight tremor. "The girl's mother," he said quietly. "She will need time. What they did to her --" He broke off, shaking his head.

"I know," I replied, the memories of the facility where we'd found Mazida still fresh in my mind. The guards hadn't expected us. They certainly hadn't expected the level of violence we'd brought with us. "But she's stronger than she looks."

"Like daughter, like mother," Samurai commented, his dark gaze following Zara and Mazida into the clubhouse. I figured he had that backward. Shouldn't it be like mother, like daughter? But either worked in this instance.

When Zara had first shown up in town, searching for the man they called the Avenging Angel to help find her missing mother, I'd considered sending her away. But there had been something in her eyes -- a determination that matched my own -- that had made me listen. And then, against my better judgment, I'd let her in. Into my home. Into my bed. Into places I'd thought were long closed off.

"Get cleaned up and get some food," I told my brothers. "It's going to be a long night."

They headed off toward their respective quarters, leaving me alone in the compound yard. I took a moment to breathe in the familiar smells of oil, leather, and dust. Home. As fucked up as it was, this place was home.

I pulled my phone from my pocket and checked it one last time. No new messages. No warnings from our contacts about movement from Tel Aviv. But that didn't mean they weren't coming. Men like the ones who'd taken Mazida didn't just let their property walk away. They'd want blood for what we'd done -- and they'd have resources to track us.

We'd be ready when they came. We always were. But first, I needed that shower, that drink -- and maybe, if the timing worked out, a few minutes alone with Zara before the storm hit.

I rode toward my house at the edge of the compound, feeling the gazes of the brothers on watch tracking my movement. They'd doubled security since we'd left. Smart move. The Devil's Boneyard had enemies before this operation. Now we had more.

As I reached my door, I glanced back in the direction of the clubhouse where Zara and her mother had disappeared. The reunion had gone as well as could be expected. The hard part was coming -- keeping them both alive when the blowback hit. But that was tomorrow's problem. For now, we'd succeeded. Mazida was home. Zara was happy.

And for a man like me, that was as close to peace as I was likely to get.

* * *

The clubhouse quieted as I made my way to the back room with Charming. The celebration of Mazida's return had given way to the sobering reality of what would follow. I ran a hand over my face, feeling the stubble of days without a razor, and took the seat at Charming's right. Havoc followed us in, his face set in stone as he closed the door behind Stripes and Samurai. Five men who'd seen enough blood to fill a swimming pool, now gathered around a scarred wooden table to plan how to avoid spilling more -- or at least, how to make sure it wasn't our blood that flowed.

Charming dropped into his chair, the leather creaking under his weight. He pulled a bottle of whiskey from the cabinet behind him and set out five glasses.

"Before we start," he said, pouring two fingers into each, "let's acknowledge our brother who brought back what he went for." He lifted his glass. "To Azrael."

The others raised their glasses, but I shook my head. "Save it. We've got bigger problems than celebrating."

Charming's eyes narrowed slightly, but he

nodded. He understood that my rejection wasn't about disrespect -- it was about priorities. He set his glass down untouched.

"Tell me what we're facing," he said, all business now.

I leaned forward, placing my forearms on the table. "We have serious consequences from Tel Aviv on our doorstep. Assuming they figure out who hit those places," I said, keeping my voice low despite the privacy of the room. Old habits. "The last facility we hit wasn't just holding Mazida. I think it was a hub for their operations. And some of the stuff I saw had US stamped on it."

Havoc cursed under his breath. At sixty-eight, our Sergeant-at-Arms still had the build of the Marine he'd once been, and the tactical mind that had kept us alive through more than one war.

"How big?" Charming asked.

"Big enough that they can't ignore it," I replied. "We took out fourteen of their men. They won't care all this shit started with Eli's fucking orders to take out three targets. In fact, he's probably made sure none of this will trace back to him. But without Shade there, we have no way of knowing about hidden cameras or any other tech they may have had in place that could track us."

Stripes took a long pull of his whiskey, his Russian accent thickening as he spoke. "Tel Aviv will send a cleanup crew. Professional. If they figure out who hit the place, they'll come for us."

"How soon?" Charming asked.

I shrugged. "Hard to say. We covered our tracks as best we could."

Havoc set his glass down with a *thud*. "Surveillance points," he said, switching immediately to operational mode. "We need eyes on every approach. Double the watch rotation, arm everyone."

"Already done," Charming said. "Since you three left, we've been on high alert. But we need more." He looked at me. "What are we talking about here? Hit squad? Full assault?"

I considered what I knew about the organization we'd just pissed off. "They won't come at us directly, not at first. They'll probe, look for weaknesses. Then they'll strike at whatever soft target they find."

"Zara and her mother," Samurai said quietly.

I nodded. "Among others. Anyone connected to the club is at risk. And, there's a chance they'll use the Devil's Minions to reach us. Maybe even team up with them."

Charming rubbed his jaw, thinking. "What if we moved our families elsewhere? Maybe reached out to other clubs?"

"Won't work," I countered. "If they're onto us, then they'll be watching for that move. Besides, Zara won't leave now that she just got her mother back. Even if you said Mazida could go with her, I don't think she'd budge."

"You control your woman," Stripes said, his tone matter-of-fact rather than judgmental.

I shot him a look that would have made a lesser man flinch. "She's not property, despite what her cut says."

Stripes held up his hands. "Make her understand the danger facing her."

He had a point, though I didn't like it. Zara had her own mind, her own will -- it was what had drawn me to her in the first place. But she also wasn't stupid. She understood danger.

"We fortify here," I said, bringing the

conversation back to strategy. "Make the compound a fortress. Wouldn't hurt to do that anyway."

Havoc nodded slowly. "Could work."

"Call in favors," Charming said. "I'll have Scratch reach out to the Dixie Reapers, see if they can spare a few bodies. Stripes, your connections with the Devil's Fury might help."

Stripes nodded. "*Da.* I'll call my granddaughter's old man. They'll send help."

I watched the exchange with a measured gaze. The alliances between clubs were complicated, built on blood and loyalty rather than written agreements. We all helped one another when the need arose. But only if we had men to spare and weren't dealing with our own issues.

"We need to have Shade watch the ports and air traffic coming in from other countries," I said. "Our best defense is early warning."

Samurai, who had been quiet for most of the conversation, finally spoke. "I have a contact in airport security at Memphis International. I doubt anyone would fly into Memphis if they're coming here, but maybe he knows someone in Miami."

Charming raised an eyebrow. "You never mentioned this contact before."

Samurai's expression remained neutral. "Never needed him before."

That was Samurai -- always with cards held close to his chest.

"Good," I said. "Get him watching arrivals. Any private jets, charter flights from Israel or connecting countries. We need names, descriptions. Then we can have Shade check into them, see if they're connected to what happened over there."

"Mazida and Zara need to be briefed. They need

- 214 -

to understand what we're up against. It's possible they'll be the first targets if things go sideways."

"You handle that," Charming said, the order clear in his tone. "For now, we defend and gather intelligence. When we have a good picture, then we decide whether we're in the clear."

The tension in Stripes' shoulders eased slightly. "So we wait," he said.

"We wait," I confirmed.

Havoc pulled out a map of the compound and surrounding area, spreading it across the table. "Let's talk specifics. I want surveillance cameras here, here, and here." He pointed to the main road and two access points through the wooded area behind the compound. "Motion sensors throughout the perimeter. Armed patrols 24/7."

I leaned in, focusing on the tactical discussion. This was familiar territory -- planning defenses, anticipating attacks. It was what had kept me alive in a world that wanted men like me dead.

For the next hour, we hammered out details. Who would take which watch shift. Where to position our best shooters. How to rotate the Prospects through security duties without leaving gaps. The conversation flowed with the efficiency of men who had done this before, who understood that thorough planning now might save lives later.

Throughout it all, I was aware of the occasional glances between Stripes and Samurai -- measuring glances that spoke of their concern. Not for the plan itself, but for me. They had seen what I'd done to the men guarding her. The level of violence had been necessary. They were watching for signs that I might be slipping, that my control might be fraying. They wouldn't find it.

I gave them nothing to worry about. My voice remained steady, my decisions calculated. The rage that had driven me during the rescue was now tightly contained, channeled into protecting what was mine.

As we finalized the details, Charming looked around the table. "Any other concerns?" he asked, his gaze settling longest on me.

I shook my head. "The plan is solid."

He nodded once. "Then we're done here. Havoc, get the security upgrades started. Stripes, make those calls. Samurai, contact your airport man. Azrael..." He paused, his gaze hardening slightly. "Take care of your woman and her mother. Make sure Mazida understands the rules while she's here."

I stood, recognizing the dismissal for what it was. "She'll understand. Zara will help her if necessary."

As we filed out of the room, Stripes caught my arm. "This girl," he said quietly, "she's important to you, *da*?"

I didn't answer immediately. Zara had crashed into my life unexpectedly, had somehow slipped past defenses I'd maintained for decades. What we had wasn't easy to define.

"She's under my protection," I finally said. "And she's... mine."

Stripes smiled slightly, the expression making the lines around his eyes deepen. "Not what I asked, but the answer is enough." He patted my arm. "Be careful, brother. The heart can make the head stupid sometimes. Especially when you can't admit your feelings even to yourself."

With that bit of Russian wisdom, he moved off toward the main room of the clubhouse. Samurai lingered a moment longer, his dark eyes thoughtful.

"They will come for her first," he said, his voice pitched for my ears only. "Not because she's a woman, but because they'll figure out she matters to you."

I nodded once, acknowledging the truth in his words. "Then they'll find out what happens to people who touch what's mine. If Tel Aviv wasn't enough of a lesson, I'll show them my darkest side."

Samurai's expression didn't change, but something like approval flickered in his eyes. He inclined his head slightly and walked away, leaving me alone in the hallway.

I took a moment to gather myself before heading back into the main room. The strategizing was done. Now came the harder part -- telling Zara the nightmare might not be over yet. That finding her mother hadn't removed the threat but possibly increased the danger. And that keeping them safe might require measures she wouldn't like.

But first, I needed to find her. In a compound preparing for war, I needed to steal a moment of peace with the woman who had, against all odds, become my reason for fighting.

Chapter Eighteen

Azrael

The operational briefing had left a weight on my shoulders that only one thing could lift. I found Zara in the main room of the clubhouse, sitting close to her mother on one of the worn leather couches. She looked up as I entered, her gaze finding mine across the crowded space. Something electric passed between us -- understanding, need, relief -- all packed into a single look. I jerked my head slightly toward the hallway, and she nodded, leaning in to say something to Mazida before standing. The brothers parted for her as she moved toward me, some with knowing smirks, others with respect. She wasn't just my woman. She was someone who had earned her place among us through her own strength.

I watched her approach, taking in the details I'd missed during the reunion. The dark circles under her eyes told me she hadn't slept well during my absence. Her hair was pulled back in a simple ponytail, revealing the delicate curve of her neck. She wore a simple black T-shirt and jeans, no makeup, no pretense. She'd never needed the extras other women used to catch a man's eye.

When she reached me, I didn't speak. Just took her hand and led her away from the noise of the main room. Down the hallway, past the meeting room where we'd just planned for war, to a small storage area with a window overlooking the compound. Not private enough for what I really wanted, but good enough for now.

I closed the door behind us, and for a moment, we just looked at each other. The dim light filtering through the dusty window cast shadows across her face, highlighting the curve of her cheekbones, the fullness of her lips.

"You found her," she said finally, her voice barely above a whisper. "You brought her back."

"I told you I would."

"I know. I never doubted." She stepped closer, close enough that I could feel the heat of her body. "But knowing isn't the same as seeing. Having."

I reached up, cupping her face in my hand. Her skin was soft under my calloused palm, a reminder of the differences between us -- differences that somehow made us fit together all the better.

"You should know what we're facing," I began, duty warring with desire.

She placed her finger against my lips. "Later. Right now, I need…"

I didn't make her finish. In one fluid motion, I pulled her against me, my mouth finding hers with the certainty of a man who knows exactly what he wants. Her lips parted instantly, welcoming me home in a way no words could match. I backed her against the wall, one hand cradling the back of her head to protect her from the impact, the other sliding down to grip her hip.

The kiss deepened, her hands finding their way under my cut, fingers pressing into my back through my T-shirt. There was desperation in her touch -- the release of fears she'd been holding since I'd left to find her mother. I could taste salt on her lips, wasn't sure if the tears were hers or mine.

For long minutes, we stayed like that, relearning each other through touch and taste. My hand moved from her hip to the small of her back, pressing her closer, feeling her soft curves against the hard planes of my body. She made a sound in the back of her throat --

half moan, half sigh -- that shot straight through me.

"Missed this," I murmured against her lips. "Missed you."

She pulled back just enough to look into my eyes. "Show me how much."

Before I could respond, a knock on the door interrupted us. I growled in frustration, keeping Zara pinned against me as I glared at the door.

"What?" I snapped.

The door cracked open to reveal Gator, his face apologetic but determined. At sixty-six, he'd seen enough of life to know when something was important enough to risk interrupting a moment like this.

"Sorry," he said, his Cajun accent thicker than usual. "Thought you'd want to know -- Mazida's looking tired. Figured she needs somewhere quiet to rest up."

I raised an eyebrow, waiting for him to get to the point.

"Mazida can stay at my place tonight," he offered, his gaze flicking between Zara and me. "Got the spare room all made up. Quiet there, away from the noise. Figure you two might want some" -- he cleared his throat --"privacy."

I felt Zara relax against me. She'd been worried about her mother, about where she would sleep tonight. The compound had limited accommodations for women who weren't club property or long-term old ladies. And after Charming had said Zara could only stay if she was mine, she probably assumed the same would be true for her mother.

"That would be great," Zara said before I could respond. "If you're sure it's not an imposition, and if she's comfortable doing that."

Gator waved off her concern. "No trouble. My

place is one of the most secure in the compound. Your mama will be safe there. And we've been talking. She doesn't seem scared of me."

I studied him for a moment, noting the careful way he avoided looking directly at Zara now that she was in my arms. Respect, or something more? It didn't matter. Gator was loyal to the club, and his offer made sense.

"She stays with you tonight," I agreed. "We'll regroup at the clubhouse in the morning. Make sure she understands the rules. I haven't had time to discuss the club with her yet."

Gator nodded. "Already explained the basics. No leaving the compound without an escort. No contact with outsiders."

"When did you do all that?" Zara asked.

"When you ran to the bathroom." Gator shrugged. "I didn't want her sitting there alone."

"And she agreed?" Zara asked, surprise evident in her voice.

"Your mama's a smart woman," Gator said with a slight smile. "She knows what's at stake."

I felt some of the tension leave my shoulders. One less battle to fight. "Tell Charming the arrangements are set," I instructed. "And make sure everyone knows we're not to be disturbed until morning."

Gator's mouth twitched in what might have been a suppressed smile. "Already done. Club's clearing out for the night -- just the usual security detail staying. The old ladies are taking Mazida over to my place now to get her settled."

Zara pulled away from me slightly. "I should go say goodnight to her."

I nodded, releasing her but following close

behind as we made our way back to the main room. It had emptied considerably in the few minutes we'd been gone. Mazida sat with Charming's old lady, the two women speaking quietly. When she saw us approach, Mazida stood, her expression softening as she took in her daughter's flushed face and slightly swollen lips.

"You are going?" she asked Zara.

Zara nodded. "Gator's offered you his spare room for tonight. It's safer for you there, and more comfortable than here."

I watched the exchange between mother and daughter with interest. In the short time since their reunion, they'd already reestablished the rhythm of their relationship -- the subtle dance of concern and independence that defined them.

"You will be all right?" Mazida asked, her gaze flicking to me with an unreadable expression.

"I'll be with Azrael," Zara said simply, as if that explained everything. And maybe it did.

Mazida studied me for a long moment, her dark eyes assessing. I met her gaze steadily, letting her see whatever she needed to see. Finally, she nodded once.

"Allah has strange ways of protecting his children," she said. "Even through the Angel of Death."

Coming from anyone else, the words might have been an insult. From her, they were acceptance -- perhaps even gratitude. I inclined my head slightly in acknowledgment.

"We'll see you tomorrow," Zara said, leaning in to hug her mother. "Get some rest."

The goodbyes were quick after that. Gator approached to escort Mazida to his place, offering his arm with a gentlemanly flourish that seemed at odds with his rough appearance. Charming caught my eye across the room and gave a single nod -- permission to go, assurance that everything was under control for the night.

I placed my hand at the small of Zara's back and guided her toward the door. Outside, the compound had settled into its nighttime routine. Security lights cast pools of yellow across the gravel, and men with guns patrolled the perimeter. The increased security was obvious to anyone who knew what to look for -- extra bodies on watch, the strategic positioning at key points around the fence line.

My bike stood where I'd left it. I swung my leg over the seat and waited for Zara to climb on behind me. Her arms wrapped around my waist, her chest pressed against my back, her thighs hugging mine. The engine roared to life beneath us, a deep, throaty growl that matched the want building inside me.

The ride to my -- *our* -- home took less than three minutes, but it was long enough for the vibration of the engine and the press of her body to reignite what Gator's interruption had dampened. I parked in the small carport and killed the engine, but neither of us moved immediately.

"I wasn't sure you'd come back," she said softly, her cheek still pressed between my shoulder blades. "I kept thinking about all the things that could go wrong."

I twisted to look at her over my shoulder. "I always come back."

She slid off the bike, her movements fluid despite the fatigue I could see in her eyes. "Until you don't."

I followed her to the door, watching as she unlocked it with the key she'd worn on a chain around her neck while I was gone. Inside, the house was exactly as I'd left it -- sparse, functional, but with touches of Zara's presence that had transformed it from a place to sleep into something that might be called a home. A throw blanket over the couch. Flowers in a mason jar on the kitchen counter. Books stacked on the coffee table.

She turned to face me as I closed and locked the door behind us. In the dim light of the single lamp she'd left on, her eyes looked almost black, pupils dilated with desire and relief and the remnants of fear.

"You brought my mother back," she said again, as if still trying to convince herself it was real.

"I told you I would."

"I know." She took a step toward me.

I crossed the distance between us in two strides. This time when I kissed her, there was no restraint. My hands found the hem of her shirt, pulling it up and over her head in one smooth motion. Her skin was warm beneath my palms as I ran them up her sides, feeling the slight curve of her waist, the swell of her breasts in the simple black bra she wore.

She was just as impatient, tugging at my cut, pushing it off my shoulders to the floor. Her fingers worked at the buttons of my shirt with practiced ease, revealing the tattoos and scars that mapped the violence of my life. She traced one of the longer scars with her fingertip, her touch featherlight.

"New?" she asked.

"Old," I replied, capturing her hand and bringing it to my lips. "Just reopened during the extraction. It's not as bad as it looks."

Her eyes darkened with concern, but I didn't give her time to dwell on it. I swept her into my arms and carried her to the bedroom, laying her on the bed with more gentleness than most would believe me capable of. She looked up at me, her dark hair spread across the pillow, her lips parted in invitation.

"Come here," she whispered.

I obeyed, lowering myself over her, careful to support my weight on my forearms. Her hands slid up my chest to my shoulders, pulling me down for another kiss that quickly turned from tender to hungry. I trailed my lips down her neck, feeling her pulse quicken beneath my mouth.

"Samir," she breathed, the name a prayer on her lips.

I paused, looking up. "I'm here."

Her smile was soft but knowing. "Then show me."

My hands roamed over her body, tracing the curves of her hips and ass as she arched into me. "You're so fucking beautiful," I groaned against her neck, my teeth grazing her skin. She shuddered beneath me, a soft moan escaping her lips as I nipped at her collarbone.

I pulled back to look at her, taking in the desire etched on her features. "Tell me what you want," I commanded, my voice rough with need.

"I want you to fuck me hard," she whispered, biting her bottom lip. "I want you to take me roughly and claim me as yours. No holding back."

My cock twitched at her words, already hardening inside my pants. "Anything for you, baby girl," I growled, reaching down to yank her jeans and panties off in one swift motion.

She gasped as I exposed her wetness to the cool air of the room. "Samir," she breathed again, this time more urgently.

I couldn't resist any longer. I had to taste her. Kneeling between her legs, I parted them wider and pressed a kiss to her swollen clit before taking it into my mouth. She cried out sharply, bucking up off the bed as I sucked on her sensitive nub while two fingers plunged inside her tight pussy.

"Fuck!" she screamed, arching off the bed again as an orgasm ripped through her body.

The room quickly filled with our moans and gasps as I devoured her pussy, as if I had been starved for years. My tongue danced around her clit, teasing and driving her wild with pleasure while my fingers thrust in and out of her wetness. She squirmed beneath me, her nails raking down my back. Her hips bucked against my face, begging for more as she lost herself completely in the sensations overtaking her body.

It was fucking delicious how much power I had over her at that moment. She was mine to control, mine to please and punish as I saw fit. A shiver ran through me as I imagined binding her wrists above her head and taking her hard from behind, claiming what was mine.

My cock throbbed in time with the rhythm of my fingers inside her tight pussy, desperate for release, but I was determined not to let myself go until she was completely undone. The scent of her arousal filled my nostrils, driving me further into the brink of madness.

"That's it, baby," I groaned against her swollen clit. "Come for me." Her body shuddered violently underneath me as she cried out my name and exploded in my mouth. I licked every last bit of her cum with my tongue before swallowing greedily.

She collapsed back onto the bed, panting heavily. I stood, kicking off my boots and pants, then covered her body with mine once more. My hands gripped tightly around her wrists and pulled them above her head. "Thank you," she whispered breathlessly.

I smirked down at her, feeling possessive. "You're welcome, sweetheart. Now it's my turn."

I couldn't help but admire the way her body trembled under my touch. She was mine now, completely at my mercy. I leaned down and captured her lips in a searing kiss, my tongue diving deep into her mouth.

"You're the prettiest fucking thing I've ever seen," I whispered against her lips. She moaned into the kiss, her body arching underneath me as she sought more contact. I trailed kisses along her jawline until I reached her soft neck, nipped at her sensitive skin, eliciting a sharp intake of breath from her.

"Please," she begged hoarsely. "I need you inside me." Her words sent a shiver of anticipation down my spine as I slid my hands down her sides.

I leaned over her chest, taking a hardened nipple into my mouth and sucking it greedily. She cried out in pleasure as I flicked my tongue over it, her hips bucking off the bed in search of release. I moved lower, kissing and nipping my way down her stomach.

"I want you to watch me," I commanded, my voice rough with lust.

I positioned myself between her legs, my hardened length rubbing against the damp folds of her pussy. I could feel her wetness seeping onto my skin as I teasingly pushed forward, only to pull back at the last second. Her gaze locked onto mine, pleading and desperate for release.

"You're going to beg for this cock, aren't you?" I whispered huskily. She nodded eagerly, her tongue darting out to wet her lips as she watched me position myself at her entrance. With one swift thrust, I buried myself inside her warmth up to the hilt.

She cried out in blissful agony as I began to

move, picking up speed until we were both lost in a whirlwind of passion and lust. Her fingernails dug into my shoulders, drawing tiny beads of blood as she met my every thrust with equal force.

"You like that, baby?" I said with a soft growl against her ear. "Do you want more?"

She nodded frantically, her body trembling underneath me. I reached down and played with her clit, circling it slowly at first before increasing the pressure and speed.

"Ahh... please," she moaned as she neared release again. "Don't stop." Her words fueled my passion even more as I slammed into her over and over again, feeling the walls of her pussy squeeze tightly around my cock.

Finally, unable to hold back any longer, I let go, groaning as I felt my hot cum shoot deep inside her. She collapsed beneath me, our chests heaving as we caught our breath. I looked down at her, feeling a sense of satisfaction wash over me. She was mine, completely and utterly.

I twisted and fell onto my back on the mattress. Zara laid her head on my chest, and I put my arm around her shoulders, allowing myself a moment of peace. Tomorrow would bring its own problems. But tonight -- tonight was ours. A stolen moment of connection in a life where such moments were rare and precious.

"What happens now?" Zara asked softly, her finger tracing lazy patterns on my chest.

I could have lied, could have told her everything would be fine. But she deserved better than platitudes. Besides, there were things she needed to know, things I'd been told to share with her.

"Now we prepare," I said, my voice a low

rumble in the darkened room. "They may come looking for payback."

She tensed slightly against me. "Because of my mother? Because of me?"

"Because of me," I corrected. "I made the call. I led the mission. The club backed my play, but the responsibility is mine."

She pushed herself up on one elbow to look at me, her expression serious in the dim light filtering through the curtains. "No regrets?"

I reached up to tuck a strand of hair behind her ear, letting my hand linger against her cheek. "No regrets."

She studied me for a long moment, as if searching for any sign of doubt. Finding none, she nodded once and settled back against my chest.

"Then we'll face it together," she said simply. "Whatever comes next."

I tightened my arm around her, knowing she couldn't possibly understand what she was committing to -- the violence, the danger, the life on constant alert. But also knowing if anyone could handle it, it would be this woman who had come looking for an avenging angel to help find her mother.

"Together," I agreed, pressing a kiss to the top of her head.

Outside, the night was quiet except for the occasional sound of boots on gravel as the security patrols made their rounds. Inside, in this small haven we'd created, I held the woman who had somehow become my reason for fighting -- and for returning.

And for the first time in longer than I could remember, I slept without dreams of blood and death. At least for tonight.

Chapter Nineteen

Azrael

The clubhouse lights were dimmed low, casting long shadows across the worn leather furniture and scarred wooden tables. My brothers and I sat in various states of attention, some nursing beers, others with hands clenched into fists, but all of them were focused on the woman sitting across from us. Mazida Quadir, her hijab pulled tight around her face as if to shield herself from the very memories she was about to share, took a deep breath that seemed to rattle through her entire body. Her dark eyes, rimmed with the remnants of fading bruises, met mine for the briefest moment before she began her story.

"Thank you for seeing me," she said, her accented voice barely above a whisper. "I would not have come, but Zara insisted. She said… she said you needed to know it was worth the cost."

Charming, our president, nodded. "Your daughter's family now. That makes you family too."

A ghost of a smile touched her lips before fading. Her fingers twisted the fabric of her long skirt. These clothes hung on her frame as if borrowed, emphasizing the weight she'd lost. Someone had gone to her place early this morning to pack a few of her things. Zara had thought it might make her mom feel more at ease.

"I'd been home for an hour," she began. "Someone knocked on the door. When I peered out, I could only see the back of a man in a suit. I thought perhaps he was lost, or at the wrong address."

I leaned forward, resting my elbows on my knees. Watching her was like watching a wounded animal, unsure whether to flee or fight.

"The man worked for my brother, Balal. Before I

could run, two more men pushed their way inside." Her voice grew hollow as she continued. "They told me Balal had been searching for me for years. That he had never forgotten the shame I brought to my family by marrying an American."

"But the bed… it looked like you'd been dragged from it, and a vase had been knocked over," I said.

Her brow furrowed. "I didn't do those things."

Well, that answered one question. Someone had gone back to her place. But I still didn't know why.

Mazida's hands trembled as she reached for the glass of water in front of her. I noticed Gator shift in his seat, his gaze never leaving her face. There was something in his expression beyond the typical protective instinct we all felt toward club family -- something more personal, more intense. It made me wonder what they'd talked about while she'd been at his house overnight.

"They drugged me," she continued after taking a sip. "When I woke, I was in a small room. My brother was there." Her voice caught on the word "brother," as if the familial connection made the betrayal that much more painful. "He told me I belonged to him now, that I would return to Tel Aviv and be properly married to a man of his choosing."

I felt my jaw tighten, memories of my own mother's bruised face surfacing unbidden. She'd endured similar controlling bullshit from men who claimed to have her best interests at heart. The parallel wasn't lost on me.

"Balal was… very angry when I refused," Mazida said, her hand unconsciously rising to her face, fingers lightly tracing a bruise on her cheekbone. "He said I was still his responsibility. That no matter how long I had been gone, my life was not my own."

Gator leaned forward, his face creased with concern. "Did he hurt you bad?" he asked, his voice softer than I'd ever heard it.

Mazida's gaze darted to him, then away. "Yes," she whispered. "When he realized I would not cooperate, he..." She paused, swallowing hard. "He beat me. Said he would beat the American out of me. That I had forgotten who I was, what I was."

The room had gone completely still. Even the usual background noises of the clubhouse -- the hum of the refrigerator, the distant sound of bikes in the compound -- seemed to have fallen silent. In that moment, there was only Mazida's voice and the collective rage building among my brothers.

"After, when I was still conscious, he told me about Carter." Her voice cracked. Carter Colton -- Zara's father. "Balal said Carter's death was not an accident. That he had arranged it, made it look like a heart attack, but it had taken him years to find us again afterward. I hadn't been able to stay in the home I'd shared with my husband. It was too painful."

"Son of a bitch," someone muttered behind me.

I watched Gator's knuckles go white as he gripped the arms of his chair. The man had always had a soft spot for mothers -- something about his own upbringing he rarely discussed. But seeing Mazida's pain seemed to be cutting him deeper than expected.

"They kept me in that room for what felt like days," she continued. "Different men would come in. They would hurt me when I refused to comply with their demands. They wanted information about Zara, about my life here. They..." She closed her eyes briefly. "They tried to break me."

I felt a familiar darkness rising within me, the kind that had gotten me my road name. The name I'd earned for the cold, calculating rage that took over when someone hurt those who couldn't protect themselves.

Her brother and his men had seen her as weak, as nothing more than property to be controlled. They'd made a fatal error. They hadn't realized she'd had people who would come for her. Of course, Mazida herself hadn't known it.

"Even though you saved me, brought me home, my brother... Balal is still out there. He will not stop. He told me... he told me he wants Zara too. Says she belongs in Tel Aviv, living under proper supervision. That he will not allow his niece to marry an American like her mother did." Her voice hardened. "I will die before I let him near my daughter."

I glanced around the room, reading the faces of my brothers. There was no question about what would happen next. This was exactly the kind of situation that bound us together -- protecting our own from outside threats.

"My brother... he has powerful friends. In Israel and here."

I watched as Gator's eyes narrowed, his gaze never leaving Mazida's face. He seemed to be studying every mark, every flinch, cataloging the damage done to her. I wondered if perhaps he'd finally found a woman who would hold his attention. Of course, that didn't mean Mazida would be interested.

"I should not have come here," Mazida said suddenly, misreading our silence. "I do not want to bring trouble to your door."

"We understand," I said firmly. The words fell from my lips without thought, driven by the memories of my mother's suffering.

I felt a familiar weight settle in my chest -- not

just anger or the desire for vengeance, but something deeper. In that moment of heavy silence, I made a silent vow. Balal Quadir would never touch Mazida again. Not while I still drew breath. Some men deserved to die, and from the sound of it, Balal had earned his death many times over.

I stood up before I'd even realized I was moving, my chair scraping harshly against the wooden floor. "I will protect you both."

The words hung in the air, heavy with promise and the weight of my own history. They all focused on me, but I kept my gaze fixed on Mazida, her face a mirror of my mother's from decades past.

Mazida looked up at me, surprise flickering across her bruised features. She hadn't expected such immediate resolve, such certainty. But she didn't know what I knew -- that the ghosts of our pasts have a way of returning, demanding justice.

"Azrael's right," Charming said. "This isn't up for debate. You already know he and your daughter are together. Which makes you his mother-in-law, or close enough. Your problems are our problems."

Around the room, heads nodded in agreement. Ripper knocked back the rest of his whiskey, setting the glass down with purpose. Magnus leaned forward, his usual relaxed posture replaced by something more predatory. But it was Gator's reaction that caught my attention. Yeah, that fucker was already invested in Mazida. I only hoped he knew what the hell he was doing.

"My brother has resources," Mazida said softly. "He has connections with a powerful crime family in Tel Aviv. I don't want to put you in danger."

I remained standing, feeling the familiar cold focus settle over me. "With all due respect, ma'am, we have our own connections."

A subtle change rippled through the room -- shoulders straightened, jaws tightened. This was what we lived for. Not just the brotherhood or the freedom of the road, but these moments when we could use our strength to shield those who needed it.

"Tell us about your brother," Charming prompted. "Everything you know about his operations, his people, how he thinks."

"I can tell you what I know from before and what I observed while I was with him recently... before he gave me to another organization as part of a deal."

As Mazida began speaking again, filling in details about Balal's criminal connections and methods, my mind drifted. I wondered what she thought about me and Zara being together. I wasn't the type of man most mothers wanted their daughters to date, much less live with.

"He will send more men," Mazida was saying, her fingers nervously tracing the edge of her hijab. "He told me he would never stop looking, that I would always belong to him. But I belong to no one. Not anymore."

"Damn straight," Gator murmured, speaking for the first time since Mazida had begun her story. There was admiration in his tone. Recognition of her strength.

Charming leaned forward, resting his forearms on his knees. "We need to decide how to handle this. Defensive is good, but it won't solve the problem."

"We need to send a message," Magnus suggested, his voice calm but his gaze cold.

"What about drawing him out?" I suggested, the plan forming as I spoke. "If Balal is as obsessed with controlling his sister as it sounds, he won't stop. He'll send more men or come himself eventually. We can use that."

The room fell silent as everyone considered this approach. I could see the calculations happening behind each man's eyes -- weighing risks, considering angles.

"It's too dangerous," Mazida protested. "I won't be bait for my brother."

"Not you," I clarified. "Information. Controlled leaks about your whereabouts, your routine. We create opportunities that aren't really there."

Charming nodded slowly. "Could work. We'd need to be careful though. Make sure Mazida and Zara are actually somewhere completely different."

"My house," Gator said suddenly. "Mazida can keep staying with me. I've got the space, and no one would think to look there."

I studied him closely, trying to read the motivation behind his offer. Gator was a private man -- his home was his sanctuary. Offering it up wasn't something he did lightly. One night had been strange enough, but this was entirely different.

"You sure about that?" Charming asked, clearly thinking the same thing.

Gator nodded, his attention still on Mazida. "Absolutely. Place has good sightlines. Easy to secure." He finally looked away from her to address Charming directly. "Plus, I've got nothing else going on. Can keep an eye on things 24/7."

It made sense from a tactical perspective, but there was more to it than that. I'd seen that look before -- men who recognized something in a woman that called to them. Not just attraction, but a deeper pull.

"I don't want to impose," Mazida said softly.

"You wouldn't be," Gator replied, his voice gentler than I'd ever heard it. "It would be my honor to help."

The room fell silent again, but this time the silence held a different quality -- like we were all witnessing something unexpected unfold between these two damaged souls.

Charming cleared his throat. "All right, that's settled then. Gator's place for Mazida. And Zara will obviously be with Azrael."

"And Balal?" Magnus asked, bringing us back to the original problem.

I felt my expression harden. "Like I said, we draw him out. Make him think he's got a chance at grabbing Mazida again. But when he makes his move..." I let the sentence hang unfinished.

"We end the threat permanently," Charming finished for me, his voice matter-of-fact.

Mazida's head snapped up, her dark eyes wide. "You mean kill him."

It wasn't a question, but I answered anyway. "Yes."

I expected protest, hesitation at least. He was her brother, after all. Blood. But Mazida's expression shifted, hardened in a way that reminded me again of my mother in her rare moments of defiance.

"He killed my husband," she said quietly. "Threatened my daughter. And he will never stop. If this is what must be done, then let it be done."

The weight of her permission settled over us like a blessing and a burden both. This wasn't just club business anymore. It was justice.

"We'll need intel," Ripper said, breaking the heavy moment. "Shade can dig into your brother's movements, track when he might come stateside."

As the room broke into tactical discussions, I watched Gator move to sit closer to Mazida. He didn't touch her, didn't crowd her space, but positioned himself like a shield between her and the door. It was subtle, probably unconscious on his part, but it spoke volumes.

"You okay with all this?" I asked, dropping into the empty seat beside her.

Mazida considered the question, her hands folded tightly in her lap. "I left my home country to escape men who thought they owned me. I'd fallen in love, got married. Then my husband brought me to this country. We built a life here, raised my daughter to be strong and independent." She looked up at me, old pain and new determination stamped on her features. "I will not let my brother take that away. Not after everything it cost me to build it."

I nodded, understanding completely. Some choices weren't really choices at all, but necessities.

"Your mother," she said suddenly, her perception catching me off guard. "She suffered similarly, didn't she? I see it in your eyes when you look at me."

The question hit me like a physical blow. I rarely spoke of my mother, had buried those memories deep. But Mazida had seen through me with the perception of someone who recognized a fellow survivor.

"Yes," I admitted, my voice rough. "My mother was gang-raped. Ended up pregnant with me. Her family threw her out since she was no longer of use to them as a bargaining chip."

"And she didn't survive it," Mazida guessed quietly.

"She did, but... Cancer eventually took her from me."

Mazida reached out tentatively, her hand hovering near mine before gently touching my knuckles. "Then I am doubly grateful for your protection. You're fighting old battles as well as new ones."

Her insight was uncomfortable but accurate. I'd joined the Devils' Boneyard seeking brotherhood but had found purpose in our code -- protecting those who couldn't protect themselves, standing against men like those who had hurt my mother. Like Balal.

"We won't fail," I promised her, and myself.

Across the room, Charming called us back to order, laying out the beginnings of a plan. As everyone focused on his words, I caught Gator's eye. A silent message passed between us -- an understanding, brother to brother. Whatever his reasons, whatever drew him to Mazida, I knew he would protect her with his life if necessary. And I would do the same for both women.

* * *

The clubhouse had mostly emptied out after our meeting with Mazida. Charming had taken her to Gator's place personally, with three brothers riding escort. I found myself drawn to the back corner of the building where a soft blue glow spilled from beneath a partially closed door. Without knocking, I pushed it open to find Shade hunched over his laptop, the light from the screen reflecting off his glasses. His fingers moved across the keyboard with practiced efficiency, lines of code scrolling past faster than I could track them.

"You got anything yet?" I asked, dropping into the chair beside him.

Shade didn't look up, still focused on the screen. "Depends on what you mean by 'anything.'" His voice was low, slightly raspy from too many cigarettes and not enough sleep. "Got plenty of somethings. Just trying to figure out which somethings matter."

The room he'd claimed as his workspace was a study in organized chaos. Three monitors of varying sizes were arranged in a semicircle on the desk, each displaying different information. Hard drives and various electronic components I couldn't name were stacked on shelves along the wall. The air smelled of coffee and the faint ozone scent of overheated electronics.

I leaned back in my chair, giving him space to work. Shade didn't like being rushed or crowded, especially when he was digging through digital rabbit holes.

"Balal Quadir," he said finally, pushing his glasses up with one finger. "Interesting character. Officially, he runs an import/export business specializing in Middle Eastern textiles and art. Unofficially..." He clicked something, and one of the side monitors filled with images -- surveillance photos, news clippings, police reports.

"As you already know, unofficially, he's connected to the biggest crime syndicate in Tel Aviv," Shade continued. "Not just connected -- embedded. Married the oldest daughter fifteen years ago. Since then, he's been their primary connection to a network of antiquities smuggling that stretches across the Middle East. In addition, he's known to also trade in young girls from time to time, selling them off as brides to wealthy clients."

I studied the photos, trying to get a sense of the man. Balal Quadir looked nothing like his sister. Where Mazida had a softness to her features despite her strength, Balal's face was all hard angles and cold calculation. In most of the photos, he wore expensive suits and a perpetual scowl.

"Interpol has a file on him," Shade said, pulling up another window. "Never enough evidence to charge him with anything major, but he's been questioned in connection with everything from art theft to human trafficking."

"If that fucker comes over here and tries that shit, he'll find out why people fear me."

Shade nodded, his fingers never stopping their movement across the keyboard.

"What about his reach?" I asked. "Mazida said he has connections here in the States."

"Working on that," Shade muttered, switching to another program. "There's definitely movement. His company has a satellite office in New York. Shipments coming in monthly through there and through Miami."

"Legit shipments?"

A humorless smile flickered across Shade's face. "On paper, sure. But there's a pattern to the customs inspections -- or rather, to the lack of them. Someone's being paid off."

I wasn't surprised. Money opened doors, especially in ports where underpaid officials handled thousands of containers daily.

"Here's where it gets interesting," Shade said, pulling up an email chain. The text was in Hebrew, but he scrolled to a translation he'd already prepared. "This was sent right before Mazida was grabbed."

I leaned closer, reading the translated message:

Target confirmed at location. Proceeding as discussed. Local assets in place to assist with extraction and transport. Will confirm when package is secure.

"Local assets," I said, the implications immediately clear. "He's got people here. Not just in

New York or Miami."

"Exactly." Shade clicked through several more screens, pulling up what looked like bank records. "Found these transfers to a shell company based in Phoenix. Five payments over the last six months, each for exactly $25,000. Same for Colorado Springs, and again in Panama City."

"Retainer payments," I guessed. "Setting up the grab."

Shade nodded. "And this is where it gets complicated. The shell company -- Desert Sun Security Consulting -- it's owned by this man." He pulled up a driver's license photo of a hard-faced man in his fifties. "James Mercer. Former military, former FBI, now supposedly running a private security firm."

My stomach tightened. "Law enforcement connections."

"Not just any connections," Shade said, his voice dropping even lower. "Mercer still consults for the Bureau occasionally. Has friends in Homeland Security. If he's working with Balal…"

"Then Balal has eyes and ears in places we can't touch," I finished.

The implications hit me hard. This wasn't just about protecting Mazida from her brother's direct attacks. We were potentially going up against people with badges, with the authority to make our lives hell -- or worse.

"There's more," Shade said, bringing up another document. "These are flight records. Balal Quadir entered the U.S. through JFK about three hours after you got back to the U.S."

"He's here?" I straightened in my chair. "In New York?"

"Was in New York," Shade corrected. "There's a

private jet registered to one of his shell companies that flew from New York to Northwest Florida yesterday morning. No passenger manifest filed, but…"

"But it's him," I said with certainty. "He's not trusting this to his men anymore. He's coming for her himself."

Shade nodded, finally looking away from the screen. "And he's bringing friends. Customs records show four men entered with him. Listed as business associates. All Israeli citizens with military backgrounds."

I stood up, pacing the small room as I processed this information. Balal was less than an hour's drive away, with trained muscle and potential law enforcement connections. The situation had just gotten significantly more dangerous.

"We need to move Mazida," I said. "Gator's place isn't secure enough."

"It's going to have to work," Shade said. "There's nowhere to move her, and we can't be sure he hasn't already connected her to our club. He may have eyes on this place."

"What about the Mercer connection?" I asked. "If he's got FBI ties, he might be able to track club movements."

Shade's mouth tightened into a thin line. "That's the other thing. Found some chatter on encrypted channels. Not enough to get specifics, but enough to know they're looking at known associates of Zara. I have a feeling Balal suspects his niece sent someone after her mother."

"Son of a bitch," I muttered. I leaned against the wall, thinking through our options. "Keep digging into Mercer. Find out everything -- his habits, his weaknesses, anyone he's close to that might be leverage. Do we know why they didn't try to take Zara when they grabbed Mazida?"

"No. Only thing I can figure is they weren't sure where she was at the time, or she was in a place that was too crowded or secure for them to grab her." He paused. "And Balal?"

"Track his movements. I want to know where he's staying, who he's meeting with. If he's in town, there'll be a trail."

"On it." Shade paused, glancing up at me over his glasses. "This is bigger than we thought, Azrael. I mean, we knew they had connections, but this is... It's insane everything they have access to."

I met his gaze steadily. "We have connections too."

I turned to leave, needing to report these findings to Charming. Balal Quadir had made a critical error in coming here personally. He thought he was the hunter, but he'd just put himself within our reach.

And unlike his sister, he wouldn't be escaping.

Chapter Twenty

Azrael

The first rays of sunlight hadn't even broken over the horizon when the rumble of performance engines shattered the pre-dawn silence. I rolled out of bed, grabbing my gun from the nightstand in one fluid motion. Balal Quadir had finally made his move, and from the sound of it, he'd brought an army. Mazida was still sleeping at Gator's house. I hoped like hell she stayed out of sight.

I shoved my feet into my boots, not bothering with socks, and pulled a shirt over my head as I moved to the window. Six black SUVs and three sports cars tore down the street outside the compound, moving fast toward the front gate. My phone vibrated and I quickly answered.

"Rally at the front. Get the Prospects to the clubhouse roof with rifles." I hung up without waiting for a response. Ripper knew what to do.

The compound's new alarm began to wail as I strapped on my shoulder holster and grabbed my AR-15 from the gun safe. By the time I reached the clubhouse, brothers were pouring out of their homes, many half-dressed but all armed.

"Balal Quadir's here for his sister," I announced, moving toward the front entrance. "Anyone gets past us, she's as good as dead. No one gets through."

The first shots rang out before any of us had a chance to take cover. Glass shattered as bullets tore through windows. I dropped to a crouch and signaled for the others to take cover. My brothers dispersed, finding positions behind vehicles, around the sides of buildings, or anywhere that might stop a bullet.

"Azrael! The bastards are using armor-piercing

rounds!" one of the Prospects shouted from the rooftop. "Check the club truck. Through and through."

I glanced at the trucks and saw he was right. The bullets tore through the vehicle like a knife sliding through butter.

Balal's men had positioned themselves behind their vehicles, using the engines as cover. Smart, but not smart enough. I spotted gas cans in the bed of a pickup parked near the clubhouse.

"Cover me," I called out, then sprinted toward the vehicle. Bullets whizzed past my head, close enough that I could feel their heat.

From my position, I had a clear shot at the gas cans. I ran to the truck, grabbed two of the cans, and tossed them toward the gate. Then I aimed, exhaled slowly, and squeezed the trigger on my gun. The explosion rocked the compound, sending two of Balal's vehicles airborne in a ball of flame, and our gate flew off, landing more than ten yards away. Screams filled the air as burning men staggered from the wreckage.

I used the distraction to move closer, ducking behind a battered Chevy as more gunfire erupted. My brothers were returning fire now, the rapid staccato of automatic weapons drowning out the screams of the wounded.

Chaos appeared at my side, his face smeared with blood that wasn't his own. "One of the Prospects isn't going to make it," he said, his voice flat. "Took one through the neck."

Anger surged through me. Just a kid, probably no older than twenty. "Which one?"

"Damien."

I nodded, committing the debt to memory. Balal would pay for every drop of blood spilled today. Jesus. Damien was just a kid. Not even eighteen yet.

"Where's Balal?" I asked, scanning the battlefield.

"Haven't seen him. Probably letting his men do the dying for him."

A grenade sailed over our cover, landing a few feet away. I grabbed Chaos by his cut and hurled us both behind a club vehicle as the world exploded. My ears rang, and dust filled my lungs. I spat blood onto the ground, not sure if it was from my mouth or my lungs.

"You good?" I asked, checking Chaos for injuries.

He nodded, though his eyes seemed unfocused. "Just ringing," he shouted, probably unable to hear his own voice.

I patted his shoulder and peered around our cover. Three of Balal's men were advancing, taking advantage of the grenade's aftermath. I lined up my sights and dropped them one by one, clean shots through the head. No need to waste ammunition.

The rain that had threatened all night finally broke, falling in sheets that turned the asphalt and gravel slick with blood and water. I used the downpour as cover to move closer to the main gate, or where it used to be. Most of Balal's forces had concentrated there.

From my new position, I could see across the compound to where several of my brothers had taken refuge. They were pinned down, taking heavy fire from a group of Balal's men who had somehow flanked them.

"Chaos," I called out. "Southeast corner of the compound. Our boys need help."

"On it," came the immediate response.

I watched as Chaos and three others broke cover, moving in a coordinated pattern toward our trapped brothers. They were good, but Balal's men were professionals. Two of my brothers went down before they reached the building.

"Fuck," I growled, adjusting my position to provide covering fire. My finger tightened on the trigger, sending a spray of bullets toward Balal's men. One dropped, then another, giving Chaos the opening he needed to reach them.

A bullet ripped through my arm, the hot pain momentarily stealing my breath. I twisted around to find one of Balal's men standing just a few feet away, his gun trained on my head. I rolled as he fired again, the bullet embedding itself in the ground where I'd been. I came up with my knife in hand, driving it deep into his thigh. He screamed, his gun wavering just enough for me to grab his wrist and force it upward. His final shot went into the sky as I slit his throat in one smooth motion.

Blood sprayed across my face, warm and metallic. I wiped it from my eyes with my sleeve and retrieved my rifle. The wound in my arm throbbed, but the bullet had passed clean through muscle. I'd live.

An explosion rocked the compound, sending debris flying. For a moment, my heart stopped, thinking of Chaos and the others. Then I saw them making their way toward the clubhouse, dragging wounded brothers with them.

Movement caught my eye. A tall figure in an expensive suit stood observing the carnage, flanked by bodyguards. Balal. The old man hadn't even bothered to arm himself, so confident was he in his men's ability to handle us.

Our gaze met across the battlefield, and even at that distance, I could see the cold calculation in his gaze. He wasn't here just for Mazida. He wanted to send a message, to crush anyone who dared stand between him and what he considered his property.

I started moving toward him, no longer caring about cover or caution. Rage propelled me forward, each step fueled by the memory of Mazida's bruised face. By the Prospect bleeding out. By every brother who'd fallen today.

Balal's bodyguards noticed my approach and raised their weapons. I didn't slow down. Bullets tore through the air around me, one grazing my cheek, another ripping through my side. I barely felt them. All I saw was Balal, his composed expression finally showing a flicker of concern as I closed the distance.

One of his bodyguards moved to block my path. I shot him point-blank in the chest, not even breaking stride as he crumpled. The second guard was smarter, aiming for my legs, but I was moving too fast, too erratically. His shots went wide, and then I was on him, driving my knife up under his chin. The ten-inch blade scraped bone before finding the softness of his brain. It looked like he'd used his intelligent muscle for the main fight and kept the weaker ones beside him. Big mistake.

By the time I looked up, Balal was retreating toward one of the few intact vehicles, a sleek black Mercedes. I raised my gun, but a burst of automatic fire from my right forced me to dive for cover. When I got back to my feet, the Mercedes was already speeding away, leaving half his men to continue the fight or die trying.

"Azrael!" Chaos's voice barely reached me over all the noise. "They're pulling back!"

Sure enough, Balal's remaining forces were disengaging, climbing into vehicles or fleeing on foot. Not a retreat, I realized. A tactical withdrawal. Balal had seen enough to know he couldn't take us all at once. He'd be back with more men, better intelligence.

I staggered back toward the clubhouse, the adrenaline fading enough for me to feel every wound. My brothers emerged from various positions, bloody and battered but still standing. We'd lost one, maybe two. Hard to tell in the chaos.

Ripper met me at the entrance, his face grim. "Two dead, three wounded bad enough they need a hospital."

I nodded, surveying the destruction. Bodies littered the ground, mostly theirs, except two: one of the prospects and Shadow. The club would take the loss hard. Especially Shadow. He'd been with the club for over twenty years. There wasn't a single man in the Devil's Boneyard who didn't have fond memories of him. Now that's all we'd have left.

Looking around once more, I took it all in. The carnage. Destruction. Vehicles burned, casting an orange glow against the lightening sky. The rain continued to fall, washing blood into the gutters.

"He'll be back," I said, wincing as I probed the wound in my side. Not deep, but it needed stitches.

"For Mazida?"

"For all of us now." I spat blood onto the pavement. "This wasn't just about his sister anymore. This was a statement."

Chaos looked across the devastated compound and nodded slowly. "What's the play?"

I thought of Mazida, safely tucked away in Gator's house. Thought of the fear that would consume her if she knew her brother had found her. Although, she'd likely heard all the commotion and put two and two together. Hopefully, Gator was keeping her calm.

"We don't wait for him to come back," I said, my

decision crystallizing. "We find him first. And this time, we finish it."

Sirens wailed in the distance, growing louder. The police would be here soon, not that they'd do anything but take statements and pretend to care. This part of town belonged to us, and everyone knew it. Still, we couldn't be out in the open like this when they arrived.

"Get the wounded to the clubhouse," I ordered. I couldn't send them to a hospital without making sure it wasn't going to cause trouble for us. We had a doctor in the club for a reason. "And get Doc over here."

Chaos nodded and moved off to relay the orders. I took one last look at the battlefield that had once been our home. Balal had brought war to our doorstep, thinking to catch us unprepared. He'd underestimated us once. He wouldn't make that mistake again.

* * *

Five hours later, I found Balal Quadir exactly where Shade said he'd be -- holed up in an abandoned textile factory on the edge of town. The rain had stopped, leaving behind a heavy mist that clung to the broken windows and rusted metal of the derelict building. I parked my bike three blocks away and approached on foot, my body still aching from this morning's firefight. The fresh wounds I'd sustained hurt like a bitch, but pain was an old friend. What mattered was finishing what Balal had started. For Mazida. For my fallen brothers. For the promise I'd made to protect those under my care.

There were times I hated being right. This was one of them. After the failed assault on our compound, he'd retreated to regroup and call in reinforcements from Tel Aviv. But he'd made a critical mistake -- dismissing most of his surviving guards to lick their wounds, keeping only his most trusted men with him. Maybe he thought we'd need time to recover. Maybe his arrogance blinded him to the threat. Either way, it was the opening I needed.

I circled the building, noting the black Mercedes parked by a loading dock. Fresh tire tracks in the mud showed where other vehicles had come and gone. I counted two men patrolling the perimeter, moving with the practiced precision of professionals. Former military, probably Mossad.

I waited until the guards crossed paths, then moved. My knife entered the first man's kidney before he registered my presence. I clamped my hand over his mouth as he sagged against me, lowering him silently to the ground. The second guard turned at the wrong moment, catching a glimpse of movement. He reached for his weapon, but I was already closing the distance. His gun cleared the holster just as I launched myself at him, my shoulder slamming into his chest, driving him against the factory wall. The breath rushed from his lungs in a pained gasp. I grabbed his wrist, twisting until something snapped. The gun clattered to the ground as I drove my knee into his groin, then my elbow into his temple. He dropped like a stone.

I picked up his gun -- a Jericho 941, Israeli-made. Fitting. I checked the magazine, then tucked it into my waistband as a backup. My own weapon felt more reliable in my hands as I approached the factory's side entrance.

The door creaked as I eased it open, but the sound was swallowed by the cavernous space beyond. The factory floor stretched before me, populated by the skeletal remains of industrial looms and cutting tables. Weak light filtered through broken windows, casting long shadows across the concrete floor. The air smelled of rust, mildew, and cigarette smoke.

I moved from shadow to shadow, ears straining for any sound that didn't belong to the settling building. A voice echoed from somewhere ahead -- Balal, speaking rapid-fire Arabic into a phone. I couldn't make out the words, but the tone was clear. He was angry, demanding.

I followed the voice to a former office space overlooking the factory floor. Through a gap in the partially closed blinds, I could see Balal pacing, one hand gesturing emphatically as he spoke. A bodyguard stood by the door, arms crossed, expression bored.

I had two options: wait for Balal to finish his call and hope to catch him alone, or go in now and deal with both of them. The decision was made for me when Balal ended his call and barked an order at his guard, who nodded and left the office, heading in my direction.

I pressed myself against the wall, waiting until the guard passed my position before stepping out behind him. My arm locked around his throat, cutting off both air and sound as I dragged him backward into the shadows. He thrashed, an elbow catching me in the ribs where the bullet had grazed me earlier. Pain flared white-hot, but I didn't loosen my grip. His struggles weakened, then stopped altogether as unconsciousness claimed him. I lowered him to the ground, checking to make sure he was still breathing before continuing toward the office.

Balal stood at the window now, his back to the door as he stared out at the ruined factory floor. The years had not been kind to him. His hair was streaked with gray, and his broad shoulders had begun to stoop. But the set of his stance still radiated the confidence of a man accustomed to being obeyed.

I pushed the door open slowly, wincing at the creak of hinges. Balal didn't turn.

"I told you I didn't want to be disturbed," he said in Arabic, his tone clipped with irritation.

"Hello, Balal," I replied in English, shutting the door behind me.

He stiffened, then turned, his face a mask of controlled surprise.

"Azrael," he said, my road name sounding strange in his accented English. "I should have known you'd come yourself."

"You should have stayed away from my town," I replied, keeping my gun trained on his chest. "Away from your sister."

A flicker of genuine emotion crossed his face at the mention of Mazida. "My sister belongs with her family, not with American bikers who don't understand our ways."

"Your 'ways' make her little more than an animal, a slave," I said, feeling the old rage bubbling up.

Balal waved a dismissive hand. "Mazida dishonored our family name by running away with that boy. Consequences were necessary."

"Consequences?" I took a step forward, fighting the urge to put a bullet between his eyes right then.

His expression hardened. "Our business is not yours, American. Step aside, tell me where she is, and perhaps I will let your club survive what comes next."

I laughed, a sound without humor. "You think you're in a position to make threats?" I gestured with my gun. "On your knees."

Instead of complying, Balal lunged for something on the desk beside him. I fired, the bullet shattering the wooden surface inches from his hand. He froze, then slowly straightened, a cold smile spreading across his face.

"You won't kill me," he said with certainty. "Mazida would never forgive you."

"I'm willing to take that chance." I kept the gun aimed at his center mass.

"Are you?" His smile widened. "Family is everything to my people."

"Really? Is that why you pretty much sold your sister to the highest bidder? Your sister is a person. Not currency."

Balal's hand shot out, knocking the gun aside as he closed the distance between us. I recovered quickly, blocking his follow-up strike and countering with a punch to his solar plexus. He grunted but didn't go down, instead grabbing my wounded side and digging his fingers into the injury.

Pain exploded through my body. I head-butted him, feeling cartilage give way as his nose broke under the impact. He stumbled back, blood streaming down his face, giving me enough space to bring my gun to bear again. But he was faster than I expected, kicking the weapon from my hand before I could aim. The gun skittered across the floor, disappearing under a filing cabinet.

"Not so confident without your weapon, are you?" Balal wiped blood from his face, his smile now a crimson smear.

I drew my knife. "Don't need a gun to kill you."

He laughed, pulling a blade of his own from inside his jacket. "In my country, we give boys their first knife at twelve. How old were you when you first held one, American?"

"Eight," I replied, circling slowly. "My mother's boyfriend tried to hit her. I put it through his hand."

Something like respect flickered in Balal's eyes before he lunged, his knife slashing in a practiced arc toward my throat. I stepped inside his reach, catching his wrist and driving my own blade toward his kidney. He twisted, my knife slicing through his expensive suit but missing flesh. His knee came up, catching me in the thigh with enough force to numb my leg momentarily.

We broke apart, both breathing heavily, reassessing. Blood dripped from a cut on my forearm where his blade had found a target. Balal's suit was torn in several places, but he seemed largely unscathed.

"You fight well," he admitted, "for a biker."

"You fight like someone used to letting others do his dirty work," I countered.

Rage flashed across his face. He attacked again, this time with less control. I used his momentum against him, sidestepping and sending him crashing into the desk. Wood splintered under the impact. Before he could recover, I was on him, driving my fist into his kidney, then his jaw. My knife hand came down, aiming for his shoulder to disable his arm, but he rolled at the last second. My blade embedded itself in the wooden desk.

Balal kicked out, catching me in the stomach. Air rushed from my lungs as I staggered back. He seized the advantage, tackling me through the office door onto the factory floor beyond. We hit the concrete hard, his weight driving what little air remained from my body. Stars danced across my vision as my head cracked against the floor.

His hands found my throat, thumbs pressing into my windpipe with practiced precision. I bucked, trying to dislodge him, but he had the advantage of position and weight.

"I should thank you," he said, his face inches from mine as he squeezed. "You've made this personal. Before, I only wanted my sister back. Now, I'm going to enjoy watching your club burn to the ground."

Darkness crept into the edges of my vision. My lungs screamed for air. I reached desperately for anything I could use as a weapon, my fingers finding only smooth concrete. Then they brushed against something metal -- a broken piece of machinery, its edge jagged and sharp.

I gripped it and swung blindly. Metal connected with the side of Balal's head with a sickening *crack*. His grip on my throat loosened as blood poured from the gash along his temple. I hit him again, harder, feeling bone give way beneath the makeshift weapon. He toppled sideways, no longer a coordinated threat but still conscious, still dangerous.

I rolled to my hands and knees, sucking in painful breaths through my bruised throat. Balal lay sprawled a few feet away, his hand fumbling inside his jacket. I lunged for him, catching his wrist as he pulled out a small pistol. We struggled for control of the weapon, our blood making our grips slippery and uncertain.

The gun discharged, the shot deafening in the enclosed space. I felt the bullet's heat as it passed inches from my face. With a surge of desperate strength, I slammed Balal's hand against the concrete floor once, twice, three times until his fingers went slack and the gun fell free.

I grabbed the pistol and pressed it to his forehead. "Give me one reason not to end you right now," I rasped, my voice a painful whisper.

Balal looked up at me, blood covering half his

face, one eye swollen shut. For the first time, I saw fear in his remaining eye.

"Mazida," he said, his voice weak. "She needs her family."

"She has family," I replied. "Us. The club. People who actually give a shit about her well-being."

"You don't understand our world," he insisted. "There are others who will come for her. Worse than me."

I pressed the gun harder against his skin. "Let them come."

His good eye searched my face, looking for weakness, for hesitation. Finding none. Despite everything, Mazida might not thank me for executing her brother, monster though he was. Even if she'd seemed to understand his death was necessary, I wondered if the reality would make her feel differently.

I made my decision. Standing, I kept the gun trained on him as I pulled zip ties from my pocket. "Hands behind your back."

He complied without resistance, his strength seemingly spent. I secured his wrists tightly, then hauled him to a sitting position against a nearby pillar.

"I'm taking you back to the compound," I told him. "Then we decide if you live or die."

Balal nodded wearily, his one good eye already calculating, planning. Even defeated, he was dangerous. But he was also my best chance at understanding the true threat to Mazida.

I pulled out my phone and called Chaos. "It's done," I said when he answered. "Bring the van to the old textile factory. And call Doc -- we're going to need him."

"Balal?" Chaos asked.

"Alive, for now." I glanced at the bloody, battered man slumped against the pillar.

"We're ten minutes out."

I hung up and returned to Balal, checking his bindings. He watched me through his swollen eye, his breathing labored but steady.

"You're making the right choice," he said quietly.

I gripped his jaw, forcing him to look directly at me. "Understand something. The only reason you're still breathing is because I'm letting my President decide what to do with you. Nothing more."

Fear flashed across his face, quickly masked by a pained attempt at dignity. But we both knew the truth. For the first time in his life, Balal Quadir was at someone else's mercy. And mercy wasn't something I was known for.

Chapter Twenty-One

Azrael
One Week Later

I leaned against the back wall, arms folded across my chest, watching as Charming took his place at the head of the table. The fluorescent lights flickered overhead, casting harsh shadows across the faces of my brothers. Nobody spoke. We all knew why we'd been called here tonight.

Every officer and patched member of the Devil's Boneyard gathered around the table. Some sat, others stood. A few nursed beers, but most remained sober, understanding the gravity of tonight's meeting.

Charming cleared his throat, and the room went silent. Even the ice in the glasses stopped clinking.

"Brothers, it's done. Balal Quadir's body has been shipped back to his people in Tel Aviv. A clear message that the Devil's Boneyard doesn't fuck around when someone threatens one of our own."

Murmurs of approval rippled through the room. I nodded, feeling a cold satisfaction settle in my gut. Balal had deserved worse than what we gave him, but time constraints meant we couldn't get too creative. In the end, Ripper had been the one to kill him. As much as I'd wanted to do it, Charming had thought I should step back since the man was technically part of my family.

"Mazida is safe," Charming continued. "Her brother won't be trying to drag her back to Israel anymore. Or anywhere else, for that matter."

I caught Gator's eye across the room. His face remained impassive, but I caught the slight twitch of his lips. Mazida had been his to protect since the moment she'd stepped onto our compound.

"The question now," Charming said, leaning forward and planting his palms on the table, "is how we prevent this kind of shit from happening again. We've got other women under our protection. We need to make sure no one gets any ideas about coming after what's ours."

"What are you suggesting?" one of the newer members asked from the far end of the table.

Charming's eyes narrowed slightly. "Enhanced security protocols. More men on rotation at the compound gates. Background checks on anyone who comes within a mile of our properties. And" -- he paused, scanning the room --"stronger alliances with clubs who've proven themselves trustworthy, and perhaps finding some new allies."

The last part caused a few eyebrows to raise.

"Which clubs?" I asked, straightening from my position against the wall.

Charming nodded at me. "The Dixie Reapers for one. Thanks to Scratch and Irish, we already have ties with them. Through Stripes, we're connected to the Devil's Fury. But there are other clubs in Florida. Ones closer to home, and some as far south as Miami."

I had a feeling he meant the Twisted Tides MC when he mentioned Miami. They'd helped out the Reapers recently. Now they were on Charming's radar.

"I'm putting it to a vote," Charming announced. "All in favor of implementing the new security measures, tap your fists."

The sound of knuckles against wood filled the room as nearly every man signaled his approval. Only two abstained, both newer Prospects who hadn't earned voting rights yet.

"And the alliances?" Charming continued.

This time, the response was slower, more

measured. Men exchanged glances, weighing the implications. Finally, knuckles began rapping against the wooden surface, mine included. The rhythm was less unified but no less determined.

"It's settled then," Charming said, satisfaction evident in his voice. "I'll reach out to the clubs tomorrow. We'll start working out the details."

The tension in the room eased slightly, but I knew we weren't done. There were other matters to discuss, other consequences of our actions against Balal that needed addressing.

As if reading my thoughts, Stripes pushed himself away from the metal pillar he'd been leaning against and stepped forward.

"I have news," he announced, his gravelly voice carrying across the room. "My contacts in Tel Aviv have confirmed that Balal's associates have backed down. They're claiming no knowledge of his 'unauthorized expedition' to retrieve his sister." Stripes made air quotes around the words, his contempt evident.

"They're letting him swing in the wind?" someone asked.

Stripes nodded. "*Da*. Apparently, Balal acted without permission from his superiors. They don't want trouble with American MCs. Bad for business."

A wave of dark laughter rolled through the room. Glasses clinked as men raised their drinks in sardonic toasts.

"Fucking typical," I muttered, though loud enough for those nearby to hear. "Guess his friends weren't as loyal as he thought."

"No honor among thieves," Stripes agreed, his blue eyes twinkling with grim amusement. "Except us, of course."

More laughter, genuine this time. The brotherhood we shared might be built on violence and intimidation to the outside world, but among ourselves, loyalty was everything. Balal had never understood that. He'd seen Mazida as property, something to be controlled. We saw her as family from the moment I'd claimed her daughter.

"What about the Israeli family?" another brother asked. "They still a threat?"

Stripes shook his head. "Not for now. They've got their hands full with some internal power struggle. Balal's death actually works in their favor. One less contender for the throne."

I exchanged a look with Charming. We both knew better than to trust the calm. In our world, threats never truly disappeared. They just retreated until a better opportunity presented itself.

"We'll keep our eyes open," Charming said, echoing my thoughts. "But for now, it seems we've bought ourselves some breathing room."

The relief in the room was palpable. Men's shoulders relaxed, postures eased. The past few weeks had been a constant state of high alert, with everyone pulling double shifts to ensure Mazida's safety and prepare for potential retaliation from Balal's associates.

"One more thing," Charming said, his tone shifting to something lighter. "I think it's time we had ourselves a proper celebration. It's been too damn long since this club had anything to feel good about."

A chorus of agreement rose from the assembled men. The prospect of letting loose after weeks of tension was enough to bring genuine smiles to even the hardest faces.

"Tomorrow night," Charming continued. "Full patch members and their women only. Tell your old ladies to dust off their party clothes. Prospects will man the gate and the bar."

The meeting began to break up naturally then, men drifting into smaller groups, conversations shifting from club business to personal matters. I moved toward the bar in the main room, suddenly craving something stronger than beer.

As I poured myself two fingers of whiskey, I felt a presence beside me. Gator reached for a bottle of bourbon, his expression more relaxed than I'd seen it in weeks.

"You good?" I asked, keeping my voice low.

He nodded, a slight smile playing at the corners of his mouth. "Better than good, brother."

I understood. With Balal dead and his organization backing off, Mazida was truly free for the first time since she'd arrived in our world. And that meant Gator could finally move forward with what had been building between them.

"Glad to hear it," I said, raising my glass in a silent toast.

Around us, the clubhouse hummed with renewed energy. Men who'd been wound tight for weeks were finally unwinding, the weight of constant vigilance lifting from their shoulders. Tomorrow we'd celebrate properly, but tonight, this moment of quiet satisfaction was enough.

I sipped my whiskey and watched my brothers, feeling a fierce pride surge through me. We'd faced a threat and eliminated it, protecting our own in the process. In our world, there was no greater victory.

Beer flowed freely now, glasses clinking and bottles hissing as caps were twisted off. I stood near the corner, rolling my shoulders to release the tension that had built there during the formal proceedings.

Around me, my brothers laughed and cursed, their voices growing louder with each passing minute. The threat was gone. Balal was dead. For the first time in weeks, we could breathe without looking over our shoulders.

Charming had moved to a worn leather couch against the far wall, deep in conversation with two of our oldest members. The lines around his eyes had softened, the perpetual furrow between his brows smoothed out by relief and good bourbon. He caught my eye across the room and raised his glass in a silent salute. I nodded back, acknowledging what we both knew -- we'd dodged a bullet this time.

"Fuck, it feels good to be off high alert," said a voice to my right. I turned to find Stripes beside me, nursing a glass of clear liquid that I knew wasn't water.

"Been a while since anyone had a full night's sleep," I agreed, tipping my glass back and letting the last of the whiskey slide down my throat.

Stripes chuckled, the sound like gravel underfoot. "You know what they say. No rest for the wicked. And we are very wicked men, my friend."

I couldn't argue with that. The things Ripper had done to Balal before sending his body back to Tel Aviv would have turned a regular person's stomach. I'd participated without hesitation, until Charming had pulled me back. My only regret being that we couldn't make it last longer. The man had planned to force his own sister back into a life of servitude, had threatened our club, had broken our unspoken code. Death had been a mercy he hadn't deserved.

The celebration was gaining momentum around us. Someone had cranked up the music, and classic rock battled with the growing volume of conversation. Two Prospects worked behind the bar, keeping glasses filled and collecting empties, eager to prove their worth even during a party.

I noticed Gator standing slightly apart, staring into his untouched whiskey. Unlike the rest of us, he seemed to be growing more tense rather than less as the night progressed. His jaw worked back and forth, a sure sign he was chewing on something in his mind.

"What's going on with him?" I asked Stripes, nodding toward Gator.

Stripes' face creased into a knowing smile. "Ah. I think our friend is gathering his courage."

"For what?"

"Watch and see," Stripes said, tapping the side of his nose.

As if he'd heard us, Gator suddenly downed his whiskey in one swallow and set the glass on the nearest flat surface. He squared his shoulders and took a deep breath. Then, with a deliberate stride, he moved toward the center of the room.

The change in his bearing was subtle but impossible to miss if you knew what to look for. This was something I'd rarely seen in him before -- the man beneath the cut, stepping forward with something personal on the line.

He didn't speak at first, just stood there, his presence gradually drawing attention. One by one, conversations died down as brothers noticed him standing there, waiting. Within a minute, the room had quieted enough that the only sounds were the low hum of the jukebox and the distant rumble of motorcycles on the highway outside.

"Got something to say, brother?" Charming asked, breaking the silence.

Gator nodded, his gaze scanning the room, taking in each face before he spoke. When he finally did, his voice was lower and more measured than usual, forcing everyone to lean in slightly to catch his words.

"You all know what we've been dealing with," he began. "Balal Quadir and his threat to Mazida."

Murmurs of agreement rippled through the room. Everyone knew. Everyone had played their part in ensuring her safety and Balal's demise.

"What you might not know," Gator continued, "is that I asked Mazida a question yesterday. Asked her what she wanted, now that she's truly free."

The room went completely silent then. I could hear my own heartbeat, could feel the collective breath being held. It wasn't often that a brother laid himself bare like this, showing vulnerability in front of the club.

Gator's lips curved into the beginning of a smile, something so genuine it transformed his face.

"Mazida has agreed to be mine," he announced, the pride in his voice unmistakable. "She's chosen to stay, not just under our protection, but as my woman."

The roar that followed nearly shook the foundations of the clubhouse. Men surged forward, slapping Gator on the back, offering congratulations and crude jokes in equal measure. Bottles were raised, toasts shouted over the din. The celebration that had been building suddenly found its focal point, its reason to explode into something wilder and more joyous.

I hung back, watching as my brothers surrounded Gator. At sixty-six, he'd been a confirmed bachelor for as long as I'd known him. Women came and went in his life, but none had been granted old lady status. None had been important enough to announce to the club. Until Mazida.

"Did you know?" I asked Stripes, who remained

beside me, watching the celebration with the same detached amusement.

"I suspected," he replied. "The way he looked at her... man my age recognizes that look." He tapped his chest. "It starts here, not lower. The kind that changes a man for good."

I nodded, thinking about the transformation I'd witnessed in Gator over the past few days. When Mazida had first arrived, Gator had been just another brother offering security. But something had changed between them during those long watches, those tense days when Balal's threat hung over all of us.

"She's good for him," I said, surprised to find I meant it.

"*Da*," Stripes agreed. "And he for her. A woman like that, one who grew up knowing only control and fear, needs a man who understands strength is not about dominance. Much like her first love, I'm sure."

Charming had made his way to Gator now, pulling him into a brief but fierce embrace before stepping back to speak. I couldn't hear the words over the noise, but the respect in his posture told me all I needed to know. This wasn't just a celebration of a brother finding his woman -- it was a celebration of everything the club stood for. Protection. Loyalty. Family.

The party shifted into a higher gear after that. More bottles appeared, music got louder, laughter became more raucous. The weight that had been pressing on all of us hadn't just lifted -- it had been flung away, replaced by a collective sense of triumph.

I pushed away from the wall, deciding to offer my own congratulations to Gator. As I made my way across the room, I noticed the men had broken into smaller clusters, their body language relaxed but energized. In one corner, three brothers were animatedly discussing plans for expanded security at the compound gates. Near the pool table, another group speculated about the fallout in Tel Aviv from Balal's death. Everywhere, beneath the celebration, was the unspoken acknowledgment: we had faced a threat and eliminated it, together.

Gator spotted me approaching and broke away from the group surrounding him.

"About time you stopped lurking in the shadows," he said, clapping me on the shoulder hard enough to make me grateful for the solid muscle there.

"Just enjoying the show," I replied. "Congratulations, brother. Didn't think anyone would ever pin your ass down."

Gator's laugh was genuine, his eyes crinkling at the corners. "Neither did I. But Mazida..." He shook his head, suddenly at a loss for words.

"She's something special," I finished for him.

"That she is." I'd never heard softness in his voice like that before. "Know what she said when I asked her? Said she'd never thought she'd want to settle down again, that she'd thought Carter was her one and only. Said I made her believe she deserved better than gathering dust like an unwanted toy."

I nodded, understanding the significance. "She's right."

"Damn straight she is," Gator agreed. "You know, when it came to ending Balal, I heard you were particularly creative with the knife."

I shrugged, not bothering to deny it. "Man threatens one of ours, he gets what's coming."

"One of ours," Gator repeated, satisfaction evident in his tone. "That's exactly what she is now."

More brothers approached then, pulling Gator

back into the celebration. I drifted toward the bar, grabbed another beer, and found myself beside Charming, who was watching the proceedings with the satisfied air of a man seeing his family thrive.

"Good night for the club," he remarked without looking at me.

"Been a while since we had one," I agreed.

Charming nodded. "We needed this. Not just Balal's death, but this." He gestured toward Gator, now laughing in the midst of a circle of brothers.

Around us, the party continued to gain momentum. Men who had been tense and vigilant for weeks were now loose-limbed and loud, their relief manifesting in increasingly boisterous celebration. The scent of leather and cigarettes hung heavy in the air, punctuated by the sharp tang of spilled beer and whiskey.

In the corner, someone had pulled out a deck of cards, starting an impromptu poker game that was generating good-natured cursing and laughter. Nearest the door, a group had gathered around Stripes as he regaled them with stories from his past, his Russian accent becoming more pronounced with each drink.

I absorbed it all, feeling a fierce pride in these men, in what we'd built and what we'd defended. The Devil's Boneyard wasn't just a club -- it was a brotherhood forged in fire and blood, strengthened by each challenge we overcame together.

"You know," Charming said thoughtfully, interrupting my thoughts, "this thing with Gator and Mazida -- it's more than just a man finding his woman."

I raised an eyebrow, waiting for him to continue.

"It's a statement," he went on. "To any other fuckers who might think about coming after what's ours. Balal tried to reclaim his sister, and now he's dead and she belongs to one of us." He took a sip of his drink, satisfaction evident in his expression. "Poetic justice, wouldn't you say?"

I couldn't help but smile at that. "Didn't know you were such a poet, Charming."

He chuckled, the sound low and dangerous. "There's poetry in everything we do, brother. Just not the kind they teach in schools."

Epilogue

Azrael
Two Months Later

I stood in the center of our ceremonial circle. The hanging lanterns cast long shadows across the packed dirt, illuminating patches of leather cuts and faces. My brothers. My family. They'd come to witness something none of them thought they'd ever see -- Azrael, the Angel of Death, pledging himself to a woman. The air smelled of motor oil, leather, and the sweet incense Mazida had insisted on burning "to keep evil spirits away." I almost smiled at that. In our world, we were the evil spirits most people ran from.

The clubhouse yard had been transformed. Persian rugs covered sections of the ground, creating islands of rich color amid the dust and gravel. Lanterns hung from the surrounding trees, their flames dancing in the light evening breeze. The mix of biker grit and Middle Eastern elegance would have seemed bizarre to outsiders, but to me, it was the perfect representation of who I was -- the son of Nadia Hamdi, raised on stories of her homeland before she was brutalized and left with a child she never expected.

My brothers had formed a loose circle around me, their leather cuts displaying the Devil's Boneyard insignia with pride. Allied clubs stood among them -- Dixie Reapers, Twisted Tides, even a few Savage Raptors who'd made the trip from a few states over. In our world, this was as close to a formal wedding as it got. No priests. No paperwork. Just witnesses and vows that meant more than any government document ever could.

My gaze found Cinder, standing tall despite his eighty-plus years. Our former president nodded at me, his white beard catching the golden light. When I'd told him about Zara, he'd just laughed and said, "About damn time someone brought that cold heart of yours back to life."

Cold heart. That's what they all thought I had. Maybe they were right. I'd spent years being the club's executioner, the one they sent when someone needed to disappear permanently. I was good at it. Too good, maybe. The Middle Eastern blood that made others distrust me hadn't been an issue for this club. They'd only seen the man I was, and the one I could become. I was different. Dangerous. Dedicated to a code of justice that extended beyond what most men could stomach. Which made me a perfect fit for this brotherhood.

Then Zara Colton had walked into my life, asking for the man they called the avenging angel.

I watched Zara step into the circle now, led by Meg, Cinder's old lady. My breath caught in my throat. She wore a dress of deep burgundy that hugged her curves before flowing to her ankles. Gold bracelets adorned her wrists, and a delicate chain with a Devil's Boneyard pendant rested against her collarbone -- my gift to her when she'd agreed to be my wife and not just my old lady.

The hunt for Mazida had bonded us in ways I couldn't have imagined. Zara had seen sides of me that I'd never shown anyone -- the rage, the ruthlessness, but also the pain I carried.

I'd never believed I deserved someone like her. Still didn't. But here she was, walking toward me, her eyes never leaving mine as the circle of bikers parted to let her through.

"Look at her," Cinder murmured from beside me. "She's got fire in her eyes, boy."

Zara had that same quiet strength my mother had possessed -- the kind that couldn't be broken, only tempered by the heat of suffering.

She reached me, and Meg stepped back. The yard fell silent.

"Brothers and sisters," Cinder's voice rang out, gruff but clear. "We gather to witness the joining of Azrael and Zara. Not in the eyes of any god or government, but in the eyes of their family -- us."

I took Zara's hands in mine, surprised to find my own were trembling slightly. I, who had faced down death more times than I could count, was nervous about speaking vows to this small woman who barely reached my shoulder.

"In our world," Cinder continued, "we make our own rules, our own families. Today, these two choose each other, binding their lives together by choice and blood."

At those words, I released Zara's hands and reached for the cuff in my pocket. Hammered silver with delicate Arabic calligraphy woven through patterns of interlocking chains. My mother's last gift to me, something she'd worn every day.

A murmur went through the crowd. No one had seen it before, and I had to admit it was a work of art.

I carefully held it between my fingers. The silver caught the lantern light, throwing patterns across Zara's face.

"This belonged to my mother," I said, my voice lower and softer than usual. "She gave it to me before she died, told me to save it for someone worth sharing my soul with." I paused, swallowing hard against the emotion threatening to choke me. "I never thought I'd find that person."

Zara's eyes glistened with unshed tears, but her

gaze remained steady on mine. Strong. Unflinching.

"The writing," I continued, turning the band so she could see the calligraphy, "says 'Justice through love.' My mother believed that true justice could only come from a place of love for humanity. Not hatred, not vengeance. Love." I took a deep breath, feeling more exposed than I'd ever been. "I've spent my life dealing out justice, Zara. But it wasn't until you that I remembered the love part."

A single tear escaped, trailing down her cheek. I reached up and swept it away with my thumb.

"Zara, will you be my partner in this life? Will you stand with me, ride with me, fight with me until death takes us?"

My hand brushed against hers as I held out the band, feeling the subtle tremble of her small frame. Around us, the circle of bikers stood silent, waiting.

"Yes," she said, her voice clear and unwavering despite her tears. "Until death and whatever comes after."

I slipped the band onto her wrist, where it fit as though it had been made for her. Then I reached into my cut pocket and pulled out a second band -- wider, heavier, but with the same intertwined patterns and script.

"I had this made to match," I said quietly. "So I could wear your mark as you wear mine."

She took it from me, her fingers warm against my palm, and slid it onto my wrist. The metal was cool against my skin, but it warmed quickly, becoming a part of me as she had.

"By the witness of your brothers and sisters," Cinder's voice broke through the moment, "you are now joined. Those who ride together, stay together."

Then, as if on cue, engines roared to life. Brothers

who had parked their bikes around the perimeter revved their motors in approval, the growl of Harleys creating a symphony of mechanical power that vibrated through the ground beneath our feet.

I pulled Zara to me, one hand at the small of her back, the other tangling in her hair as I claimed her mouth with mine. The kiss was equal parts tenderness and possession, a promise of both protection and passion. When we finally broke apart, the cheers had grown louder, punctuated by whistles and the continued roar of engines.

"You sure about this?" I asked her, our foreheads touching, my words for her alone. "Life with me won't be easy."

She smiled, fierce and beautiful. "I didn't come looking for easy, Azrael. I came looking for you."

Around us, the celebration was already beginning. Tables laden with food appeared as if by magic, bottles were opened, music started playing. But for that moment, we remained in our own world, lost in each other's gaze as the chaos of our family swirled around us.

I had been called the Angel of Death for so long that I'd forgotten what it felt like to bring life instead. But with Zara's hands in mine and my mother's band around her wrist, I remembered. This wasn't an ending. It was a beginning.

Bonus: Azrael (Devil's Boneyard MC 13)
Deleted Scene

Zara

What the club had created for our wedding day took my breath away. String lights draped from trees created constellations against the dark sky. Rich fabrics in deep jewel tones -- burgundy, emerald, sapphire -- hung on handmade panels. The polished chrome of parked motorcycles gleamed. This wasn't just a biker party. And it wasn't just a Middle Eastern celebration space either. It was something entirely new -- something that belonged to Azrael and me alone.

"You like it?" Meg appeared beside me, her hand squeezing my arm.

"It's… perfect." My voice caught as I took in more details -- the brass lanterns casting pools of warm light, the scattered rose petals mixed with motorcycle parts repurposed as centerpieces.

"The girls worked all night." By "girls," she meant the other old ladies -- the partners and wives of club members who formed their own hierarchy.

"Where is she?" I asked, searching the room for my mother's familiar face.

"Mazida's helping in the back," Meg said. "She insisted on preparing the special bread herself. Said it wouldn't be a proper wedding without it."

My throat tightened. "And Azrael?"

Meg's smile turned sly. "Pacing like a caged animal out back with the boys. Cinder threatened to tie him to a chair if he doesn't settle down."

The image made me laugh -- my fierce, deadly Azrael, the man who made hardened criminals beg for mercy, nervous about a wedding ceremony.

"Come on." Meg tugged me toward the

clubhouse. "Time to get you ready. Can't keep the Angel of Death waiting at the altar, or he might start taking souls to pass the time."

I laughed, as she'd intended. The women's preparation room had once been a bedroom but now held mirrors, clothing racks, and the makings of a bridal suite. Clarity, Scratch's wife, immediately pushed me into a chair and began working on my hair while Jordan, married to the club's Sergeant-at-Arms, Havoc, laid out my outfit.

"Not too much makeup," my mother said, entering with flour-dusted hands. "My daughter has no need to hide her beauty."

Seeing her standing there, proud despite the lingering shadows in her eyes, I felt tears threatening. I'd lost my mother for a while, but I'd also found Azrael.

"No crying," Clarity scolded, dabbing at my eyes with a tissue. "I'll never get your eyeliner right if you start now."

"Sorry," I whispered, blinking back the emotion. "Just thinking about how much has changed."

"That's what these men do," Jordan said, smoothing out my dress. "They charge into your life like a fucking hurricane, turn everything upside down, and somehow leave it better than it was before."

The women laughed, a knowing sound that embraced me in its solidarity. They understood what it meant to love a man who lived partly in the shadows.

My wedding outfit wasn't traditional by any standard. A deep burgundy, fitted through the bodice then flaring slightly at the hips, ending just above my ankles. My mother approached with something in her hands -- a delicate gold headpiece with tiny bells that chimed softly as she placed it on my head. "This was mine at my wedding," she said quietly. "Before everything changed. I saved it for you."

"It's beautiful, Mom," I whispered, reaching up to touch the delicate metalwork.

"A queen should have a crown," she replied, cupping my cheek. "And you, my Zara, have always been a queen."

An hour later, I stood at the entrance to the main room, my heart hammering against my ribs. The sound of motorcycles outside announced the arrival of more guests -- members from allied clubs coming to witness the union of Azrael to his bride. "Ready?" Meg appeared at my side again, offering her arm.

I nodded, not trusting my voice. We'd decided against traditional bridal music. Instead, when we appeared in the doorway of the clubhouse, a brother named Magnus hit a single, resonating note on a massive gong someone had picked up from who knew where. The sound vibrated through the space, silencing all conversation.

Every head turned toward me. I forced myself to stand tall, channeling both the strength of the biker women who'd taken me under their wings and the dignity my mother had somehow maintained even after her kidnapping.

Then I saw him, and everything else faded away.

Azrael stood, tall and proud, his powerful frame impossible to miss even among the crowd of bikers. He wore black jeans and a crisp white shirt open at the throat, revealing the edges of tattoos that told stories of his past. Over it, he wore his cut -- the leather vest that proclaimed his membership in the Devil's Boneyard, adorned with patches. His dark gaze found mine across the space, and I saw in his eyes a mixture of fierce possession and breathtaking vulnerability that made my knees weak.

This deadly man was mine. And I was his.

Meg guided me through the parting crowd. As we passed, women reached out to touch my arm or dress -- gestures of welcome and blessing. The men nodded respectfully, some touching their hearts in the traditional Middle Eastern gesture of honor that Azrael had taught them.

When we reached the front, Meg placed my hand in Azrael's, and I felt his fingers tighten around mine. His palm was warm, slightly calloused from years of hard work and harder fights. "You're beautiful," he murmured, his gaze never leaving mine.

"So are you," I whispered back, earning a small smile that transformed his usually stern face.

Cinder cleared his throat, and the area fell silent again. When he spoke, his voice was gruff but carried easily through the space.

The wedding itself seemed to pass in a blur. My heart pounded so hard, I worried everyone could hear it. When it was all said and done, and I was finally his in every way possible, I felt happier than I ever had before.

Azrael kept his arm around me as we accepted congratulations, his body a solid presence at my side. Despite the noise and crowd, he leaned down to speak directly in my ear. "No regrets?" he asked, a rare uncertainty in his voice.

I turned to face him, framing his face with my hands. "Not a single one."

Overhead, I saw the first fireworks explode against the night sky -- brilliant bursts of color and light arranged by the club as a surprise. Each explosion sent vibrations through the ground beneath our feet, matching the pounding of my heart.

As Azrael pulled me close again, I caught sight of my mother across the way, standing with Meg and Clarity. She raised her glass to me, her eyes shining with tears and pride.

In that moment, as fireworks continued to illuminate the sky and Azrael's warmth enveloped me, I realized the Devil's Boneyard hadn't just given me back my mother or given me a husband. They'd given us both a home where our broken pieces fit perfectly into the larger pattern of their beautiful family.

I wrapped my arms around Azrael's neck and pulled him down for another kiss, claiming him as fiercely as he'd claimed me. Around us, the celebration erupted in another wave of cheers and catcalls, the bikers delighting in our display. "I love you," I whispered against his lips when we finally came up for air. "My avenging angel."

His answering smile was both tender and predatory. "And I love you, my queen." His hands tightened possessively at my waist. "Now, how soon can we slip away from our own wedding?"

I laughed, feeling lighter than I had in years. "Soon," I promised. "But first, we dance."

As he led me to the cleared space serving as a dance floor, the music shifted to something slower, more sensual. Azrael pulled me against him, moving with surprising grace for such a powerful man. Over his shoulder, I watched our new family celebrating around us -- dangerous men and fierce women who had accepted us as their own.

This wasn't the life I'd imagined for myself, but standing in the arms of my avenging angel while fireworks illuminated our future, I couldn't imagine wanting anything else.

Harley Wylde

Harley Wylde is an accomplished author known for her captivating MC Romances. With an unwavering commitment to sensual storytelling, Wylde immerses her readers in an exciting world of fierce men and irresistible women. Her works exude passion, danger, and gritty realism, while still managing to end on a satisfying note each time.

When not crafting her tales, Wylde spends her time brainstorming new plotlines, indulging in a hot cup of Starbucks, or delving into a good book. She has a particular affinity for supernatural horror literature and movies. Visit Wylde's website to learn more about her works and upcoming events, and don't forget to sign up for her newsletter to receive exclusive discounts and other exciting perks.

Harley at Changeling: changelingpress.com/harley-wylde-a-196

Bad Boys Multiverse

Contemporary MC, Organized Crime, and Crossovers
A Bad Boy Romance
Dixie Reapers MC
Devil's Boneyard MC
Hades Abyss MC
Devil's Fury MC
Reckless Kings MC
Savage Raptors MC
Swift Angels MC
Owned by the Mob
Bryson Corners
Underland MC

Paranormal MC
Devoted Guardians MC
Balor's Saints MC

Print and Audio:
Dixie Reapers MC Print
Dixie Reapers MC Audio
Devil's Boneyard MC Audio
Hades Abyss MC Audio
Devil's Fury MC Audio

Changeling Press LLC

Contemporary Action Adventure, Sci-Fi, Steampunk, Dark Fantasy, Urban Fantasy, Paranormal, and BDSM Romance available in e-book, audio, and print format at ChangelingPress.com -- MC Romance, Werewolves, Vampires, Dragons, Shapeshifters and Horror -- Tales from the edge of your imagination.

Where can I get Changeling Press Books?

Changeling Press e-books are available at ChangelingPress.com, Amazon, Apple Books, Barnes & Noble, Kobo, Smashwords, and other online retailers, including Everand Subscription and Kobo Subscription Services. Print books are available at Amazon, Barnes and Noble, and by ISBN special order through your local bookstores.

Changeling Press LLC

ChangelingPress.com